# THE AFTERLIFE OF THE PARTY

## ALSO BY DARCY MARKS

*Grounded for All Eternity*

Darcy Marks

# THE AFTERLIFE OF THE PARTY

ALADDIN

New York  London  Toronto  Sydney  New Delhi

ALADDIN
An imprint of Simon & Schuster Children's Publishing Division
1230 Avenue of the Americas, New York, New York 10020
First Aladdin hardcover edition July 2023
Text copyright © 2023 by Darcy Richardson Miller
Jacket illustration copyright © 2023 by Sara Luna
All rights reserved, including the right of reproduction in whole or in part in any form.
ALADDIN and related logo are registered trademarks of Simon & Schuster, Inc.
For information about special discounts for bulk purchases, please contact Simon & Schuster Special Sales at 1-866-506-1949 or business@simonandschuster.com.
The Simon & Schuster Speakers Bureau can bring authors to your live event.
For more information or to book an event contact the Simon & Schuster Speakers Bureau at 1-866-248-3049 or visit our website at www.simonspeakers.com.
Jacket designed by Karin Paprocki
Interior designed by Mike Rosamilia
The text of this book was set in Fournier Pro.
Manufactured in the United States of America 0623 FFG
2 4 6 8 10 9 7 5 3 1
Library of Congress Control Number 2023932361
ISBN 9781534483392 (hc)
ISBN 9781534483415 (ebook)

*To everyone who saw something of themselves*
*in Malachi's story. I'm glad you're here.*

## COMMAND

### MALACHI

*Track: Command*
*Interests: Anything I'm not supposed*
*to do*
*Fear: Fate, failing*

## INTELLIGENCE

### LILITH

*Track: Intelligence*
*Favorite Activity: Knowing things,*
*teasing Mal*
*Fear: Imperfection*

## MAGICIAN

### CROWLEY

*Track: Magician*
*Interests: All things comics*
*Fear: Like I would tell you*

## ENFORCER

### ALEISTER

*Track: Enforcer*
*Favorite Activity: Competing, sports*
*of all kinds*
*Fear: Nothing to fear with good friends!*

*Dear Divine Being of Creation,*

*You are cordially invited to the gala of the millennia! In order to foster goodwill and create friendships that will last our nearly eternal lives, we, the celestials of the paradise otherwise known as Heaven, invite you and your families to a mixer to be held in the hallowed halls of our beloved great hereafter.*

*Our golden gates will open for the first time in eons to welcome you, the denizens of the infernal realm, into our home, where we may live, laugh, and love in mutual respect.*

*Please join us for food, fun, and dancing at a date and time to be agreed upon shortly.*

*~C*

# ONE

From the outside, the shop looked perfectly normal for something that had just appeared one day on a crowded street with no empty lots. It settled at the end of a row of my favorite stores, somehow lining up perfectly with the street like it belonged there, even though it shouldn't have even fit.

Glamourie had stood empty for weeks. Only a small gap between the blue velvet curtains allowed any snooping of the vacant interior, while the sign above had displayed the name of the shop in swooping silver glittery letters . . . and nothing else.

The endless rumors of Hell's new resident from Faerie had kicked up immediately.

Interdimensional travel was heavily regulated, as I now

knew firsthand, but interdimensional *residency* was an entirely different thing altogether. When Morgan arrived from Faerie, it constituted BIG NEWS.

Speculation was everywhere. Why was one of the fae coming to live here? What was the shop going to be? Was it the start of a secret invasion? Who knew!

Morgan was seen around town in a sequence of brief sightings, but they hadn't said a word to anyone. One day they posted a countdown on the door of the shop. Day by day the pages fell to the ground, each bringing us closer to what everyone assumed would be the grand opening and finally the answer to so many questions.

As the days ticked down, there was just one problem: I was STILL grounded.

After our unplanned visit to Salem, my squad and I had been in as much trouble as you'd expect from us sneaking off to another dimension and almost causing the apocalypse. Which is to say, a lot.

We had been questioned again and again—Aleister included, though he thought it was pretty unfair to have to deal with the consequences when he hadn't even gotten to enjoy the mayhem in the first place—by increasingly higher-level people, until eventually we'd been brought as a group to face the Powers That Be.

The group of intimidating elites had sat at a table, as we'd all taken chairs at one of our own. Their table had been polished black wood with elaborately carved legs, framed by dramatic flame sconces. Ours had been a folding table that had looked like it got brought out for bake sales, with folding chairs just slightly too short.

We had exchanged panicked looks at the PTB's stern shadowed expressions, certain that we were heading to a very eternal grounding. But after yet another recitation of the facts, at least the version my squad and I had all agreed to tell, a man came in pushing a cart of snacks.

"Excellent," said the man at the far left, clapping his hands. "I missed lunch."

And with that the entire vibe changed. True, I vaguely wondered if taking the cupcake was a trap, but when nothing happened, I let the worries about eternal punishment fade away and sat a little more slumped in my seat.

The Powers That Be reassured us, between sips of cider and bites of snacks, that they figured it had all been an accident on our parts rather than any malicious intent, and that this interrogation was all about following the proper procedure. Unfortunately, exchanging victorious grins with my squad was one of the last good times we'd have for a while.

We were happily received by our parents when we left

the room, with enormous, relieved hugs, but once they realized we weren't actually being sent to the Cage, they decided that if the PTB weren't going to punish us, it was their job to do it.

I ended up with Methuselah as a babysitter for literally every time my parents were not home, which should have been punishment enough. But oh no, it didn't stop there. It was school and home only. No Faust's. No Choirs of Hell. No Frozen Over. Not even Burn This Book, even though I told my parents that reading was fundamental and people who didn't read were highly suspect. They didn't completely block us from seeing each other, but we weren't allowed to hang out without supervision.

Like we were littles.

Seriously. It was awful.

And I suspected it wasn't so great for the parents either, a fact we may have exploited just a teensy, tiny bit.

As our supervised antics ramped up, there were more than a few rubbed foreheads and grumbles, rolled eyes and exasperated sighs from whoever was stuck in charge of us for the moment. By the time we were all pleading to be let off this punishment from—well, you know where—our parents were ready to surrender.

It only took a bit more nudging, a few well-placed phrases

of apology, and our constant begging to attend the grand opening of the mysterious Glamourie with everyone else, and our grounding came to an end, not with a bang but with a parental whimper.

Yeah, we were pretty good.

That first breath outside on our way to the grand opening was just as good as the one I had taken when I had walked through the forest with my friends that Samhain night. Ahh, freedom.

The celebration at Glamourie featured massive amounts of food, live music, and incredible displays of magic. After the over-the-top party, the revelation that the shop was a salon was a bit of a letdown. Well, at least until Morgan's work started appearing around town.

Now Glamourie was hopping, and I had a standing weekly appointment. How, you may ask, was I able to do this on my woefully meager allowance? Luckily for me, Morgan apparently wasn't in it for the money. At my first appointment Morgan declared me "fun," and that was that. They announced they'd get their infernal denarius from boring people and stretch their creative muscles on me.

Flamelight flickered across the glass front as I stood on the sidewalk outside, and as I always did, I tried to find the seam where Glamourie's brick walls met Choirs of Hell's—

the music store next to it, and formerly the last shop on this street. But as always, the fit was perfect.

I had a theory that the shop was actually a pocket dimension that Morgan conjured with faerie magic, but I still wasn't sure how that worked. I just knew that pocket dimensions were small bits of extra space, not existing in this dimension but not big enough to be their own.

The bell chimed with a sound unlike any other shop bell I had heard, sophisticated and pure, as I pushed open the wreath-decorated door and entered the best and brightest salon in all of Hell.

"Ah, there's my favorite customer!" called Morgan over their shoulder. "Have a seat. I'll be done in a sec."

I waved and threw myself into an open chair, sending it spinning. Ever since our grounding had ended, I had become obsessed with the new salon. It was a welcome distraction from the endless parental lectures on my "recklessness," and how I could have been stranded in the mortal coil or snatched off to Heaven forever, and I was never, ever, ever supposed to go through a gate, authorized or otherwise, from now until the end of time . . . or something.

The lectures had been occasionally interspersed with grudging pride in how my squad had managed to recapture an escaped soul without a morningstar, something fully trained powers couldn't even do. Powers were what our class of angels were called, and the only ones living in Hell. Mom seemed more concerned about the possibility of me being lost forever, which was nice, but Dad seemed pleased that under pressure I had done what I was supposed to do.

Dad and I had always butted heads about *destiny*, and after witnessing my epic speech to the forces of Heaven, he had seemed to breathe a sigh of relief. Not that he approved of everything I did, but he wasn't as uptight, now that he believed I was falling into line.

I scowled at the thought and sent the chair spinning again, watching colors streak by and letting myself be surrounded by the heady scent of Morgan's magic, or possibly whatever incense they had burning.

When the spinning began to slow, I put my foot out to stop the chair and studied myself in the elaborate mirror while I waited for Morgan to finish up with their client. The purple tint to my hair was pretty much gone, and the cat's-eye slit to my pupils hadn't really held up at all. The first time I got angry, the resulting flames in my eyes wiped the glamour clear. I smiled as I thought about how Morgan's magic had looked before it had worn off. It had only been an illusion, but it had been an illusion that had made sure I didn't blend into the background.

This was especially important because the return from Salem had led me straight into the start of a new school year. *The* new school year. I may have had no choice in accepting my fated track at school and being separated from my squad mates, but that didn't mean I had to be like everyone else.

There was probably something deeply psychological to be revealed there, but whatever. My trip to the mortal realm may have made me face some things I didn't want to face, but I was still very much me, and I had done enough personal reflection over the last forty-two days, thank you very much.

Morgan whipped the sparkling cape off their current client with a flourish, and the movement caught my eye, bringing me back to the present.

"Voilà, my dear," they said. "What do you think?"

"Perfect!" the faun said, examining his rhinestone-covered horns in the mirror.

The faun was dressed in the latest fashions, with piercings up and down his ears, and was exactly the type of trendy I wanted to be. If my parents and teachers thought I was going to live in a field uniform when I was an adult, they were crazy.

"Lovely," Morgan said, standing back to admire their work. Today Morgan had tan skin and gold eyes, with hair the color of flames running down their back in elaborate braids. "Now, come back whenever the stones fall loose or lose their shine, and we'll dazzle them up, and of course if you change your mind about the hooves . . ."

"I just might do that," said the faun. He touched his horns once more before smiling in wonder. Morgan had that effect.

Before Morgan had arrived, I'd been only vaguely aware of Faerie as a dimension of wild creatures and mysterious beings. I had learned a lot since then from incessantly picking Morgan's brain, and reading everything I could find, though I still considered "wild" and "mysterious" to be pretty accurate.

The fae came in all shapes and sizes, some of which, like the brownie we had seen in Salem, were more animalistic, while others were people just like us. Faerie was broadly separated into two courts, the Seelie and the Unseelie, sometimes called the Summer and Winter Courts. After meeting my heavenly counterparts, I had a new appreciation for the divide.

Morgan had been in the inner circle of the Unseelie Court, but after eons they had decided they'd had enough of political intrigue and needed a change. With no interest in the boring mortal realm where their talents would be stifled—their words, not mine—Morgan had toured the dimensions available to them and decided that my great hereafter was their kind of people. They settled in Hades, opened a shop, and changed the local fashion for the better.

That high court impressiveness was still there, though,

and Mom said it was like having an archangel cut your hair, except the way she said it was like it was a colossal waste of time and not something amazingly cool. Morgan was doing what they loved, something I could appreciate.

"What's it going to be today, Malachi?" Morgan smiled as they turned their attention to me.

Morgan changed their appearance even more than I did—so who was just having a teenage rebellion, DAD?—and they had taken to dressing in red and green as Yule approached. I didn't know if their clothes were glamour or something they'd brought from Faerie, but the fabrics were like nothing I had seen here. I couldn't help smiling in return.

"I'm thinking . . . blue flames." I felt a tiny rush of freedom, just saying the words.

"I like your style."

# TWO

The bells over the door of Frozen Over were tinkly and vaguely childish and didn't sound anything like Glamourie's. But that sound meant you were getting ice cream, and it was hard to be in a bad mood when you knew you were getting ice cream. The chime turned my friends' heads, and it was a bonus that my appointments with Morgan always had me running a little late. All the better to make a dramatic entrance.

"What did you do this time?" Crowley said, throwing his hands up in exasperation.

"Awesome!" yelled Aleister. "You do you, dude!"

"Your dad's going to kill you," Lilith said, but she didn't

look overly worried. She turned her attention back to the sundae in her hand, clearly looking for an angle of attack that wouldn't send the whipped cream spilling over the edge.

I did a little turn, showing off my latest look, grinned, and took my spot in line with an extra bounce in my step. I looked over the array of options in the case, scanned the entire menu, debated the benefits of fruit verses spice, and then ordered the same thing I always ordered.

"Two scoops chili cinnamon chocolate, extra whipped cream, please," I said to the yeti at the counter, whose blue skin was visible through spiky white hair that remained completely motionless no matter how quickly he moved.

I got a few looks from the people nearby as I waited, and my wings puffed in pride before I could control them. I didn't stress about it, though; the movement made the blue flames skirting the feathers' edges look that much more dramatic. I ran my fingers through my hair, knowing the flames there would flare too.

"Thanks!" I said, grabbing my frozen goodness from the new kid at the counter, who was immediately sent to scoop something else. I skirted around the tables to my friends and watched gleefully as a few people moved aside in clear terror of my flaming wings.

Lilith gingerly reached her hand just above the flames,

and I held very still. My stomach tingled like it usually did when Lilith was close, but then she realized the flames gave off no heat and ruffled my hair.

"Hey!" I grumbled. "Leave it."

"Maybe I should go to Glamourie," Lilith said.

"Your mom would love that," Crowley scoffed. "Besides, I think Mal's just showing how much he wishes he were me."

Crowley activated his magic and let the red swirl of power run up and down his arms in a mimicry of the blue flames Morgan had glamoured onto my wings and hair.

"You wish," I said, shoving a spoon full of whipped cream into my mouth. "Whad I mid?"

"Well, we were talking about your atrocious manners," Crowley said, letting his magic fade away. "But I suppose we'll have to talk about something else now."

"We were just comparing notes on our school days," Lilith said, kicking Crowley gently. "I may not make it out of this year without spending time in the Pit."

"Dina?" I asked, swallowing the ice cream in my mouth way too fast, and sending a jagged arrow of pain to just behind my eye. "Ow."

"Yes!" Lilith exclaimed. "If I have to hear her know-it-all voice one more time . . . UGH!"

We were all still adjusting to our new school situation,

which had us separated into our "appropriate" tracks. For me, that meant a Command track filled with people who wouldn't know fun if it bit them in the butt. Crowley was spending all his time studying the arcane, and boiling frogs or whatever magicians did. Aleister seemed to spend all his time working out, and for Lilith? Her track meant more time stuck with her nemesis.

"She can't be in all of your classes," Aleister said. "Can't you just ignore her?"

"Yes," Lilith said, slamming her empty ice cream cup down on the table. "I could do that! If I wasn't assigned a partner project with her!"

"Ooohh."

"Ouch."

"That's . . ."

"Yeah! Exactly!" Lilith said, throwing her arms up into the air. "I'm heading to the Pit for sure."

"Or," I said. "And hear me out. Have you thought of not killing her?"

Lilith struck a pensive pose. "I've thought about it. I don't think I have the self-control."

Which, of course, was a complete lie.

"What about you guys?" Lilith asked. "Distract me, please. I have to meet with her tomorrow, and I just can't."

"I love my classes," Aleister said, as cheerful as ever. He passed his nearly empty cup under the table.

I leaned back to glance under the blue table and was met with glowing red eyes, accompanied by a happy drooling grin. I hadn't realized Damien was here, but I wasn't surprised that Aleister had brought his dog. Frozen Over was pet friendly, and Damien wasn't even the only pet there.

A cat with shiny eyes and a scaled tail was perched on their owner's shoulder, sending a forked tongue into a cup the woman held up. And a fluffy black something or other with bat wings was darting in and out of an imp's long trench coat.

"We've been sparring all week," Aleister said. "It's awesome. I haven't opened a book since the school year started. I wish I could have done this ages ago."

"Sounds awful," Crowley said. "We've been doing nothing but books, and my Enochian is spot-on."

"Nice!" Lilith said, and they high-fived over the table.

I still wasn't used to us having to catch each other up. It was so weird to think about us living completely different lives all day.

"Well, I survived yet another day of bossy camp," I said. "But the important question is, Are we all going to the concert tomorrow at Choirs of Hell?"

"Yeah," Crowley said. "Who's opening for Nephilim?"

"Some new band," I said. "Dark Knights? Something like that, anyway. Everyone in?"

"You know it!" Aleister said. "The dads said yes. Think I can bring Damien?"

"Probably no on the hellhound, but yes, I will be there," Lilith said, gathering her backpack over her shoulder and tossing the empty ice cream cup into a trash can off to the side. The cup immediately burst into flames. "And I will desperately need sugar when I get there. Three hours with Dina, Lucifer help me."

"You're leaving already?" I asked. "I just got here!"

"Homework," Lilith said.

"Yeah, me too," Crowley said, gathering his own belongings.

"Not me!" Aleister crowed. "I'm getting another one. Watch Damien for me?"

"Yeah," I said, waving to Crowley and Lilith as they left. Damien thumped his massive head into my lap, and I scratched behind his soft ear in the way that made his tail thump hard against the floor.

The ice cream shop was crowded, and I recognized a few faces, including a kid with a neat fade and a sling around his black feathered wing. For once we weren't the only powers here.

I knew of Azael. Everyone heard about him after he broke his wing a few months ago. He was in my track this year. I still didn't know him, but when Beliel had attacked Azael after his injury, the gossip had been epic. Azael's wing was now just barely supported by a light sling, so I supposed it was getting better, but there was no way he was flying with it.

I shuddered. I had spent one day wingless; that was plenty long enough. Azael was sitting with a girl who must have been the one Beliel had been after. I didn't recognize her, but she looked like she could hold her own.

"Who are you looking at?" Aleister said, throwing himself into his seat. "Oh, Sidney?"

"The one with Azael?"

"Yeah, she's in my weapons class. She's pretty good. No, Damien! Down!"

Aleister wrestled his ice cream from his overly eager hound. I was absolutely no help at all as I leaned back and laughed in my chair.

"Hey!" yelled the guy behind the counter. "Control the hound or leave."

We left.

And Damien ate half the ice cream.

The flames in the sky were their normal cozy glow as we walked; they hadn't been raised to alert since Samuel Parris, the manipulator whose butt we totally kicked in Salem, had escaped. The black sky and flickering oranges and reds of home had been a huge relief when I'd first gotten back, and I still appreciated them more than I had before. My eyes had pleasantly forgotten the strain of a bright blue sky, and although the adventure had been fun, if you ignored all the parts where I thought I was going to die, I wasn't in any rush to leave home again.

A leaf climbed up Damien's back, and I swatted it away while Aleister regaled me with a hundred and one reasons why he loved his new classes. As much as I had dreaded splitting into our tracks, I was happy it seemed to be working out for some of us, even if I was possibly a little jealous.

". . . and then he said we could—"

"Awesome!" I interrupted as we approached the spot where our paths diverged to our different houses. "COH tomorrow night?"

"Dude, yes!" Aleister said, and held out his hand for the overly complicated handshake he had recently come up with. I had only just gotten the hang of it and managed to complete it on the first try. Score! "C'mon, boy!"

Aleister took off in a run, and Damien immediately chased after him, his claws sending sparks into the air whenever they hit the cobblestones. Unlike me, Aleister actually enjoyed running, and probably would have even had fun while running for his life. Too bad he had missed our trip to the mortal world.

I, on the other hand, had spent enough time running while I was wingless in Salem, thank you. I flapped my wings to take to the sky, the movement sending the glamoured blue flames flaring in a dramatic whoosh as I launched into the air. I rolled lazily and saluted a neighbor who was flying nearby. I regretted it almost immediately. That was parent-level uncool.

After a quick flight I dropped down, landed lightly in my yard, and grabbed the mail from the box at the side of the door. I caught movement out of the corner of my eye for a second, and looked back to the street in time to see the edge of a long black cloak pass by. Huh. Maybe I needed a cloak.

"I'm home!" I called out, and tossed the mail onto the table.

"What did you do this time?"

"Nice, right?" I grinned broadly and ruffled my hair. The blue flames clung to my fingers for a second as I dropped my hand.

My dad opened his mouth, and then snapped it shut. He shook his head and went back into the kitchen. "Dinner is in five."

I flew up the stairs to my room and tossed my backpack onto my bed. With five minutes till dinner, burgers by the smell of it, my plan was to go right back down the stairs, but a glow from the corner of my room caught my eye. My stomach twisted in excitement, and I closed my door as silently as I could. I pushed off the T-shirt that was currently hiding the box and picked it up.

It was a wooden box I had scavenged from Alighieri's. The box had once contained a spell book or maybe bootleg movies, who knows, but Dante, the owner of Alighieri's, was going to just throw it away, and I had thought it looked cool. Since Dante only occasionally paid any attention at all, he'd let me have it with a shrug. It had been simple to convert it into my own interdimensional mailbox. The edges glowed faintly, and I flipped the lid open. As soon as I picked up the paper inside, the light, which was alerting me to a new letter, went out.

Shortly after I'd returned home from the mortal realm, Cassandra, a seraph from Heaven who had tried to kidnap me but had turned out to be kinda okay in the end, had sent me a letter. That had given me the idea to try to contact my new human friend, and it had only taken a few failed attempts to figure out how to send my own cross-dimensional communications. It had taken Sean longer to learn how to respond, which had given me time to completely second-guess myself, but ever since then, we had been writing back and forth.

It was a little low magic, but what could you do? I wasn't Crowley, who as a magician had his own internal magical energy source that could be channeled and manipulated. I needed runes, ingredients, and a lot of intention to power my admittedly basic communication method. But hey, if it worked, it worked.

*Mal—*

"Mal!" yelled my dad. "Dinner!"

"Brimstone," I muttered, and then refolded the letter before pushing it under my pillow. "Coming!"

My glamoured flames spread behind me like a phoenix as I soared down the stairs. These things were awesome. Maybe *this* was the real me? And for a second, I was brought back to the auras of the humans in the mortal world and the way Sean glowed blue.

"Wow," said Mom. "I could see that glow before you came into the room. I'm glad to see they don't stay that bright all the time."

"Yeah, Morgan did a great job." I spread my left wing just a little to see delicate blue flames edging my feathers. When I wasn't in motion, the look was much more subtle.

"Still not sure about—" Dad started to mutter, before Mom shot him a look and he switched course. "How was school?"

I repressed a sigh.

It had become an unspoken agreement that Dad would not make as big a fuss as he wanted to about my ever-changing look, and the fact that I was allowing a fae to cast magic on me to do it, as long as I went along with my new track education with minimal argument.

23

We launched the same conversation we always had. Dad wanted desperately for me to say something positive about my classes. Depending on my mood, I either said something vaguely complimentary or raged about how terrible everything was.

I was in the middle of acknowledging that one of my teachers was kinda cool and our latest lesson had been almost interesting when the doorbell chimed.

"I'll get it," I said, hopping out of my chair with a silent thank-you for the distraction. I was so relieved to be out of the conversation that I flung open the door without looking. "What can I . . . do . . ."

On my doorstep was a supremely uncomfortable-looking angel, and not the local kind.

# THREE

The angel's white wings practically glowed in the dim light of home. He didn't look that much older than me, just older enough to be considered an actual adult. He was tall and lanky and had a wispy beard that wasn't growing in fully. And even though he wasn't wearing armor, or the blazingly white gown Cassandra had worn, I still assumed he was wearing a uniform of some sort, since it looked official in a way that fashion never did.

"Uh—um," stuttered the angel. "Are your . . . I mean, are there adults?"

I raised an eyebrow. "Are there adults?" I repeated. "Like, here, or in all of Hell? Or maybe I am one and you just insulted me."

The angel stared at me, no doubt wondering if I was serious, and probably trying to decide if he had made a fatal mistake. I wished Cassandra could see this. It would be good for her ego to realize how much she knew already. Maybe she'd feel less like a screwup. I had received more letters from the seraph, and woo-boy, there were issues in Heaven.

"Uh, I'm looking for Commander Chayyliel," the angel said hesitantly, looking down at a scroll in his hands. "I was told he lived here."

He?

"Mom!" I called, and the already pale angel visibly blanched. "It's for you!"

"Who is it, Mal?" asked Mom. Her posture changed so quickly, I almost laughed, but I managed to suppress it to a devilish smirk instead.

"I don't know," I said. I was probably enjoying the angel's discomfort a little too much, but it was such a nice change to be on this side of the equation. "He didn't give me his name."

"Can I help you?" Mom snapped as she made her way toward the door, shoulders back, chin up, and striding like the commander she was.

"Are you . . . ?" started the angel, before coming to the conclusion that he was done being played with. He straightened his spine and cleared his throat. "Commander,

I have—I'm sorry, but is your son supposed to be on fire?"

I stifled a laugh. My mom rolled her eyes.

"It's—it's a thing," she said, waving her hand vaguely. "Is there a reason why you're here?"

"Yes, ma'am," he said, and thrust a wrapped scroll forward. The paper sparkled, and I recognized the scent of vanilla and snow from where I was standing. The scroll was wrapped in ribbons of lavender, teal, and pale blue that each ended with sparkling crystals. "I've been tasked with giving you this."

My mother took the scroll with two fingers like it would bite her. She sniffed, and her lip curled, like the scent of Heaven personally offended her. In that moment I was forcibly reminded that when I had filled my parents in on my adventures in the mortal realm, I had neglected to mention the side trip to Heaven. At the time, I'd figured I was in more than enough trouble as it was, and I was not willing to gamble that they would blame the seraphim more than me. Besides, my parents didn't need to know everything.

"Has something happened?" my dad asked from the entryway to the dining room. He crossed his arms and leaned against the doorway. "Is there a problem?"

"Oh, no," said the messenger, shaking his head. "It's not like that! It's for the whole family. It's a good thing!"

The messenger looked from face to face, eager to please.

I felt a little bad that I had messed with him, but it had been very gentle teasing, and I was sure things would only get worse as he went to his next stops.

"I do have more to deliver. . . ."

"Of course," Mom said. She shook her head and took a big breath, and then, with apparently great effort, she softened and even managed a smile. "Thank you."

"Oh!" The messenger seemed surprised, and then flushed a bright pink that reminded me of the shade I got when Lilith complimented my new looks. "I wasn't expecting—I mean—of course, you're welcome."

And then they just stared at each other in an awkward silence that made a laugh rise in my throat. I managed to squash it down, since bringing attention to myself would only make things more awkward. Especially since I had been not so subtly raising my pocket mirror to record the standoff.

"You can go," Mom said. "Unless there's something else?"

"Yes," said the messenger. "I mean, no, there's nothing. Right, goodbye."

He looked like he was trying to figure out how to leave the house without turning his back to us, and when he finally turned, I saw the bag hanging over his shoulder. Lavender and blue crystals dangled out of the opening in a way that reminded me of Morgan's salon and sparkling hooves.

I closed the door behind the angel and spun on the spot.
"What's it say?" I asked.

Dad looked over Mom's shoulder as she pulled at the
ribbons, but no matter which way she fidgeted at the ornate
ribbons, they just pulled tighter. Mom swore, pulled out a
blade, and cut the satin, sending crystals bouncing across
the floor.

"Aww," I said. "I could've done something with those."

"Crowley can fix them," she muttered, unfurling the scroll
in her hands. The scent of vanilla and lavender grew stronger,
and sparkling flakes of something rose from the scroll, disappearing as they went. A rainbow prism of lights reflected
over my parents' faces as they read.

"What does it say?" I asked. "C'mon, you've got to tell me.
He said it was for the whole family. That includes me."

"They can't be serious," Dad said.

"Well, it's not like there's not a need," Mom said, grimacing slightly.

"What does it say?" I asked. "Let me see. You can't tell me
that's work; I know it's not."

"It's not work," Mom agreed. "But . . . I'm not certain you
need to see it."

"That's not fair," I said. "That guy had an entire bag of
those things. Everyone is going to be talking about it. Dad,

what kind of leader can I be if I don't even know what's happening? Knowing is half the battle!"

It was a low blow, calling on duty. Mom might be totally able to ignore something like that, but I knew Dad wouldn't be.

"He's right," Dad said. "Everyone's going to know."

"Fine," Mom said. "But we don't even know if we'll be going, so don't get ahead of yourself."

She held the paper out to me, and I snatched it before they could change their minds.

The script was metallic gold, and fluttery and overly embellished, and I didn't even need to get to the word "mixer" to know that it had been written by Cassandra.

> *You are cordially invited to the gala of the millennia!*
> *In order to foster goodwill and create friendships that will last …*

In her first act of unforced rebellion, Cassandra, my attempted-kidnapper-turned-friend, had sent me a letter violating all sorts of rules for official interdimensional communication, claiming that she was trying to set up a get-together between Heaven and Hell. Never in a million years had I thought she would actually manage it.

"You are cordially invited," I said in a singsong voice. "That means me too, right?"

"I haven't heard anything about this yet," Mom said. "Which means that nothing is decided."

"What do you mean nothing is decided?" I asked. "We have to go! This is amazing."

"How is this amazing?" Dad asked. "We have jobs to do."

"Argh! But we can have vacations, too!"

"Didn't you already have one?" Dad raised his eyebrow.

"That's not fair," I said, pointing at him as respectfully as I could. "I've already been punished for that, so clean slate. And it should be noted that I did my job there, even though it wasn't even my job yet, and we never got our vacation time back. We just started school once he was safely back in his circle. Plus, I've been the perfect little soldier, going to my track without a fuss."

"Without a fuss?"

"With only a minuscule amount of fuss," I corrected. "Which is way more than you should have expected. This will be fun! And besides, the other side is a victim of their own propaganda. I wouldn't have had nearly as much trouble on Earth if Heaven knew what they were talking about."

"This isn't a decision *we* are making," Mom said. "I'm sure it's going to be the topic of conversation tomorrow, and the decision will come from the top."

31

"Isn't that you?" I asked.

"You know it's not," Mom said. "Come on, let's finish dinner."

The angelic messenger and sparkling scroll did a good job of distracting Dad from my new style, which was a plus. If it were up to him, my hair would be three inches shorter, and my clothes would be a field training uniform . . . every day. He had no idea what he was talking about when it came to fashion, but now he wasn't talking about it at all, which was even better.

As much as I tried to pry a commitment from Mom, she wasn't budging. I held my pocket mirror under the table and discreetly gestured with my fingers to send the video I had taken out to my squad. We were going to be talking about this.

I had fought hard against going to Heaven when Cassandra had been after us, but that had been when I was going to be kidnapped forever. But this? This was something else entirely. Poking around in another great hereafter without worrying about getting stuck? Oh yeah, we were doing this.

By the time I flew up to my room, my mirror was loaded with messages, and a full-blown conversation between my squad had started without me. Apparently, Mom wasn't the first one to have gotten the invite. Aleister had missed our accidental expedition to Heaven and was thrilled to get his chance to see it firsthand, and Lilith had all sorts of theories about what might have inspired the invitation. It wasn't until a fist against my door warned me to go to sleep or else that I put my mirror away. My friends' holograms vanished as I flashed them a sheepish look and closed my pocket mirror. My room immediately went dark.

An interdimensional mixer with Heaven.

This. Was. Amazing.

We were going to own the place.

# FOUR

I landed in front of my school the next morning with a burst of glamoured blue glory. The flames immediately retreated to their subtle flickering, but I had made my spectacular entrance, and really, wasn't that what mattered?

I flashed a smile and a wink at a couple of people and hiked my bag over my shoulder. A couple of the try-hards in my year rolled their eyes. Whatever. They didn't want to be like me? That was fine. I didn't want to be like them, either.

The truth was, the people I was closest to were my squad. I knew people in my track but hadn't really gotten to where I had any connections with them beyond knowing their faces. I missed seeking out Lilith or Aleister when I got to school.

Heck, even walking the halls with Crowley would have been welcome, but instead I just pretended I was so cool that I didn't need anyone else to hang out with.

With a shocking burst of insight, I realized that that was what Crowley typically did. Huh.

Well, I had the concert to look forward to, and an interdimensional party on my mind, so I figured I could get through the day without too much effort.

"That's pretty cool."

I turned, surprised at the sincere tone. Azael gestured to my wings and hair. "Did your magician do it?"

"No," I said. How had I never asked Crowley if this was something he was capable of? On the other hand, would I really trust Crowley with my appearance? Probably not. "But I should probably ask him if he can, now that I think about it. Morgan at Glamourie did it."

"Oh, the fae," he said. "Is that who's been changing your hair and doing the tattoo stuff?"

I hiked my bag up farther onto my shoulder. I hadn't realized Azael, or anyone else for that matter, had paid attention to my changing fashion. At least not beyond the first *Unholy night, what is he wearing?* reaction.

"Yeah, have you been?" I asked.

"Nah," Azael said. "I'm not sure my parents would let

me, and I wouldn't even know what to do."

"Yeah, my mom had her squad's Intelligence investigate before I could go," I said, rolling my eyes. "Dad still isn't convinced, but I think that has more to do with the look than any worry about danger. Morgan has good ideas even if you don't know what to do. The dragon tattoo I had a couple of weeks ago was their idea."

"The one that kept moving and transformed into a phoenix?" Azael asked. "That was cool."

"Yeah," I said, smiling. "I thought so too."

An ear-piercing siren rang out across the courtyard.

"I've got to go," Azael said. "I have Art of War. But the flames are cool too. Maybe not dragon cool, but, you know, cool."

"Thanks," I said.

Azael waved awkwardly, and I waved back, then set off across the courtyard through the swarm of my classmates moving to their various lectures. My chat with Azael meant I still hadn't hit my locker, and I didn't want to lug this bag all day. I slipped it off my shoulder to free my wings, and twisted my way between bodies. Once I was through the doorway, I started to fly.

"No flying in the hallways!" yelled a teacher.

"Watch it," snarled somebody else as I dropped to the floor as gracefully as possible.

"Sorry," I said.

"I know you," said the voice, and I turned. She was a carbon copy of most of the other students in my track, straitlaced and just slightly full of herself. Her hair was pulled back into a tight bun, and freckles stood out on her pale skin. "You let the prisoner loose."

I knew that people had heard about our adventures in Salem. It had certainly added to my cred in certain groups. But we had been cleared by the Powers That Be of any wrongdoing. Besides, I hadn't let him escape—I wasn't Parris's guard—but I *had* gotten him back. I was hardly to blame for his escape. But this girl I didn't even know certainly seemed to believe I was.

She leaned closer, a venomous expression on her face, and I leaned back with my upper body, trying to keep some distance. Her dark eyes flickered with a touch of flame.

"Some of us are onto you," she sneered.

"Onto what?" I asked, finally finding my voice. "It's called 'fashion.' I know you're not familiar—"

"*Fashion,*" she scoffed. "If you're trying to distract us or make us think you're a fool by dressing like that, it's not working. We know what you're doing. We know about Chaos."

The girl spun on the spot and left me standing stunned.

My classmate was a nutter.

# FIVE

In all honesty I was a bit shaken by being challenged, even though my classmate was clearly mental, and grossed out that some of her spit had ended up on my face.

Ugh!

I wiped my hand across my face and ruffled my wings. Okay, clearly she was a conspiracy theorist, and probably a complete outlier. I was still getting to know people in my new school, and I was willing to bet she had a reputation for being crazy. I just hadn't been here long enough to hear about it yet.

I took the last two steps to my black locker and pressed my palm to the surface. The runic variation of my name glowed bright red, and a small sound told me my locker had opened.

I pulled the door open and hung my backpack on the hook inside. I grabbed the notebook for my first class just as the second wail warned me that if I didn't move my butt, I'd be late to class. I slammed the locker shut, booked it to my first lecture of the day, and slid into my seat just as my teacher stood from his desk.

"Good morning," said Professor Jophiel. "As you remember, we were discussing the division of the great hereafters in the first expansion."

He swiped his hand across the mirror that covered a large portion of the wall at the front of the class, and with a few complicated hand gestures, the surface fogged and swirled. After a moment a map of the great hereafters took form. It was large and complicated, and my eye immediately went to Hell, and then to Heaven. But there was so much more to the map.

There were small offshoots and dimensions that overlapped or twisted between and around others. Still more that seemed unconnected on first view, but nothing in creation was really unconnected, so the way they interacted with the other great hereafters was more subtle. I wondered if I could steer the conversation to the invitation that had arrived at my house last night, but before I could speak, the image zoomed in further.

"Purgatory or the Gray is ruled by who?" asked the professor.

"Anubis," recited most of the class, while I said, "The Jackal."

"Correct," said Jophiel, though he raised his eyebrow at me before he continued in a much sterner-sounding tone. "I wouldn't call him 'Jackal' to his face. At least not until you're on much friendlier terms, not that I've ever heard of that happening."

I shifted in my seat as Jophiel maintained eye contact for an uncomfortably long period of time—okay, seriously, was he trying to read my mind?—before he turned his gaze away and resumed teaching in a more normal voice.

"Purgatory plays a key role in the judging and distribution of souls into their proper eternal homes. Before the establishment of Purgatory, the division was much less clear. Souls ended up in Heaven and brought chaos and ruin. Souls came to Hell, and the punishment of those not yet damned led to a destabilization in the energy inherent in keeping the balance between good and evil. As you all know, the balance is the be-all and end-all, the key to keeping everything in order. If the balance falls, Chaos will undoubtedly take its place as ruler, and chaos will reign."

The classroom remained silent. Jophiel gave one of those sweeps of the room that required every one of us to meet his eyes. It may have been my imagination, or paranoia from my weird encounter in the hall, or the recent stare-down, but it seemed like he held my gaze a bit longer than he did everyone else's.

This didn't help my anxiety. At. All. Did people really think I was up to something? Our names had been fully cleared, but I was starting to get the feeling that some of my fellow hellions didn't agree with the decision. People didn't really think I helped Parris, did they?

Nah, I was being paranoid because of that weird girl.

My stomach twisted uneasily as my teacher directed his attention back to the mirror. He made an intricate gesture, and scenes of Purgatory flashed across the surface. The scales, a feather, gray swirling auras of ghostly souls, a door of flames and a door of white, and then the images stopped on a slender hound head, large, with pointed ears, and eyes that even on this false image looked as if they were seeing through us. He was wearing the traditional golden snake headpiece and holding a staff that I knew channeled his power.

"Why was Anubis selected?" asked Jophiel.

More silence.

"Did we just need someone there?" Jophiel pressed. "Draw straws? What?"

I lifted my hand from my desk, just high enough that if he didn't call on me, it wouldn't be obvious that I had volunteered. After all, I wasn't 100 percent on this.

"Malachi," Jophiel called, taking a seat on the edge of his desk.

"Anubis has the gift of pure sight," I said softly at first, but when my teacher didn't make a *Dear Lucifer, are you stupid* look, my voice grew a bit stronger. "He's not swayed by artifice or glamour and isn't convinced by sympathy or bribery, so he always judges true."

"Very good," Jophiel said, and he actually looked impressed. "Purgatory is an essential part of the system. It's also the part that would be most susceptible to influence, *if* Anubis was not in charge. Thankfully, we don't have to worry about that."

Class continued, and I managed to sail on the high of grudging approval from my teacher, rather than being brought down by the dread that he and maybe a bunch of others thought I was a bad guy.

But I was surprised that there was no mention of the invitations. Was it possible that I was the only one who knew about them? Maybe it was just my squad who was invited. After all, we personally knew Cassandra. Did she think we were the only ones who lived here?

No, that messenger had had a whole bag of invitations.

Was it possible that my classmates were just rule-following try-hards and wouldn't bring it up because it wasn't on the syllabus? That was a very real possibility.

I considered that as I tossed my books back into my locker and headed for lunch. The dining hall was in the center of the academic complex. There were six separate stone archways that brought all of the various hallways into the main dining area, and I entered through one of them and looked around.

The room was already swarming with my fellow students, and unlike my old dining hall, with one food station that we all impatiently lined up at, this hall gave us a choice of stations. It was my favorite part of my new track, and while not as good as the food at Faust's, my favorite café, it was a decent substitute.

What went well with hidden secrets? Hmm . . . barbecue.

I joined the line, which moved quickly, and selected from steaming trays that smelled sweet and spicy and vaguely mysterious.

I grabbed my now full tray and pretended I knew exactly where I was going, like I was on a mission to join up with friends. Instead I ended up at the same corner table I had been sitting at since school had started.

Alone. As usual.

I hadn't been here long enough to make new friends to sit with, but it had apparently been long enough for me to develop a routine.

Ugh, I was boring and unpopular. This was a new feeling

for me, and my mind was starting to reel from the injustice of it when a voice interrupted my thoughts.

"Is it okay if I sit here?"

I looked up, and for the second time that day I was looking at Azael. Was I giving off neediness vibes? Or just looking extra cool today? Probably a toss-up.

"Here?" I asked, eloquently. "Oh, yeah, sure."

"Thanks," Azael said. "I haven't really figured out who's, you know . . . not . . . so *intense*, but a friend of mine said one of your friends was pretty cool, so . . ."

"Yeah," I agreed, knowing exactly what he was trying to say. "A lot of them are a bit . . . much. Was it that friend you were with at Frozen Over? My friend Aleister said he knew her."

"Yeah, it was. She thought you might be worth talking to," Azael said, smiling sheepishly. "No offense. It's that people here can be . . . I mean, I don't think it's everyone. I just haven't figured out who's who yet."

"Tell me about it," I agreed. "It can be a little . . ." Lonely.

I almost asked him if he ever thought the universe had gotten things wrong. That he was really supposed to be something else, *anything* else. But even as I thought it, I wasn't entirely convinced of that anymore.

If working with my squad to capture Parris had taught me anything, it was that as much as I wanted to fight it, I did have some inherent take-charge tendencies. Did Azael? I hadn't even realized what his designation was until we had started the school year.

But I didn't want to risk sitting alone at lunch forever. So instead of asking anything too serious, I took an overly big bite of my barbecue sandwich.

"What is this?" I muttered. "And how is it so good?"

"Don't know," Azael said. "Best not to think about it."

I made a noncommittal noise and then, reaching for something safe to say, asked, "How's the wing?"

"Better," he said. "The healers say I can take the sling off today if my appointment goes well."

"You'll be able to fly again?" I asked.

"Eventually," he said, grimacing. "It might take a while, though."

That made sense. Was this boring? Was I boring?

"Hey," I said, debating on whether or how to even ask. But I swore that if I didn't get to talk about Heaven, I was going to scream. "Did you have any . . . visitors last night?"

"Sidney—the girl I was with at the ice cream place—came over," he said innocently. "Why?"

"Oh, uh, just wondering."

Cassandra knew there were other people in Hell, right? I was fairly sure she did, but now I had been quiet for too long and it was getting awkward, and Azael was never going to sit with me again. *Think, brain, think. Conversation, you can do it.*

"Is Sidney your girlfriend?" I asked.

Azael started coughing, and frantically grabbed the cider in front of him. He chugged it down and took a deep breath before shooting me a look. "What?"

"Sidney," I said, starting to doubt whether this was the safe topic I had thought it was. "Is she your—"

"No, brimstone, no!" Azael protested. "She's just a friend!"

"Okay," I said, holding my hands up in surrender. "My bad."

"No, sorry," Azael said. He took another sip of his drink and sighed heavily. "It's not your fault. Everyone thinks that."

"Well, Beliel anyway," I said, referencing our former classmate who had been sentenced to fifty years under the Styx for attacking Azael.

"Beliel's an idiot," Azael said, and for the first time since I had met him, there was a spark of fire in his eyes. "You heard about that, huh?"

"Everyone heard about that," I scoffed.

"Well, there never seem to be any secrets here," Azael said, with a smirk nowhere near as good as mine. More like Smirk 101, but still respectable. "You know what that's like."

"Tell me about it," I said, rolling my eyes. Across the room

I saw the girl who had accosted me earlier, and I gestured with my chin. "Do you know who that is?"

"Who?" Azael asked, turning in his seat. "The one with the dark hair?"

"Yeah," I said. "Freckles, murdery eyes."

"Um, yeah, I think her name is Rachel."

"Do you know if she has any sort of reputation, like, I don't know . . . prone to conspiracy theories?"

"No," Azael said. "Pretty sure she's head of the third-year class. Why?"

"Huh," I said. "No reason."

Over the course of lunch, I learned that Azael had broken his wing playing Red Rover; he had known Sidney since they were tiny, and they were best friends; and although he knew the members of his future squad, he hadn't really connected with any of them enough to be friends. Sidney was assigned to another squad entirely. I also learned that he had a long history with Beliel and was ecstatic that he wouldn't have to deal with him for another fifty years.

I tried hinting around, but if he knew anything about the mixer in Heaven, he didn't give any signs, and despite what Azael thought about secrets being public knowledge, there were parts of our adventure known only to my squad.

By the time lunch was over, I had come to the solid

conclusion that I was thankfully not the only person in my school who wasn't a complete stiff.

The rest of the day dragged in the way that only happens when you have something to look forward to when you're done. And it dragged even longer when the group project we were assigned in our last period got stuck in a spiral because no one would agree to anyone else's idea.

"Can we just pick one?" I growled. "Throw a dart or something. Draw it out of a bag, whatever."

"That wouldn't show very good leadership skills," said Uriel.

"Exactly," argued Zachariah. "Which is why I say we use my idea, if you know what's good for yourself."

"Force. An excellent leadership skill," I said with strained patience. "The idea is to get us to work together as a team. You know, like, actually listen and take input from other people."

I could have sworn I saw the teacher smirk at that, but maybe she was just enjoying my misery. I got the impression that Professor Ruth enjoyed misery.

"Fine, we should follow my idea," said group member number three with a crew cut, whose name I hadn't bothered to learn yet. "The origin of the Dominion Accord."

"That's boring," I said.

And the yelling started again.

# SIX

Eventually the day ended, like they typically do, with zero progress toward group unity, but that was a problem for future Mal. Current Mal was home at last, and had a concert to get ready for! I checked myself out in the mirror in my room, and ruffled my hair with some gel, making it artfully messy in that way that looks like it took no effort at all but actually takes a lot. I gave it one final flick, and the blue flames flared for just a moment before they settled.

I had on my newest Nephilim T-shirt, with the image from their last holovid front and center. The flames on my wings matched the blue highlights on the shirt. My hair was finally perfect, and when I slapped some bracelets onto my wrist, I was ready for the concert.

"Going to the concert!" I yelled as I soared down the stairs.

"Hold up!" yelled Dad.

I groaned and dropped my head in defeat. My hand on the doorknob, so close to freedom.

"Yes?" I asked innocently.

"Don't *yes* me," Dad said. "You know the drill. Where are you going? Who is going to be there? When will you be back?"

"Choirs of Hell, everyone, later."

"Try again," Dad said, looking unimpressed at my brevity.

"Dad, I'm going to be late!" I groaned.

"Then you'd better hurry," Dad said.

"The Nephilim concert in the alley next to COH. Everyone from my squad will be there, plus everyone with any musical taste. Concert starts at five p.m. There will be crappy opening bands and then the good opening band and then the actual band. I'll fly home after."

"Which will be when?"

"I don't know," I said. "Later."

"Counteroffer," said Dad. "You will message me when the concert is done, and I will meet you there."

"Dad!" I objected, groaning loudly and thumping my

head against the door. I might as well just bring my stuffie, if my dad was going to fly me home.

"I thought you were going to be late," Dad said lightly. Jerk.

"Counter counteroffer," I said, spinning around from the door. "I will message you when it's finished and fly part of the way with Aleister, and then fly the two blocks home from there. If I'm not back at a reasonable time, you can release the search party."

Dad considered. "Counter counter-counteroffer. You will message me at nine p.m. whether the concert is over or not."

"Deal," I said.

"Have fun," Dad called, and by the time the door swung shut behind me, I was already airborne.

I dropped down at the corner of Perdition and Hellfire. I had made good time even with Dad's desire to parent, and I wanted to enjoy the excitement of a good show that was already spreading across Perdition Boulevard like the very best kind of contagion.

This was my favorite area of my hometown, and it was currently decorated with ivy and holly for Yule. It was the shopping district of the cool. Faust's and its amazing apple cider donuts; Burn This Book with its extensive comic section and comfy reading areas; Frozen Over, our current hangout; and of course Glamourie on its newly appeared corner.

As if those things weren't enough of a selling point, Choirs of Hell and the alleyway where they put on the best concerts in all of Hades was right in the middle.

A new art installation had taken root recently over the pedestrian area. There were paper dragons arched over the cobbled streets so that walking down the sidewalk was like walking under a canopy. One artist had positioned the dragon's head to hold the flame streetlamp in its mouth. They were each moving subtly so that the rustle of paper was continuous, but as I got closer and closer to the music shop and the stage in the alley, the sound of excited voices became more prevalent, until the rustle of the dragons above was too quiet to hear.

"Mal! Mal! Over here. MAL!"

It took me a second to find where the voice was coming from, but then Aleister took wing and hovered over the crowd, waving his hand frantically while screaming my name, and that was kind of hard to miss. He was making such a scene, I almost wanted to pretend I didn't know who he was, but then Aleister would only get louder and louder, so I waved in acknowledgment and felt my face get red in response. Thank malice, Crowley yanked Aleister's foot to the ground, so I didn't have to die of embarrassment.

People were still standing in their own groups, loosely filling out the alley between Choirs of Hell and Burn This

Book. I knew that when the band appeared, the crowd would move closer to the stage, but at the moment everyone was just enjoying hanging out with their various groups. This wasn't my first concert, but I hadn't been to enough for the novelty to wear off.

Besides the stage at the end of the alleyway, there were booths set up selling merch for each of the bands, stands for food and drinks, and one that was selling magic trinkets that would send fireworks or noise into the air.

There was a booth on my right that immediately attracted my attention with smoking drinks and rising flames, and sparkling swirls of magic. I stared for just a moment before turning away from my friends and slipping over, in between a couple of much larger bodies.

I reached a hand out, a swirling liquid galaxy in a fancy glass within my grasp, before a clawed hand pushed it away.

"Not a chance, kid," growled the oni at the counter.

"Come on, Enko!" I said, recognizing the oni from his normal job at Burn This Book. "Be cool!"

"You're supposed to use that one," growled Enko, gesturing with a head nod to a nearby tent crowded with kids. I could see tails being stepped on from here, and there was no way I was letting my feathers get near a litter of bast tweens.

Our split this year into our different tracks may have been

new, but it wasn't the first separation we had gone through. When I'd first started school, it had been a mix of everyone who lived in Hades, not just the angels who lived there. It had only been a few years since I'd started attending school with just my black-feathered brethren, but apparently it was long enough for me not to recognize anyone at the kid tent.

"Come on," I whined. "Look at that mess. Don't make me go over there."

The oni glared at me, but when he took a deep breath, I knew I had won. I smiled broadly. "I have three friends."

The drinks didn't have the same depth and sparkle to them without whatever it was they were putting in them for the adults, but I didn't care. They were awesome. I pulled coins from my dwindling allowance out of my pocket and put them on the bar.

"Thanks, Enko!"

I juggled the four drinks in my arms and, amazingly enough, made it through the waiting crowds to my friends without spilling any on my awesome T-shirt. Although, there had been a near miss when a gremlin had decided to dart between my legs on its way to cause trouble.

"Who's the best?" I asked triumphantly.

"Are those real?" Aleister asked incredulously.

"Don't be ridiculous," I said, handing him one.

Crowley made a show of looking to where the younger kids were embarrassing themselves at the food tent, and then looked back at me, raising an eyebrow.

"Please," I scoffed. "I have my ways. Now thank me for spending my hard-earned allowance on your ungrateful butt."

"Thank you, dear leader," Crowley mocked.

"Thanks!" Lilith chirped, and then kissed me on the cheek. My face grew blazing hot, and I knew it was an embarrassing shade of red. Which, of course, was the exact reason why she did that stuff. To torture me. Because Lilith was evil, perfect and evil.

"Stop it," I grumbled, not meaning it for a second.

A kiss on the cheek was worth Crowley's snicker. And okay, yeah, maybe stopping the embarrassing part would be nice, but a part of me was relieved that the teasing and the torment hadn't changed even though we weren't at the same school anymore.

We finished our swirling galaxy drinks and tossed the cups into a nearby bin, which erupted with a sudden whoosh of purple-tinted flames, moments before the whine of a guitar called everyone forward in a huge press of bodies. My glamoured wings flared where people touched, and several people jumped back in response. I laughed. Crowley shook his head but took advantage of the space to move forward.

Sure, we could take to the sky and watch from above, and as I looked up, I noticed several adults who had done exactly that, sitting on the seats high above the alley. But I liked being on the ground close to the stage. It made me feel like part of the crowd, like we were all in this together.

Lilith grabbed my hand and pulled me even closer toward the stage, and I jerked my eyes down, noticing a gap in front of us that hadn't been there before.

I wasn't sure who the opening band was, but I recognized the guitarist from the skate park and was pretty sure she lived on the street behind me. That wasn't too shocking. The first band was usually local. The claws on her hand were painted red and silver, and when they plucked the strings, they sent swirls of sparks into the air. I wondered if it was Morgan's work or if it was the guitar itself. Maybe it was her own magic?

The drummer let loose, and the sound thumped in my chest like a second heartbeat. The lead singer didn't have the best voice, but what she lacked in ability she made up for in energy, and her tail thrashed along to the melody.

"That was awesome!" Lilith yelled as soon as the band took its final bow.

Since there was more to come, we did our best to keep our spots. We took turns getting snacks during the teardown and the setup for the next band, which took forever because apparently that's how long it takes to stand around an empty stage and position things just so, so that most of us were still guarding our spots as we waited for the main act itself.

Anytime there was an opening, we'd edge forward just a bit, and by the time the second opener, the Dark Knights, had finished performing, not only did I have a new favorite band but we had slunk our way into a spot an arm's length from the stage. Crowley was getting water when a hard shove sent me tumbling into Lilith, who jostled into Aleister, who thankfully stopped us from falling.

"What the heck!" I turned on the spot, to see sickly yellow eyes in an enormous, angry face.

"Out of the way," snorted the orc, raising his head and trying to look tougher than he was. His tusks almost reached my hair, he was standing so close. Rude.

"I don't think so," I scoffed. "We were here first."

"Well, we're here now."

Oh goodie, the orc had friends. Teenagers that were bigger than us with wispy beards, and disproportionate horns, and zero fashion sense.

"Congratulations," Lilith said, rolling her eyes. "You made it."

Muscle-head's reptilian friend flicked a forked tongue out, almost touching my face, and I leaned back in disgust. "This is our spot now," he said.

"No way," said Aleister.

The orc shoved me with a hand like a sledgehammer. My wings expanded as I tried to keep my footing. There were some complaints from the nearby concertgoers, and I felt a few feathers bend even as the glamoured flames flared at the contact. My eyes lit with unholy fire.

Who did this guy think he was? Besides, COH concerts always had security. This could really only go so far before someone bigger and stronger—and with an actual right to tell people what to do—would send these guys packing. We just needed to hold off until then.

The stage crew for Nephilim was almost finished, and the noise from the sound check made a wave of excitement wash across the crowd.

"What is your problem?" I asked the biggest one. "You should have gotten here sooner if you wanted to be closer."

"And you should just take to the sky, feathers," Muscle-head said. He puffed out his chest like this was the height of wit. "You're taking up ground space. You birds think you're so much better than us, huh?"

"Yes," said Crowley. "Better than you? Certainly. Smarter, cleaner, smell better . . . I could go on, but why don't you just *go on*. Over there." Crowley made an imperious wave like their presence didn't matter at all. This dismissal was epically cool and also, at the same time, horrifically bad.

Muscle-head's group of friends apparently took offense at, well, all of that, and while the sound check ramped up and the crowd surged forward, our would-be bullies tried to displace us. Fighting the surge of the crowd while keeping our own position close to the stage and fighting off these power-hungry teenagers was much harder than attending a fun concert should be.

And they were being so obnoxious!

Why couldn't everyone just come here for the music? Why did I have to deal with idiots who still thought powers belonged near the Pit, away from all the other residents? We were as much a part of the community here as anyone else.

I jerked my elbow away from clawed hands, but when I went to make my own move, suddenly there was nothing in front of me.

"Break it up," snapped the security guard who had pulled Muscle-head away from me. "Don't make us rethink these all-ages shows. C'mon, guys, behave yourselves."

The guard glared at all of us, me and my squad included, which, come on, what?

"We just want to watch the show," I protested.

"Watch it from up there!" snarled the orc. He turned to another security guard. "They can watch from up there. Why are they allowed to take our spaces?"

"Your spaces? We were here first," Lilith said. Her arms

crossed over her chest. "We bought tickets, and this is our neighborhood too."

A bubble of open space had formed around us with the arrival of the security guards, but I knew it wouldn't last. And I really wanted to see this show. They wouldn't really listen to these morons, would they?

"Were they here first?" asked the guard.

"What does that matter?" asked Muscle-head's reptilian friend. "They can watch from up there. We can't."

"That doesn't matter," said the guard. "You can't just force them to move. Behave yourselves or you'll be out."

"You're going to side with *them*?" spat Muscle-head, yanking his arm out of the guard's grip.

The other guard leveled a suspicious glare in our direction. "Any more trouble, and you're out too."

I rustled my wings, trying to shake off the negativity that had ruined my good mood. It didn't happen often. Hades was a pretty cool place to live. It was artistic and modern, and I had always thought that the great thing about living here was that we rarely dealt with idiots who thought us being angels meant that we didn't belong.

Rarely, but not never.

Brimstone. I had been looking forward to this concert all week.

"Don't worry about it," said Aleister. "They're idiots. C'mon, it's starting. Shake it off, bro!"

I took a deep breath and let it out. I looked at my friends. Crowley looked pissed, and Lilith had a pinch to her expression that meant she hadn't shaken it off either.

But then Nephilim took the stage.

The audience roared, howled, and screeched in excitement, and that was hard to ignore. A shiver went up my spine in the best possible way. I loved this band, and I was finally getting to see them live and in person. When Cain took the stage, my knees tried to buckle, and my heart raced, and my stomach twisted, because, unholy night! That was Cain. Right there! In person! Aleister was right. Screw those guys.

By the end of the first song, I had forgotten all about our run-in with Muscle-head and friends. The excitement from before was back, and then some. This was shaping up to be one of the best nights ever!

My shirt was sticking to my skin by the time Nephilim took their "final" bow, which everyone knows isn't really the final bow. As the band left the stage, I looked at the instruments significantly left behind, and then exchanged wide grins with my squad.

The noise became deafening. Rising and rising until the stomping, clapping, howling, and chanting was all there was.

Some people had purchased the fireworks and noisemakers and had clearly been waiting for just this moment to let them explode. Sparks flew. The band let the noise carry on, and then the lights that were draped across the top of the alley walls and around the stage began flashing in time with the chants of "Nephilim! Nephilim!"

Finally, when I thought the surrounding buildings would collapse from the noise, Nephilim retook the stage in an explosion of fireworks and smoke. The chanting changed to screams and applause, and the band members wore enormous smiles as they reclaimed their instruments.

"Okay, okay," said Cain. "I suppose we can do a couple more. I think you know this one, and if you do, I expect you to sing along."

With a quick drumbeat and a wail of Seth's guitar, Nephilim started playing "Jabberwocky," their most popular song.

"Yes!" I yelled, and even with the band playing loudly and joyously, my friends heard me and smiled in my direction.

"Like they weren't going to play it," said Crowley beside me, and I just shrugged and grinned and turned my attention back to the stage.

At first I thought it was the music, or the crowd. Maybe there were loose cobblestones that made a bad combination with the dancing of too many excited people. But the rumbling became too much to ignore. The singing dropped off first, and then the guitar fell silent. The drums stopped a moment later, but the rumbling didn't. Murmurs and grumbles of confusion rose, and the ground shook, and continued shaking until it was hard to keep our balance. A curse came over the loudspeaker as Cain almost fell.

"Clear the area!" security ordered, their voices magically amplified, and for several confusing moments people didn't seem to know which way to go.

Sure, this was an alley, with the stage blocking one end and the only other way out behind us, but there were booths of merchandise scattered around, and ropes where ticket checks had happened, and people were slow to move in an organized manner. We exchanged glances, gave quick nods of agreement, and once our wings had the room to move, we took to the sky.

The ones who had been watching the show from their perches were in the air, as were many more who had decided the easiest way out was up. From up here the only signs that the ground was shaking were the stumbling of people below; the aggressive waving of tree branches; and other hanging objects like flags, paper dragons, and lights being jerked to and fro.

But *why* was the ground shaking? That didn't happen here, and I couldn't help thinking of the time I had felt the ground shake in Salem when a juiced-up Parris had made the dead rise. Had Parris gotten out? Had someone else? Someone stronger this time?

I looked frantically beyond our neighborhood to the flames and distant areas to search for any sign that trouble was brewing like before, but the fence was its normal height, and the flames were low just like every day. If there was something going wrong in the Pit, or some other cosmic threat to us, the security measures would have sent the flames and the fence skyward to protect the residents of Hell. Looking to the horizon, everything appeared normal.

I don't know what it was that made me look up. The sky should have been a solid, cozy black. It wasn't quite. There was no big adjustment to the level of light or a dramatic display of *different*, but where there should have been nothing but black, there were instead swirls of deep olive green and gold. What was that?

The flap of large wings moved my attention back to our airspace, which was rapidly getting more crowded. If I didn't start paying attention, I was going to be making an unpleasant landing.

"C'mon," I said, calling out over the noise to my friends.

Most people who had the option had left the ground far behind, and there were too many people for us to fly easily.

We swooped and swerved around other people as we made our way out of the alley, and found a relatively open space to land in next to the circular fountain nearby.

By the time we hit the ground, the shaking had stopped. I looked up and tried to see through the crowded sky, but I could barely make out the blackness at the top, never mind anything weird. Leathery black wings swooped to the left, and through the gap left behind I could see sky that looked . . . completely normal. Black and cozy, just like it was supposed to be.

"What just happened?" I asked.

"Magic gone wrong?" asked Aleister, and we all turned our attention to Crowley, who looked deep in thought. "I've never felt the ground shake."

"I have," Crowley said darkly, and we exchanged significant looks. "I suppose it could have been a magic mishap, but I don't know."

"Something from the Pit?" asked Lilith, clearly worrying about the same thing I had been. "Demonic energy?"

"No way," said Aleister. "The Pit is spirit-tight. Nothing comes out. I mean, besides that Parris mess. There are serious mystical barriers that I'm still not totally clear on, plus a bunch of other levels of protection in place to keep any demonic stuff in there. It wouldn't affect us."

"Maybe my mom will know," Lilith said.

"You can ask her now," I said, nodding to a frantically searching woman who I recognized from the millions of times we had all piled into Lilith's house to hang out. Her hair was in a ponytail instead of her typical bun, and . . . was that a tie-dyed T-shirt? And . . . pajama pants?

"Oh, brimstone," Lilith said, going even paler than normal. "What is she wearing?"

"Lily!" yelled Lilith's mom, rushing to us through the crowd. "Are you okay?"

"Mother," Lilith said, horror clear in her voice. "What are you wearing?"

"Oh, Lily," Lilith's mom groaned. "Really. It was my night off. You know that."

"You couldn't have changed first?"

"C'mon, *Lily*," I teased. "It was her night off."

Lilith shot me a glare, but Aleister and Crowley snickered, so I took it for a win.

"Are you all okay?" Lilith's mom asked.

"Yes, ma'am," said Aleister.

Crowley and I nodded in agreement.

"What *was* that?" I asked.

"That's what I'm going to find out," Lilith's mother said. Even standing there with her tie-dyed shirt and fluffy pajama pants, she looked strict and intimidating. She was Lucifer's right hand, after all.

And in moments, Lilith's mom wasn't the only parent we had to deal with.

"Mal," said my dad, looking frazzled as he approached the decorative half wall where we were still gathered. "Are you okay?"

"All good," I said. "But this was not the plan."

"Plans change," Dad said wryly.

I would have objected to him coming out to get me like I was a baby, but it was honestly a nice change of pace to see him worried instead of irritated. Plus, unlike Lilith's mom, he was fully dressed, so I had that going for me too.

"Hale, any idea what that was?" asked Dad. Lilith's mom's name was Haylel, but I had never heard anyone call her that.

"I'm not sure yet," said Lilith's mom. "But I see a meeting in my future. Oh, for the loathe of . . ."

She pulled out her pocket mirror and waved Lilith along as she started talking. I wondered if she'd go to Lucifer's office in slippers.

"Bye, guys," Lilith said, waving over her shoulder as she followed her mom.

"Boys," Dad announced. "You're all coming with me."

Aleister and Crowley exchanged glances and then shrugged.

"Wait!" I said, after pushing myself off the edge of the wall where I had been sitting.

"What? Do you see something?" Dad asked, suddenly on alert.

"Well," I said, glancing at the sky without meaning to. "No, but that's kinda my point. Everything is fine and so, you know, there's no real reason to rush home, and I didn't have time to buy a T-shirt."

"A T-shirt," Dad said flatly.

"Or maybe a bracelet," I said.

We stared at each other in silence.

"I could use a new travel mug," Aleister said.

"I think I saw some journals," Crowley said thoughtfully. "I could use one for class."

"Something unknown just happened to our world, and you want to buy souvenirs," my father said, staring at us all in disbelief.

I looked back at the merchandise tables. After some hesitation, the sellers did seem to be getting back into the groove. They straightened items that had fallen, and when the security guards didn't stop them, fans started buying.

"Pleeeaaaassse," I said.

Minutes later we were making our purchases, while my dad updated the parental units with his pocket mirror. No doubt reassuring Aleister's and Crowley's parents that we hadn't been crushed by falling buildings; we were just struggling to decide between the black design with the red highlights and the purple design with the green highlights.

"All set," I announced as we carried our Nephilim merch back to my dad.

Once everything had settled down and nothing had rattled again, people had gone back to doing what they'd normally be doing after an epic concert. Music started back up in the alley, and I was pretty sure a DJ was going to be playing there later. Unless the ground decided to quake and the sky decided to have a crisis, it looked like the show would go on.

Some people went into restaurants nearby. Others went into Choirs of Hell or made their way over to the food stands, which had started cooking food and pouring drinks once again. I even thought I saw Morgan talking animatedly to someone in a long black cloak, but the space was so crowded with people and carts and tents that when I did a double check, I couldn't find them again.

If it weren't for a few flags hanging askew, one paper dragon art piece that looked like it had decided to climb down the pole it was attached to, and the fact that instead of scattering across the area, the security guards were grouped together deep in conversation, you would never have known anything had happened at all.

In fact, as we flew back to where our streets converged, we excitedly compared notes about the amazingness of the concert, and all the weirdness, and wondering about what had caused it, were easily outweighed by the excitement of having seen one of my favorite bands live.

Unholy night! I had actually been within ten feet of Cain? How was this my life?

# SEVEN

Mom met us where our street diverged with Crowley's, and even though everyone but my parents thought my friends would have been perfectly fine flying the rest of the way themselves, Dad accompanied Crowley to his house, while Mom and I took a detour to bring Aleister straight to his door like we were fledglings on a playdate.

We took it as seriously as it warranted and giggled and swatted at each other the entire way, like we'd done when we were little and our parents had made us be friends so they could hang out with each other.

"Thanks for playing, Mal!" Aleister said after we touched down. He waved his entire hand, fast and chaotic, so that his wings rustled. I did the same thing. My mother sighed.

"Mom, can Al come play tomorrow?" I hopped up and down on my feet, flapping my wings out of sync so that I barely left the ground.

"I promise to be really good!" Aleister said, jumping as well.

"All right, you two, say goodbye," Mom said, unimpressed with our antics.

"Bye," I said in my normal voice.

"See ya," Aleister said. "Thanks, *Mom.*"

"No wandering off," she said, pointing at him in a warning gesture.

"Of course not," he said. "*I* stay home like a good boy."

Aleister's mom opened their front door, and Damien came bounding out from where he had no doubt been lunging at the door. Aleister's mom leaned against the doorway and waved.

"Not helpful," I said under my breath, and kicked Aleister casually for good measure, before he headed into his house.

I didn't need him reminding my mom why I had been grounded forever. I smiled innocently, and she pinched the bridge of her nose with her thumb and forefinger. I petted Damien, and Aleister whistled, calling the hound to follow him back to his house.

"You're sure you're okay?" Mom asked when we were finally alone.

"Ugh," I groaned. "Of course I'm fine. It was a little rumble. Didn't you hear how amazing the concert was?"

"Sounds like you had fun, but the ground doesn't just *rumble* here," Mom said.

"Maybe it does now," I said, and knew immediately that that was very, very wrong. At Mom's disbelieving look I shrugged and smiled. "Concert was awesome."

Mom laughed, which meant I'd won. "So I heard."

Once we got home, I brought my merch up to my room, but after a few minutes of enjoying post-consumer bliss, my curiosity got the better of me. What had caused the shaking? Was I the only one who had noticed the wrong-color sky? It hadn't lasted long, and Mom and Dad hadn't mentioned it. Neither had my squad, although I hadn't asked. How far had everything extended? Was it just Hades, or had all of Hell quaked? Had it been centered over us, or was I just being self-centered?

And in a literal face-slapping moment, I realized I had finally had my squad together and we hadn't even discussed the invite to Heaven! I hadn't even pressed Mom for an update! I debated going out and asking, but my dad had just closed the front door behind him, and even though I could probably sweet-talk Mom, it wasn't likely that she'd tell me, with Dad there saying, *He doesn't need to know that, Chay. He should just do what he's told, blah, blah, blah.*

I pulled out my pocket mirror, and then thought better of it. Communication with my squad had gone super stealth during our nearly eternal grounding, and while I wasn't sure what was happening yet, this all had the feeling of the start of . . . something. It was best to be discreet.

I tossed my mirror onto my bed and pulled open the drawer to my desk. I grabbed a piece of paper and scribbled at the top, *Tomorrow. Noon meet-up! Location?* I lit the candle on my desk and held the note over the flame. It burned bright and disappeared in a puff of spice-scented smoke. I lay back on my bed and waited. A flare of light made me turn my head, and I reached out to catch the falling paper in my open hand. Lilith's bright green script scrolled across the page: *My place.*

Noon came way too soon after a long night of watching holovids of Nephilim and the Dark Knights and searching for info on the local band that had opened the show. I yawned and dragged myself out of bed. I stared at the insides of my dresser drawers, taking way too long to pick out clothes, before I grabbed the things on top and decided that was good enough.

"He lives," said Dad as I flew down the stairs and landed clumsily in the kitchen.

"Nope," I said. "This is all your imagination."

"Well, that's a relief," said Dad. "That means you're not really wearing that."

"Ha, ha." I looked down. Purple shirt, lime-green pants. I shrugged. It worked. "I'm heading to Lilith's."

"Eat something before you go," said Dad.

He never gave me a hard time when I wanted to go to Lilith's. Probably had to do with who her mom was and that he thought Lilith was a good influence on me. Although, that opinion had taken a dent when he'd realized Lilith had gone mortal-side too and hadn't done the responsible thing and told her mom about the wild opening. Eventually that became my fault too, but for one blissful second Lilith had taken some of the blame.

"Where's Mom?" I asked.

"Meeting," Dad said. "She'll be back later."

"K," I said. I didn't bother asking for information. He wouldn't give it to me anyway, and since I was on my way to Lilith's, I was hoping to get better info there. I shoved a muffin into my mouth and mumbled what could generously be called a goodbye . . . if you were feeling especially generous.

Lilith's house was a short walk and an even shorter flight. Normally on a day like today with nothing on the schedule and a beautiful breeze in the air I would have walked, and enjoyed the scurrying leaves, but I was very nearly going to be late, so I flew.

I couldn't help my gaze drifting upward, but the sky was

its normal black. In fact, everything looked normal. The flames were their normal height, the fence was down, most trees swayed in the breeze while others jerked with a little more intentional movement from whatever was crawling on them. Sky traffic was light, but ground traffic was normal.

So, the ground had rumbled? Big deal. Everything was normal now. A magician probably screwed up a spell. It was no reason to ruin an encore.

Wait a minute.

I dove to the ground.

"Hey," I yelled. I wasn't sure why he was over in this neighborhood, and it didn't matter. "Tony!"

"Aahh!" he screamed, and then spun around to face me. Once he realized it was me, he sighed in relief. "Oh, it's just you, kid. Gonna give a guy heart attack here."

"It would serve you right," I said. "You ripped me off."

"I did not such thing!" he said.

"That spark of creation was fake," I said.

"I don't know anything about that," he said. "We made a deal and I got you what you wanted."

"It. Wasn't. Real," I said, feeling like I was pointing out an obvious problem.

"Look," Tony said, looking over his shoulder. "Quality varies in my line of work. Sorry it wasn't what you expected, but I gotta go. Come by Alighieri's. I got some new games in, I'll toss you a couple for free. Okay?"

"Fine," I scoffed. "But the deal's off."

And this time Tony did look right at me. "Deals are never off, kid."

"Yeah, whatever," I said, rolling my eyes. "I have to go. Hold those games for me."

I took to the air again and watched Tony scurry away, looking over his shoulder again. Dude was weird.

# EIGHT

I landed on the sidewalk outside Lilith's house. Her mom
had all sorts of plants she had spent her time cultivating,
including moonstone moss on the sides of the walkway, which
glowed purple, blue, and green. Unfortunately, it didn't like
being landed on, or landed close to, or bothered in any way.
We had come down on it a few times when we were young, and
our landings had not been overly graceful, and a new rule had
been established and firmly enforced: we were to land on the
sidewalk and walk with "careful feet" to the house. The rule still
stood, even though we were now way too old for "careful feet."

Okay, maybe there was the one time last year when a game
got a little heated and a couple of plants may have gotten a

tiny bit pressed, but really, banning us all to the sidewalk was a bit much. I mean, the plants got better. Eventually.

I knocked on Lilith's door and walked in without waiting for an answer. I was only a little late, so even though everyone was there, they were still grabbing drinks and otherwise milling around.

"Ugh, what is all this, Lil?" Aleister asked, his head in the fridge. "Why don't you have anything good?"

"You could have brought something with you instead of sponging off me," Lilith said, nodding in my direction. "Did you—?"

"Yes," I groaned. "I *walked* to the door."

"Don't blame me," Lilith said. "If you guys didn't ruin everything—"

"I didn't ruin—"

"I was not part of the idiocy!"

"They weren't even really ruined!"

Lilith held her hand up. She cleared her throat, straightened, and put her hands on her hips. "It doesn't matter who was at fault. You are a unit, and you are all responsible for—"

We all groaned and threw whatever was close at Lilith, until she stopped the parental impersonation and started to laugh. I loved Lilith's laugh. Especially this one, which made her eyes crinkle.

Lilith had lots of different laughs. There was the one that was just a huff of a laugh, there was the snicker, and the giggle. There was the full-body laugh like the one she was doing now with the crinkle at her eyes, and every great once in a while there was the laugh that was so huge that she'd end up snorting, which was probably my favorite. That was hilarious. Still somehow cute, though.

Besides, she was the one who had crushed the plants in the first place.

"All right," interrupted Crowley. He was wearing a Dark Knight T-shirt he must have bought at the concert, though I hadn't seen him getting anything besides the Nephilim journal he supposedly wanted for school. Crowley was sneaky. "Enough with the nonsense. We have snacks, and things to talk about, no?"

"Yes!" cried Lilith before running over to the corner of her kitchen counter and grabbing something. She held it up, ribbons trailing through her fingers as familiar-looking crystals caught and reflected the light. An odd thrill of excitement rushed through me. This was real. I wasn't the only one who had gotten the invite. Well, my parents weren't the only ones. Whatever, same thing.

"We're going, right?" I asked. "What does Lucifer say?"

Lilith grimaced. "Mom's not saying," she said. She tossed

the ribbons so that they fell gracefully into her open palm, and we followed her to the basement.

Of all our houses, Lilith's basement was our favorite to hang out in. With only Lilith and her mom living there, her mom had decided they should each have their own spaces outside of their bedrooms.

Her mom had an office we theoretically weren't allowed in but had been in often enough to be familiar with the contents. In fact, Lilith's visit to the office had given us our tip to the wild opening that had led to our magically terrifying adventure in the mortal coil just weeks ago. Lilith's space was the basement. Her mom *said* she didn't go in there, but we never kept anything secret there anyway, just in case.

Lilith parted the two sliding doors covering the entrance to the basement and soared down. Unlike the steps to Faust's basement, which were designed for the wingless among us, this house was built for Lilith's mom. The opening had plenty of room to fly. I let everyone go in front of me and slid the doors closed behind us. For a moment there was darkness, but Lilith turned on the decorative lights as I walked down the stairs.

Crowley sprawled into a beanbag chair on the floor while Aleister and Lilith continued turning on lights. Over the years we had added more and more, every time we had found something cool. There were elaborately scrolled metal lanterns hanging from the beams, lit in any color we could find. Faerie lights, named because they were imbued with faerie magic, glittered across the ceiling like the fireflies that haunted our forests on peaceful nights.

There were posters of our favorite bands and games plastered across the walls, many of them covering others that we'd outgrown. There were some places on the wall squishy with layers and layers. Someday we would probably take them down and laugh at the stuff on the bottom, but while I was curious about what the bottom layers were, the thought of finding out also kind of depressed me.

There were beanbags and enormous pillows scattered on top of shag rugs that added their own layer of comfort. Lilith had added a basket to the corner to hold the blankets we had accumulated over the years. A table in the center held the hologame console, and a large mirror, which normally played our favorite obsessions but now just reflected the room back to us, was mounted on the wall.

"So," said Lilith as we settled into our spots. Not that they were assigned, of course, but yes, the oversized black beanbag was my spot.

"Ahh," I said as I let myself sink down into it. "Heaven."

"Been there, done that," Crowley said flippantly.

"I still can't believe you guys went there without me," Aleister whined.

"It wasn't like we had a choice," I said. "And we didn't see much anyway."

"This is true," Lilith said. "We only saw one room and out a window to their business district. Well, I think that's what it was."

"Maybe it wasn't," Crowley said. "Maybe they just live like that."

"That would make a lot of sense," I said. "It would explain Cassandra. She had no life skills, until she met us."

"Hey," Lilith said. "That's not cool. That's like saying we all live in the Pit. 'Torturous pit of torture,' remember?"

I flushed. Cassandra hadn't believed us when we'd said we have families and homes here, and despite exchanging several illegal letters with her, I kind of got the impression she still didn't believe it. At least a little bit. I should really know better than to do that to someone else. In fairness, the heavenly angels we had met had not been good to us. Except Cassandra. Eventually.

"Okay, yeah. I know," I said. "Sorry."

"Anyway," Lilith continued. "We didn't see much in the few minutes we were there; we were kinda begging for our lives, but I don't know. If this party or meeting or whatever goes forward, I doubt it will actually take place in Heaven."

"Wasn't that what it said, though?" Aleister asked. "The invite? That the party was going to be in Heaven, 'golden gates' and all that."

"Yeah," Crowley agreed. "But there's no way the grown-ups are letting us go there. Or even going themselves."

"You're probably right," I said, more than a little disappointed. "There's not an established level of trust yet, so it will probably be on neutral ground. No one is going to want the other side to have home-field advantage."

"Ooh," Crowley taunted. "Look who's learning tactical skills in their elite leadership school."

"Shut up," I said. "It's common sense."

"He's right," Lilith said. "But it's not opposite sides, since we're all on the same side."

"Totally," said Aleister flippantly, and we all laughed.

Technically Lilith was right, of course: both Heaven and Hell were tasked with the same basic mission. We just fulfilled it in very different ways. Heaven preserved and concentrated goodness in their paradise. On the other hand, Hell locked down evil souls, trapped the demons that those souls became, and kept them where they'd remain harmless. Despite the same mission, in practice . . . well, there had been eons of separation and bad PR. It had led to not the best of relationships. Which was of course why this party was happening. Cassandra wanted to fix things.

"I tried to pry info out of Mom," continued Lilith. "But she's all hush-hush until things are decided. It *does* sound like they're going to try to make it happen, though, if negotiations go well."

"Now, that is the first interesting thing any of you have said today," Crowley said, leaning forward so that his elbows rested on the table. "Where and when are negotiations?"

"C'mon, Lilith," I said, leaning forward myself with a glint in my eye that had nothing to do with flames. "What do you know?"

# NINE

Lilith didn't know much, as it turned out, though I didn't fault her, and probably wouldn't even if it *was* her fault. She was just so . . . Lilith. Perfect and amazing and way too beautiful to . . . whatever.

Anyway.

Even though Lilith was in the Intelligence track, she didn't know much because Lilith's mom had *also* been tracked in Intelligence, long before she became Lucifer's right-hand person. Lilith's mom might have turned a blind eye to our office snooping, but she never kept the really top secret stuff in there either.

At least not unguarded.

The alert to the opening that we had accidentally used to get into Salem had been automatically generated, and Lilith had found it before her mother had even seen it. But anything else we had ever found in that office was because her mom had wanted us to find it. She was evil like that.

We decided we'd all press the 'rents and get whatever info we could, while keeping ears out for anything about this mixer or the negotiations. We didn't know who had been invited from home or whether the mixer was even just between Heaven and Hell. Were there invites sent to other places? All the great hereafters? Other dimensions? Would there be representatives from the mortal world? It didn't seem likely, but who knew? All in all, our conversation led to more questions than actual answers.

But if there were representatives from the mortal world . . . was it possible I could see Sean again? His dad was in a secret order, after all. Those tended to have connections, even if I hadn't learned much about them.

Sean! Oh, brimstone!

He had sent a letter, and I hadn't even read it!

Brimstone, brimstone, brimstone. I couldn't believe I'd done that! I always read the letters right away. ALWAYS. But I had wanted to read the letter in peace, and it had been dinnertime, and then the messenger from Heaven had come, and that *never* happened, even more never than my favorite band coming to town, and then the ground had rumbled, and the sky had done something weird. It had been distraction after distraction, and I had forgotten.

"Dude, go!" Aleister's voice knocked me back into the present. As did Crowley's shoulder. We had transitioned from gossiping to table gaming, and it was my turn.

"Okay," I said, shaking off the cobwebs of guilt. I promised myself I would read Sean's letter as soon as I got home, and looked down at the game board. "Wait, what did you cast?"

Crowley laughed. It was an evil laugh. An evil laugh that said he had gotten away with something. And he had! I had a card to counteract what he had cast, but I had been distracted, and now that his card was out, there was nothing I could do about it.

"Should have paid attention," Lilith said in a singsong voice. She and Crowley were partners, a deadly combination if there ever was one.

"Seriously, dude, head in the game," Aleister growled. He may have been the happy-go-lucky friend in our group, but he was competitive.

Lilith's mom brought home flatbread pizza topped with ham and candied oranges, a seasonal tradition, and it was awesome. We ended up spending the entire day, and by the time Mom messaged me to see if I was alive and still living with them, the day was over.

I waved to Lilith and thanked her mom. Crowley, Aleister, and I left together. We walked a few blocks to the street where we'd part ways, Crowley still gloating about how he had beat us. When I pointed out that the only reason he had won was because he'd been paired with Lilith, he turned to me, a glint of victory in his eyes, and said, "And don't you wish you were me." I flushed, wished the ground would swallow me, tried to stammer out a rebuttal, and ultimately just decided to smack him with my wing. The flare from Morgan's glamour was just bonus. Actions speak louder than words, after all.

"Whatever, losers," Crowley said before launching into the air. "Talk soon." He rolled a lazy circle in the air and flipped us off before flying home.

"Why do we put up with him?" I asked as we turned the corner onto Stine Street.

"Assigned in toddlerhood?" Aleister asked.

I thought about Uriel in my study group from school. I couldn't imagine being friends with him, even if we had been assigned to each other.

"Or maybe we actually like him," I said.

"Yeah, that's probably it," Aleister said.

"Got time to game tomorrow?" I asked. "We still have to

get through level forty-three." Aleister and I had been working our way through *D'yavol*, a game released shortly after our parents had let us have lives again.

"Ehhh," Aleister said, and I almost stopped walking in shock. Aleister never turned me down. Ever. "Maybe."

"Why?" I asked, feeling defensive and weird. "Got something better to do?"

"Sort of," he said. His voice rose at the end like he was trying to be nice. "I made plans with Sidney and Nikolai from my weapons class? They're really cool. We're meeting up with some other people at Braham Park to play *Run, Hobgoblin, Run.*"

"Oh," I said. Braham Park? We always went to Pandemonium Park. Why was he going somewhere else?

"It would probably be okay if you came too," Aleister said. "I can ask. I'm sure it would be fine."

"Nah," I said. Pity inclusion? No thanks. "Let me know if you have time after."

"Yeah, for sure," he said. He was overexcited in a way that made me feel like he was placating me, but Aleister also had a tendency for overexcitement, so maybe I was being paranoid. "I'm sure you want to hang out with someone from your new school anyway, right?"

Not if they were the last people in all of Hell.

Was I the only one who wasn't making new friends? Besides

Azael, who seemed fine, everyone in my track sucked. None of them knew a thing about comics or music or games or anything beyond taking charge and fulfilling their mission. They all thought they were right all the time, and they never admitted to not knowing the answer, which was dumb because even Lilith, who hated not knowing the answer more than anyone else I knew, still was power enough to admit when she didn't know something.

"Nah," I said. "I'm just gonna chill."

"Okay, well . . ." Aleister stood awkwardly and smiled sheepishly. These send-offs were weird now. We always used to say *See you at school,* except we didn't now.

"I'll keep an eye out for you," I said like the confident person I was not.

"Yeah," Aleister said, smiling in relief. "Definitely. And we'll still watch for the Wild Hunt, right?"

The Wild Hunt was a Faerie original. The Hunt started in Faerie every year at Yule and traveled without concern for dimensional divides. Legend had it that if the Hunt found you outside when it passed by, you'd be compelled to join them, completely unable to resist. It sounded amazing to me, but Faerie magic was chaotic, and the Wild Hunt didn't exactly return people to where they belonged after the Hunt was done. If you joined, you were on your own.

While Yule wasn't a major holiday in Hell, not like Samhain or Beltane, we did celebrate it. And my squad and our families had a tradition of watching for the Hunt together. It never came close enough to call anyone to join, but we'd lie on our roof eating candy, or sometimes go to the hill outside of town, and try to catch a glimpse.

"Yeah, of course," I said. "It's tradition."

"Excellent!"

Yeah, excellent. I was officially relegated to holiday gatherings. Great. Just great.

# TEN

I watched Aleister take off like a bolt and kept walking down my familiar block. Old lady Shelley's hellhound growled and ran for the fence as I passed. Juliet was more bark than bite, and there was a fence between me and her. Plus, she was going blind. She probably thought I was the mailman. For some reason she hated that guy.

"Knock it off, Juliet." The hound stopped, or at least tried to, before slamming her face into the fence.

Was I the only one not fitting in? Lilith still hated Dina, which was comforting, but other than that she seemed to *like* the people she was going to school with. Aleister thought his new track was the best thing that had ever happened to him. Even Crowley had said good things about his teachers and classmates. In fact, everyone in my track seemed just as comfortable.

I ruffled my hair. The blue glow from my decorative flames sent dots of light onto the cobblestones beneath me. I sighed.

It wasn't that my friends couldn't have other friends. I wasn't that selfish. I just wanted to be their first choice. All the time. Was that so wrong?

Maybe I should try to make new friends too. But I just couldn't see it happening. What would I even do with someone like Zachariah? Study strategy? Ugh. No thank you. Dad would be happy if I did, though.

Well, he was just going to have to be unhappy.

Great, now *I* was unhappy. I had had an awesome day. Why was I ruining it by angsting? I shook my wings like I could shake off my mood, and the light flared. There. That was better. I did it again just to see the ground light up with the blue flame. The illusion flickered around each feather as I stopped the movement, then settled into the gentle effect it normally was. Motion at my side made me turn my head, and there was a figure in a cloak. Just standing there. I lifted a hand to wave, but they didn't wave back. Okay . . .

Whatever, I was being ridiculous, and I needed to stop. Besides, I had a mission. Get info out of Mom and Dad.

When I got into the house, Mom was back, but not alone like I'd been expecting.

"I'm home!" I declared, even though it was painfully obvious.

"Hello, darling," Mom said. She was holding a goblet of something, probably mulled wine, from the smell of it, and although she looked tired, she looked relaxed, too. "You remember Megara?"

"Yup. Hi," I said.

Meg had been Mom's friend for a long time. They were in separate squads, but they both had command positions and had bonded in school, so theoretically it was possible to make friends at my school. It had been a while since Meg had been to our house, but with Yule in a couple of days, there was an extra day off.

"Oh, unholy darkness," said Meg, and I prepared myself. *Why did you do that, Mal? What were you thinking? Does it really give off the image you want people to see? Don't you think you should be more serious?* "Where did you get that awesome look?"

Wait, what?

Was it just my imagination, or did she sound impressed?

"Glamourie," I said. "That place at the end of Perdition."

"Oh. Right," said Meg. "The new Unseelie. You can't beat a high-court fae for glamour, and I've always thought the

Unseelie were the best. They're much more . . . adventurous. What do you think, Chay? Think I could pull something like that off?"

"Definitely," Mom said. "And I'm sure you wouldn't be pulled into Bathin's office at all."

"Bah," Meg said. "I bet they could do one that would only last for my days off."

"I bet they could!" I said, excited to have an actual adult person on my side for once.

"Then maybe I'll have to visit Glamourie," she said. "Down the street from Faust's, right?"

"Yup!"

"I'd love to find out why they left Faerie," Mom said.

"They said they didn't like court politics," I said, giving the answer that Morgan had given to me when I'd blurted out the same question.

"Uh-huh," Meg said.

"That's what Morgan said!"

Morgan had been nothing but nice to me, so sue me if I was feeling rather defensive.

"I'm sure they did, and I'm not doubting the answer," Meg reassured me. "But to really get sick of politics, so much so that you leave an entire dimension? You have to be *involved* in politics, not just surrounded by it."

Mom tilted her glass, and they clinked.

It occurred to me that an unscrupulous person would take advantage of this relaxed vibe going on in my living room to get more information. I had been planning on going to my room, but instead I threw myself down onto the free chair, kicking my legs over the arm to use as a sort of couch.

"Did you have a good day?" asked Mom.

"Yup," I said. "You?"

"It was fine," said Mom, raising an eyebrow at me. "Thank you for asking."

Did I really never ask Mom about her day? Probably not. I'd have to be more subtle.

"What did you do?" I asked.

"Had a meeting," she said. "Ran into Megara."

"How's school, Mal?" asked Meg.

"Ugh," I said. "It's the weekend. No school today."

"Ah," said Meg with a twinkle in her eyes. "It's going well, then. Don't worry, kiddo. It's not forever."

"Thanks," I said. It might not be forever, but it *was* right now. "What was the meeting about?"

Meg laughed, and Mom nodded like she'd been waiting for that question all along.

"Stuff," said Mom. Oh, so it was going to be like that.

"Are we going to the party?" I asked, not even pausing to

wonder if it was something I should be keeping from Meg.

"That has not been decided," Mom said. "And even if it goes forward, there's no guarantee that *you* will be going."

"The messenger said it was for the family," I said. "And besides, I've already—"

I just barely managed to choke off my words. I had been going to say that I had already been to Heaven, but kinda forgot that Mom and Dad didn't know about that yet.

Or ever, if I could help it.

"Already what?" Mom said, narrowing her eyes at me.

"Already . . . picked out my outfit," I said. "Or at least drafted some ideas. I'll need Morgan's help and a way bigger allowance."

"Uh-huh," said Meg. "I don't know. This mixer idea does seem a little . . . frivolous? Although, it could be a good opportunity to try out a wild new glamour. It is supposed to be a party, after all. Assuming I read that right."

"To promote interdimensional cooperation," said Mom. "If you believe the invite."

"You don't?" I asked, surprised. For some reason that possibility hadn't occurred to me.

"I think . . . ," Mom said as she got up to refill her and Meg's glasses, and even brought back a cider for me. She *was* in a good mood! "I think that we should be cautious. It never hurts to get more information. They haven't reached out to us in millennia, so to reach out for a *party*? Seems a bit . . ."

"Childish?" filled in Meg. "Simplistic?"

"Fun," I said.

"Case in point," said Meg, but then she threw me a wink when I immediately objected.

"Maybe you just don't know how to have fun anymore," I said.

"That could be true," Meg said. "When's the last time we got together?"

"Oh, darkness, too long," said Mom.

"Okay, yeah," I said. "Blah, blah, blah. When are they going to decide?"

"I will tell you when I know," Mom said. "Isn't it your bedtime?"

"Oh," I said, standing up. "I see how it is!"

"Give me a hug," Mom said.

"Mom," I said. "Really. We have company."

But I gave her a hug anyway. I had gotten what info I was going to get, and now it was going to be boring down here.

"Good night, kiddo," called Meg.

"Night!" I said.

I wasn't even three steps up, wondering if I should be offended by being treated like a little kid, when I nearly lost my footing. I grabbed the handrail as everything rattled, pictures and mirrors and possibly Mom's goblet. The rumbling got louder, and the shaking got worse.

Mom and Meg made disconcerted noises, and then I could only hear the roaring as it got impossibly loud. But just when I thought my head would burst, it started fading away. In seconds it was quiet again and the shaking had stopped.

"Mal?" asked Mom.

"Yup. I'm good," I said, attempting to pry open my white knuckles from the handrail. "What was that?"

Neither adult responded, but I didn't think it was because they were hiding the answer.

"Seriously, what was that?" I asked again. "Is this something we're worried about?"

"No?" said Meg.

"I'm sure it's nothing," said Mom, who was being a lying liar.

I looked out the window, but the overhang from the roof didn't allow me to see up. All I could see were the glowing reds, oranges, and yellows of the horizon. If I could have seen the dark, would there have been that strange green shimmer, or would it have been just like it was supposed to be?

We all stood, waiting to see if anything else would happen, but nothing did, and as I looked around, I saw that nothing was really disturbed. For all the noise and vibration, it really hadn't been that bad. Twice in two days, though, when it had never happened before.

"Is this just a thing we're going to have to deal with from now on?" I asked.

"I'm sure it's nothing," Mom repeated. "Anyway, it seems to be done now. Bedtime."

"Uh-huh," I said. "Okay, good night."

I took a few steps, and even though the staircase stayed stable, I decided to launch myself the rest of the way on my wings. Couldn't shake me off-balance if I wasn't touching the ground. I was smart like that.

I closed my bedroom door behind me, my shiny new poster of Nephilim looking pristine and perfect on the back of it. I dropped my sweatshirt onto the floor, pulled off my new T-shirt, and threw it vaguely in the direction of my laundry basket. I kicked down my pants in a ridiculous dance that probably would have been more ridiculous if I wasn't using my wings to keep my balance, and then flopped onto my bed and considered. I had no plans tomorrow . . . apparently. And now my world was unstable.

That seemed a little too on point.

I rolled over and groaned in frustration, but when my hand reached under my pillow, it met something that should not have been there. For a second I thought it might have been alive, which was a stupid thought, though I guessed it was possible, if I had left my window open. I lifted my head. Nope, window closed. I pulled up the pillow.

Oh, brimstone! I was such an idiot!

I sat up and unfolded the letter as quickly as I could without ripping the paper.

*Mal—*

*Sorry for not writing sooner. Things have been ... weird. I mean, first it was the normal "hard to open a portal to Hell without Dad noticing" thing, but then stuff went strange. Not necessarily bad. I mean, I'm fine. But ... man, I don't even know why I'm writing like this. Is anything weird going on over there? Something that shouldn't be happening? Charity's magic is wonky, and I keep seeing things. You know, the whole psychic thing? Anyway, I keep having visions I can't figure out yet, but they don't look good.*

*And you're in them.*

*But that may not be bad! I haven't figured it out yet. Anyway, can you write back and just,*

*I don't know, tell me everything is normal over
there and that I'm completely overreacting?*
—Sean

Huh. That didn't sound all that promising, but as always happened when I got a letter from Sean, I felt a little thrill go through my stomach. Not only was he still thinking about me but he was having visions that I was starring in. That had to mean we'd see each other again, right?

Or maybe it meant I was dying.

I reread his letter, and then read it again. Seemed like a toss-up.

Was I messed up that this hint of adventure, with the possibility of immortal peril, made me feel better? I might not have made new friends in my track, but I had made a friend in a completely other dimension.

Which my friends knew about, of course. I mean, most of my squad had been there.

It's just that once we'd gotten home and I'd gotten the letter from Cassandra and I had reached out to Sean and he had responded, well, I hadn't exactly told my squad. I know, I should have learned my lesson when all my secrets had come out into the open in Salem and my friends had been pissed.

And I did learn my lesson!

I meant to mention the letters a few times. But it didn't really have anything to do with them, and despite what they might think, I was allowed to have my own secrets. It was nothing like the spark of creation thing. That was potentially destiny changing and, although my squad had had to point it out, wouldn't have just impacted me. Making it so that I wasn't a power with a cosmic destiny? Yeah, that was slightly different than this. It wasn't like me talking to a human affected them, what with them busy with all their new friends who weren't me, doing stupid things I wouldn't want to do anyway.

But what to say to Sean?

I pulled out a sheet of paper and fountain pen, my favorite bloodred ink ready to go. And then I stopped. I was fine. I mean, okay, I was being all angsty and dealing with fitting in or not wanting to fit in or whatever in my new school, but that wasn't what Sean was asking. I wasn't hurt, so I could reassure him of that. I was home and no one was threatening to kill me or kidnap me, so already I was way better off than the last time we had been together.

But the ground had shaken twice in two days, and there was possibly a weird change to the sky, although I had only seen it that one time. And then of course we had also gotten a live, in the flesh, visit from a heavenly angel. Was that weird? Well, yes, but was it the weird that Sean was asking about?

I tapped the pen against my desk, thinking.

When it was all done, my letter to Sean was embarrassingly long. I would never have said any of this in person, but for some reason that blank page was just calling for me to keep going.

I told him about the messenger, the mixer that still hadn't been decided, the shaking ground, and even the swirl in the sky that I might or might not have seen. And then I went completely off the rails and told him about the idiots I went to school with and how everyone in the squad seemed to be adjusting to being apart except for me, that everyone loved their new tracks, even Crowley, who didn't love anything. I told him about the concert, the opening band I wanted to learn more about. I told him about Morgan and my flames and my thoughts of what to try next. I told him everything.

I put my pen down and read my letter. Oh, yeah, no. This could never see the light of day.

I grabbed a fresh piece of paper.

*Sean—*

*Depends on what you mean by weirdness.*
*Apparently, Cassandra made good on the*
*threat to get us all together for social hour. We*
*had a messenger from Heaven for the first time*
*ever show up at our house. And the ground*

*has shaken twice in the last two days. That's*
*never happened here. I thought maybe there*
*was something weird in the sky during the first*
*one, but I can't be sure. What's going on with*
*Charity's magic? What did you see? Is there*
*anything I can do to help?*
*—Malachi*

Yeah, that was better. Sane and to the point and not nearly as pathetic. I yawned. I put the letter on my desk and left the pen in the well. I'd send it tomorrow. It didn't take a ton of effort, but it was nothing like sending a quick flare to my friends, and none of the stuff I needed to send the letter between dimensions was near me. It was in a box in the back of my closet. I thought about getting it, but my bed was comfy, and I really didn't want to get up. Spilling my guts in the first, not-to-ever-be-sent letter had taken a while and far too much energy. I'd send the rewrite tomorrow.

What was a few more hours anyway?

# ELEVEN

I woke up late. No alarm. No parents nagging. Nowhere to go. No friends.

Okay, that was a bit much. And also untrue. I was being melodramatic, and I was better than that.

I kicked off my blankets and stared at the ceiling for a minute before dragging myself out of bed. I pulled on a pair of black sweatpants that might or might not have been clean and my favorite oversized sweatshirt with the big dramatic hood. Wonderful for mischief and brooding alike.

I could already smell something amazing coming from downstairs. One of the parents had cooked, and I was hoping there was a lot of whatever it was. I glided down the stairs and stumbled my way into a chair. Dad raised an unimpressed eyebrow. I stared right back. I took a piece of bacon off a plate and shoved it into my mouth. Dad snorted a laugh, so I was in the clear.

"Hey, Mal," Mom said. "What are your plans for this Yuletide Eve?"

Gee, thanks, Mom. Awesome job distracting me.

"I don't know," I hedged.

"Well," she said. "I was thinking that since I actually have the day off, maybe we could have some Mom-Mal time? I need to stop by Hell If I Sew. We could check out Dorian's, see if they have anything new that might work for some hypothetical event that may or may not happen."

"Uh, yes!"

Dorian's was one of my favorite clothing stores, and Mom knew it. If there was anyone in Hell who had more fashion sense than Morgan, it was Dorian Gray. I hardly ever went there, though. His stuff tended to be just a tad outside the realm of my allowance, but if Mom was inviting, then Mom was paying.

"Does that mean you want to come?" Mom asked, a know-it-all smirk on her face.

"Obviously," I said. "Don't patronize me."

I shoved an apple pancake into my mouth and said something that vaguely resembled, "I'll get ready and be down in a second" but probably sounded more like "Mmfmhfsdfdss."

I also had a letter to send, but they didn't need to know about that.

"Ten minutes!" called my mom, which did not give me much time.

I flew up the stairs, went straight to my room, and kicked the door closed. The ritual to send Sean my letter wasn't complicated, but I did need to focus. Crowley could probably do it without thinking and with far fewer ingredients, but he was a magician, and I was not. I caught my reflection in the mirror. This could not stand. These clothes were fine for wallowing in my house. They were not fine for being seen at Dorian's.

I grabbed what I needed to send my letter to Sean, and after only a few minutes of concentration and a few phrases in Enochian, I was holding the letter over the flame of a yellow candle. I said the final word, and my letter went up in a huge flash of green flame. Done!

I dug through my closet and drawers, and at nine minutes and fifty-nine seconds I was soaring down the stairs, my glamoured blue flames going nicely with my blue plaid skinny pants, my hair back to perfect.

"Let's go!" I said.

I suppose some people might have been embarrassed to be shopping with their mom, but Mom had the money and was generally cool enough not to be overly mushy in public. Plus, if I played my cards right, I'd get lunch out at an actual restaurant instead of the sandwich I'd have to get myself when we went home, and we might even be able to stop at Faust's for apple cider donuts.

Our stop at Hell If I Sew, to pick up whatever, was thankfully quick. I barely noticed, only looking up from my pocket mirror once during the wait, and in no time flat we were approaching the gilded door of Dorian's.

My mom shook her head and muttered something that sounded suspiciously like "tacky" under her breath.

"Blasphemer," I said. Mom laughed.

We each pulled open a door and entered the clothing store. The carpet was so thick, I felt like I was sinking.

"Welcome, welcome," announced the one and only Dorian Gray.

Dorian was another one of our special residents. Like Faust he had been human in life; unlike Faust he hadn't made a deal. In a confusing turn of events that no one was quite clear on, Dorian had ended up nearly immortal, with a painting that had aged instead of him. That had only worked for so long. A human soul may be eternal, but the body is not, even one painted onto canvas. Eventually the problem had been rectified, and somehow Dorian had negotiated himself a new life in Hell rather than eternal rest. And unlike Faust, Dorian never seemed to have the problem of maintaining a body. I had a sneaking suspicion it was because he was never not focusing on himself.

"May I help you?" Dorian asked.

"Hi, Dorian," I said. "Anything new?"

"Ah, yes." Dorian frowned. "If you're sure you don't want to look at the classics, well, then, go on. Over there. There are some . . . modern styles, if you're interested in that sort of thing. Probably even some things from Faerie."

"Thank you," Mom said.

Dorian didn't design all the clothes, which was probably a good thing. He was always dressed in clothes that had way more lace than I would ever be caught in. But there were some local designers that provided cutting-edge stuff, with the benefit that they remembered to put slit options in the tops for wings, something Dorian always forgot no matter how long he'd lived here.

I was trying on a possible choice in one of the dressing rooms when I heard a familiar voice coming from the next stall.

"I told you I don't care," Morgan said.

"You should," said an unfamiliar voice, with a melodic tone that meant they had to be from Faerie too. "It will affect—"

"It is none of my business," Morgan said, steel in their voice. "I told you. I live here now. I have a salon; you should visit."

"A salon," sputtered the other voice. "Lord Accolon, please. If you don't help—"

"I said no," Morgan snapped, and then they took a breath so loudly that I heard it in my dressing room. "And don't call me that; I am not that person anymore. It's probably an overreaction. It doesn't always mean anything serious."

"This time—"

"No," Morgan said. "This is not my problem." And then there was a sound like the curtain sliding open, and another sound I couldn't identify. I thought they might have left, but then there was a heavy sigh and a muttered, "I'm not the one to fix it anyway."

I waited, straining my ears to hear anything more, which was probably why I jumped when my mom called out, "Mal, do those pants fit? Because they looked a little small around—"

"Yes," I called before Mom decided to elaborate. "I'll be out in a second."

My dad was already suspicious of Morgan, and I knew others were too. I wasn't sure what I'd just heard, but it wouldn't make people trust them more. It didn't matter. I trusted Morgan.

Didn't I?

By the time we left Dorian's, I was three outfits richer, and starving. Mom took pity, especially when I pointed out, "We never really spend time together anymore, Mom, and I'm growing up so quickly."

We grabbed lunch at Baphomet's BBQ and sat outside under a flaming lamp decoratively wrapped with holly and a red bow. The breeze picked up, and leaves skittered across the cobblestones—several of the legged variety took off after a gremlin that was running frantically with something clenched in its tiny arms. I wasn't sure what there possibly was to steal from leaves, but if anyone could figure it out, it would be a gremlin.

We ordered a ton. I ate so much, I was ready to burst, while my mom just smiled and shook her head, and I actually did feel better. Maybe I just needed to get out of the house to get some perspective.

I wiped my face vaguely clean and leaned back in my chair with a massive sigh. Movement near the host stand caught my attention, and I saw a familiar face. Azael walked up with his family. He looked uncomfortable. Not that I ever really saw Azael comfortable. Even when we'd sat together at school this past week, he hadn't looked completely relaxed. We made eye contact and I waved. He waved back, raising his hand only up to his waist and dropping it quickly.

"Who's that?" Mom asked.

"Azael," I said. "He's in my new school."

"Oh, do you want to say hi?" Mom asked like I was still in kindergarten and needed her to set up a playdate.

I rolled my eyes and leveled an unimpressed glare in her direction.

She held her hands up in surrender. "I just thought it would be nice."

"Nah," I said. "I don't really know him."

"Maybe you should," she said. "You're in the same track."

I groaned. "Why should that choose my friends?"

"It doesn't," Mom said, looking like she was going to let it drop, but then I saw a look come over her face that meant we were going to have *a talk*. I really wanted to groan and pull my hair, but I knew objecting wouldn't make it stop, so I reined myself in.

Go, me.

"Look, it helps to have friends wherever you are. I love that you have a great relationship with your squad, and I hope it stays that way."

"Why wouldn't—"

"I'm not saying it won't," Mom interrupted. I crossed my arms over my chest, but I shut my mouth anyway. "I'm just saying that this is your new school for a long time, and those kids in your class now are going to be some of the people you spend the most time with later on. It wouldn't hurt to make some friends."

"How do you know I haven't?" I demanded.

"Well, beyond the fact that you're spending the day with me . . . ," Mom said. "Not that I don't love it. And not that I don't think a large part of your decision to spend the day with me was Dorian's and lunch out, but it would be nice if you had people outside of your chain of command."

"Mom," I groaned. "There's no chain of command. Lilith, Crowley, and Aleister are my friends."

"And I hope it stays that way," Mom said lightly. "Azael seems nice."

"We didn't talk to him at all," I pointed out.

"No, but you waved," she said. "Which means he's not awful."

"Fine," I said. "I'll make an effort or whatever."

"That's all I ask," Mom said. "Dessert?"

The answer of course was yes.

Baphomet's had this deep-fried ice cream thing that came out in flames, with a hard crunchy shell and whipped cream and this sugar decoration that's different every time. This time it was a moon for Yule, with a silver bell.

A chiming melody, barely audible over the people chatting, came from Mom's pocket, and she reached down to pull out her pocket mirror. She looked at it and frowned, before adjusting her posture ramrod straight and answering.

"Yes," she said, brusque and in charge. It must have been work. I went back to my ice cream but watched as her frown grew more pronounced. "That's not possible."

Okay, that had my attention. What wasn't possible? Unfortunately, since it was a work call, the conversation was concealed for security and only Mom could see and hear who was on the other end, but I could still hear *her.*

"I understand, but that's still not possible. Someone must—"

Mom rubbed her temple with her free hand. "All right, I'll be there." She looked up at me and grimaced. I guess my day was over, but at least I had gotten through dessert, so woo-hoo for me.

"What was that about?" I asked after Mom paid the check and we left for home.

"It's probably nothing," she said.

"But what did they say it was?" I asked.

Mom sighed and made a sound like she was going to say

something but stopped. Then she laughed and shook her head. "I don't know. If my Intelligence is to be believed . . ."

"What?" I demanded.

"It's ridiculous. I swear Ruby needs a vacation."

"So just tell me," I said.

Mom sighed. "If she is to be believed, then a soul slated for Heaven ended up in the fifth circle."

# TWELVE

The idea of a soul marked for Heaven ending up in Hell instead should have been laughable. That sort of thing hadn't happened since the balance between good and evil, between making and unmaking, was newly established. But then again, Mom had that weird tension at the corners of her eyes that meant she was still worried about something, even if it was just that apparently someone *believed* the soul was supposed to be in Heaven, when it was obviously supposed to be here.

I mean, *that* had to be the mistake, right? Not that the soul had ended up in the wrong place, but that someone mistakenly thought it had. After all, Anubis didn't make mistakes, but if he did? An innocent soul ending up in the fifth circle with all those wrathful souls? The idea of it was terrifying!

By the time we got home, and Mom immediately left for work, Lilith was logged on, and I eagerly joined the game she was playing. When I went up to my bedroom later that night to go to sleep, I was feeling back to normal and not at all wallowy. Mom hadn't come back from work yet, so I could only imagine that she was still yelling at her squad for the obvious mistake.

Thankfully, an extra day off for Yule meant a lazy morning, and since Mom had worked all night, a quiet house. Dad read a book and prepped Yule dinner, which we ate while Mom slept.

"C'mon, let's go," I said when it had finally gotten to be time to head out.

"All right, all right," Mom said, yawning into her hand. "I'm coming."

"You don't have to go," Dad said.

"Yes, she does," I said. "It's tradition! Let's go!"

Stoker Hill was the perfect spot for Wild Hunt watching. It was above the houses and had a flat clearing at the top where people spread out blankets or played games while we waited. The thing was, there was no guarantee that a viewing would occur. By definition the Wild Hunt was . . . well, wild, so there were always more activities planned to keep everyone entertained rather than just sitting around and waiting.

By the time we arrived, a crowd had already gathered, the air was filled with music, and littles were running around playing tag. The hill wasn't steep, so even though we had flown, there were wingless people here who had hiked to the top. Aleister was already involved in a game with a few other kids from the neighborhood.

A few adults with leathery wings and horns were lighting an enormous fire, and as they added wood, it crackled and sparked, filling the air with the smell of woodsmoke. A leaf jumped off a log just as the log was tossed into the flames, narrowly escaping burning before it ran for its life, slightly smoking.

"Save me."

And for a second, I was impressed that the *ambulafolia* had apparently learned to talk, but a tug on one of my feathers had me turning to see Lilith looking panicked. "I just saw Dina, and it doesn't matter if it's Yule. She'll want to discuss the rest of our project, and just no."

We successfully avoided Dina and met up with Crowley and his brother, Simon, who only tolerated us because his friends hadn't come. Aleister eventually joined us, sweaty and out of breath. We grabbed snacks and looked to the sky at every gasp.

One group of kids decided to make false alarms a game and ran off laughing whenever they tricked someone into thinking they'd seen the Hunt. As Aleister and Crowley scared them off, I heard a high-pitched giggle behind me, which was weird because I thought I had seen the entire group run off in the other direction.

I turned around to look for any straggling littles, but instead I saw a familiar figure sitting off by themselves in a velvet chaise that I was willing to bet had not been carried up this hill.

"C'mon," I said to my squad. As I led them over to where Morgan was sitting, I wondered if I was making a pain of myself. After all, I already had a standing appointment that I wasn't even being charged for, and my blue flame glamour was still going strong. They probably didn't want to hang out with a bunch of kids. But then again, they were alone, and this was a holiday, and we were just saying hi.

"Well, hello there!" said Morgan, and then it was really too late to debate if I was making the right call.

Today their skin was a deep brown with a faint purple sheen; their hair was long and mostly white, with a dramatic purple streak in the front. Their clothes were still red and green for Yule, but they had added a deep black cloak that literally sparkled with twinkling stars.

"Hey," I said. "These are my squad mates, Crowley, Lilith, and Aleister."

"A pleasure to meet you," Morgan said, smiling at us all.

My friends murmured greetings, and Crowley shot me a glare, though I wasn't sure why.

"What do you think?" I asked. "Is this what Yule was like for you in Faerie?"

"There are similarities," Morgan said. "Although, I don't think I've ever had to worry about little leafle picking my pockets before." Morgan withdrew their hand from the pocket of their cloak to reveal a leaf frantically running tiny legs in the air. They dropped it and it ran, zigging and zagging its way between people's legs.

"Wait," Aleister said. "What did you call it?"

"Oh, 'leafle'?" Morgan asked, and we all exchanged grins. "Like 'leaf-people.' Why, what do you call them?"

"Leaves," Aleister said.

"Or *ambulafolia*," said Lilith generously. "If you want to separate them from the kind that don't have legs."

"Hmm." Morgan seemed to consider, and then, "No. I like 'leafle.'"

"I don't think they're actually people, though," said Crowley.

"But how do you know?" asked Morgan, a spark of mischief in their eyes.

And we were all rather stumped at that.

But before we could ponder this new existential question, Morgan spoke again. "Do you all always watch for the Hunt?"

"It's tradition," Crowley said, and shrugged.

"We don't always see it, though," Aleister said.

"Have you ever joined it?" I asked.

"The Hunt?" Morgan asked. They smiled. "Once or twice."

I had a million questions about that, but before I could ask, more adults came over because apparently Morgan was not actually alone or friendless. So instead we said our goodbyes.

"Was it a good idea to give them our real names?" Crowley asked once we had gotten some space. "Names have power, you know, especially for the fae."

"Morgan wouldn't do anything like that," I said, and I was about to argue further, but just then a murmur rose from the crowd, and we looked up to see the sky changing.

From here the flamelight reached and stretched, but the black sky above was starting to shift from black to gold, and then as we watched, it expanded as the first rider became visible. Ghostly hounds and horses and elk with riders raced across the sky.

We couldn't hear the howls or hoofbeats or the shouts of the riders because the Hunt never crossed into Hell, although I had heard that they'd crossed into Hel, which, confusingly, was another dimension entirely. Here the closest we got to the Hunt was watching as it passed through the space between dimensions on its way to somewhere else. And that was what protected us from its call.

Even though I knew the Hunt wasn't actually calling me, since it wasn't traveling through Hell proper, I still felt a moment of longing. I wondered if Morgan wished they were going too.

It was like watching a holovid on silent. The horses were running full out, frothing at the mouth. The hounds dug their feet into the "ground" and threw their heads back in silent howls. The riders gestured wildly, urging their mounts on. But instead of the sounds of a hunt, all I heard was Yule music, the crackle of flames, and the wails of the passed-on contained in the Pit.

We watched in silence as the Hunt raced across the sky. It was only when the very last riderless horse disappeared from sight and the sky returned to its cozy blackness that the noise of conversation resumed, louder than even before.

A few games, songs, and snacks later, and we were all heading home. My parents and I flew off Stoker Hill and touched down along the street leading to our neighborhood. There were plenty of people still out, so I didn't think twice about the sounds of the flap of wings behind me.

My pocket mirror started alerting me almost immediately, so as my parents walked ahead, I fell behind, reading messages and watching images my friends had captured. Aleister had shared a photo of Damien with a bow on his head the color of his glowing eyes, and a strand of ivy around his neck, under his hanging tongue. I snickered and heard a high-pitched giggle behind me.

I turned, but there was no one.

I went back to my pocket mirror and kept walking. My parents were farther ahead now, but this was our neighborhood, so I wasn't worried.

It took me a few seconds, but then I heard a shuffling movement behind me, quick like leaves running across the ground but much, much heavier. I stopped. The sound stopped.

Well, that wasn't suspicious.

I took another few steps. The shuffling picked up again.

I stopped.

So did the shuffling.

I started walking again, and this time there was another giggle.

I whipped my head around, and my mouth dropped open.

There, standing in front of me, was something I had seen before, and like before, it did not belong. Well, *she* did not belong.

Bright white wings reflected oranges and reds from the flames in the sky and framed the chubby legs and arms of a tiny angel. She had her hands over her mouth, but it didn't matter, because her eyes were smiling big enough to make her joy obvious. It was the same angel I had seen in the memory of Beadle's Tavern, and while I had half joked that she'd be coming downstairs someday, today definitely was not that day.

"What are you doing here?" I breathed.

She did a weird little run with her feet but stayed in place, and a squeal of obvious glee snuck out past her fingers.

I knelt down. "How did you get here?"

"Jump," she said, jumping in place and letting her tiny wings flap a few times.

"You jumped?"

"Yes!" she said, and demonstrated her jump again.

"Okay," I said.

She couldn't stay here, and for a brief moment I considered trying to run, but in a shocking realization, it came to me that I hadn't done anything wrong. I was exactly where I belonged; she was not.

"You want to come to my house?" I asked.

"Yes!" she said again, but this time she ran and leapt at me, and wrapped her chubby arms around my neck.

"Oof," I grunted, trying to support my weight and deal

with a mouthful of curly dark hair. She tightened her grip around my neck, and I managed to get her up onto my hip, and somewhat stable as we stood. I glanced around. Thank Lucifer there was no one else here to see.

"C'mon," I said, bouncing her a little. She was heavy. Heavier than last time, anyway. Maybe gravity was different in memory spaces.

She giggled and thrust her hand out to point. "Fire, hot!"

"Yes, it is," I said, trying to quicken my pace. "You're lucky you ran into me, and not someone else."

"I find you!" the baby angel said. "Aria find Mawki."

"Mawki?" I asked. "Malachi? And your name is 'Aria'?"

"No," the angel said. "Aria!"

"Aria?" I asked.

"No!" said Not-Aria. "Aria!"

"Okay, that clears things up," I said. "Well, this is my house. Let's go in and . . . see what happens."

I opened the door and braced myself.

"Well, it's about time. What took you . . . Oh unholy night," said Dad.

"I didn't do it," I said.

# THIRTEEN

Not-Aria was enthralled by my glamour, our house, and a leaf she had somehow managed to capture and declared to be her pet. Dad watched her like I had let a gargoyle into the house, and Mom stared in shock before she slowly got working to figure out who to call about this. Eventually Meg arrived, and even Ruby, Mom's squad's Intelligence, showed up, which was saying a lot because I couldn't remember a time when Ruby had *ever* come to our house.

If Not-Aria was intimidated by a room of powers staring at her, she didn't let it show. She simply ran around on bare feet, leaving a soft shine of glimmer wherever her feathers touched. It was only when someone even further up arrived that she shrank back and plopped herself onto my lap.

"Well, she likes him," said Meg.

"Have you met this child before?" asked Ruby. "Why is she here?"

"I don't know," I said, avoiding the first part of that question. "She said she jumped."

"I jump!" she said, bouncing in my lap.

The specialist who'd arrived decided he'd take Not-Aria to the offices and call Heaven so they could retrieve their fallen angel. Which was all fine and good, except Not-Aria had other ideas and refused to budge from my lap.

Eventually our house had even more people in it, including, finally, a pair of white-winged angels from above. Not-Aria finally agreed to go with the angels, who looked flustered but not actually surprised that a baby angel had ended up in Hell, apparently of her own accord.

I waved goodbye, and when my house had cleared out, my parents both turned to stare directly at me.

"I didn't do that," I said.

"Okay, it's been a long couple of days," said Mom when Dad looked like he was going to continue asking. "Bedtime."

It was only a message from Uriel reminding me of our upcoming session for our stupid group project that brought my earlier mood back. I supposed holidays couldn't last forever. I grumbled and threw a mini temper tantrum before deciding that I should probably just surrender and pull out the book. It was on my desk somewhere. I vaguely remembered throwing it down in disgust when I had emptied my bag the other night.

I shuffled things around, threw some loose papers onto my bed, before finding the stupid book that I hadn't read yet but probably should. Or I could fake it. I put the book into my bag, ready for our meeting. I went to toss another piece of paper onto my bed, but a few words caught my eye.

*Sean—*

*Depends on what you mean by weirdness.*

Wait. No. I grabbed the letter and read it. It didn't take me long because this was the short, sane letter that I was *supposed* to have sent to Sean. It was supposed to have gone up in flames when I performed the ritual before Yule. I remember it went up in flames. Why did I have it?

I searched my desk. The other pages I had already tossed onto my bed were doodles and notes from class. I flipped through those. And then I went back to my desk and searched through it again, panic growing larger and more overwhelming by the minute. I checked under my desk and behind my bed. I shook out books. No matter where I looked, the only letter that was there was the short one I had written to Sean.

The one I had meant to send.

Noticeably missing was the one where I rambled on and on. The one where I vented every insecurity and feeling in full pathetic detail.

Oh, brimstone!

That letter was so embarrassing. I wouldn't have told ANYONE any of that. Not even with the threat of death or even worse, an eternity in the Pit.

And yet.

That letter. That epic diary of personal feelings vomit was not here. I had performed the ritual. A letter had gone up in electric green flames and been sent out across the ether to reach my intended target, and the letter I thought I had sent was sitting right here. Oh, unholy night, strike me down in celestial light.

I had sent Sean the wrong letter.

# FOURTEEN

Somehow, sleep happened.

It wasn't restful.

In between bouts of vivid dreams of humiliation, I dozed in some sort of fog, but by the time my alarm told me to get my butt out of bed, I felt like I had never fallen asleep in the first place. Worse yet, I still had my meeting for my stupid group project today.

I wondered if I could tell Mom I was sick. Nah, she'd just insist we go to a healer. Maybe I could sweet-talk her. Strike that right note where I was too pathetic to go to school but not so sick that I required a healer. I could do it. I had before.

But then what would I do all day? Wallow? Or worse yet,

what if Sean responded? He hadn't yet, but that didn't mean he wouldn't, and if I was here all day, I'd know when it came in. I'd have to read it. And if I didn't, I'd still know it was there. No, this wouldn't do.

I dragged myself out of bed and managed to pull myself together before Dad started yelling that I'd be late. My reflection was less than fantastic, and I thought the blue flames might be fading a bit. Maybe I should start planning for the next look?

See, that was something worth focusing on. What was the point in stressing? Even if Sean got the letter, what did it matter? It wasn't like I had to see Sean face-to-face. We would probably never see each other in person again, a thought that normally depressed me but had a definite upside now.

Okay, so I did something stupid and slept like crap. That seemed like punishment enough. I had a group meeting that would probably undo me, but I had new clothes, and it had been a good holiday, and I wouldn't have to face Sean.

Really, I was being ridiculous. I had lost sleep over what? Sending a longer letter than I would have liked? Big deal. Maybe he'd even be interested in my ramblings. And even if he thought I was a nutcase, he'd probably politely ignore it or chalk it up to cultural differences.

I needed to be much more worried about my stupid group

project. Theoretically we residents of Hell weren't supposed to be tortured ourselves, but group projects certainly felt like a ring of the Pit.

I only fell asleep during history, but in my defense, it was after lunch, and they decided to show a movie. Obviously I fell asleep. That wasn't even my fault, and I wasn't the only one.

As a bonus I had managed to wake up before Uriel, so when Professor Sauriel turned his attention back to the class, Uriel was the one who got the massive textbook of *A Timeline of Creation* dropped onto his study table. He woke with an unflattering snort and almost managed to fall backward, just catching himself as his wings smacked the kids on either side of him. Azael and I exchanged a grin in response.

Were we friends? Who knew? But we had spent lunch together again, so it definitely felt like I had an ally here. Mom would be proud.

By the time I landed at my doorstep that afternoon, I was feeling pretty good about the day, the lack of sleep and the reason for it notwithstanding. And maybe it was because of that lack of sleep, but the group meeting of the morning, which indeed had been terrible, was just a hazy memory.

I was so thoroughly distracted by school stuff and the hope/fear that I'd have another message from Sean that it took a second for me to register the sound of voices. Well, one voice anyway.

"It's all set," Mom said. "It took forever and more yelling than I'd like, but the soul is where it belongs."

Wait . . . I had never questioned Mom after her late work night because the problem they'd called her about clearly couldn't have been real. The thought that a soul would end up in the wrong hereafter was too ridiculous to take seriously, but was Mom saying that was what had happened?

Stealth mode activated.

I closed the door as quietly as I could and placed my bag onto the floor with the care of an experimental magician.

"We still don't know," Mom continued. "I assigned Ruby to message Anubis's people, but who knows how long it will take to get a response; you know how secretive they are. . . . Yeah, I'm sure. We checked. You don't even want to know how many times." Mom laughed. "I know. I didn't believe it either, but that soul belonged to Heaven."

There was a long stretch of quiet as I crept slightly forward. Mom sighed, and her voice grew more serious. "Yeah. That little surprise visitor didn't help. I've thought about that too. . . . No—absolutely not."

The chair squeaked as Mom stood up, and her feathers fluttered as she rustled her wings in agitation. "There's no reason to think they're related, and I refuse to jump to conclusions. . . . No, not to that, either."

Mom paced the room. "I'm not assigning a connection just because it would be convenient. Leave it to Intelligence, but right now it's just one of those random things. . . . Yes, just like the last random thing . . . Yes, and the other one. All of them are random! I'll talk to you later. . . . Yes. Later. Bye."

Mom sighed, and since the conversation was now officially over, I needed to make a proper entrance or Mom would suspect me of eavesdropping. Which, I mean, fair, but still. I grabbed my bag and quickly slid back to the door and opened it before slamming it behind me.

"Mal?" called Mom.

"Yup," I said. "What are you doing home?" I dropped my bag for the second time.

"Ugh," Mom said. "I had to go in extremely early, so I'm actually going to head to bed for a nap, if you're okay by yourself."

"Of course," I scoffed. I thought we had established that I did not need a babysitter, but Mom and Dad seemed to forget that far too often for my liking.

"Hey, Mom," I called.

"Yes?"

"The baby got home all right, right?" I asked.

"Yes, she did."

"And, um . . ." C'mon, Mal, be subtle. Just had to ask without making her think I had been listening. "I mean, they were obviously wrong, right, about the other thing?"

"The other thing?"

"You know, before Yule?"

*Nailed it.*

Mom hesitated, and I had a feeling she wasn't going to tell me the truth.

"C'mon, Mom," I said. "You already told me what they said. You can't leave me hanging like that."

Mom sighed. "Everyone makes mistakes, even the Jackal," she said lightly, which was all well and good, except that was a thing that didn't happen. Like, ever. "It happens."

We'd just had an entire unit on why that thing did not happen. The Jackal never made mistakes, which was why he had the job in the first place. So how did the soul end up in the wrong place? And what did whoever Mom had been talking to think it was connected to?

"Now, I'm sorry, sweetie, but I really need a nap. Dad's going to pick up food for dinner."

"Okay," I said.

"Stop worrying about it," Mom said, and kissed my head.

What was left of the glamoured blue flames flared gently before Mom chuckled and messed up my hair.

"Hey," I protested. It was the one downfall of this look; everyone was constantly messing with my hair.

"Sorry," Mom said, not sounding sorry at all. "Get your work done."

"I will," I said.

Mom went up the stairs, and I grabbed a snack from the kitchen before sprawling in the living room. I waved the mirror awake and requested a reality show that wouldn't distract me from my work.

I wrote part of an essay that was mostly going to need to be rewritten, before giving up entirely. My brain was too scattered to focus.

WHAT WAS HAPPENING?

# FIFTEEN

I slammed my locker shut with an enormous yawn and an almost pep in my step. We were meeting at Faust's today. Apple cider donuts. Yum.

I thought about inviting Azael along, then thought about how I would feel if one of my squad showed up with one of their new friends to our almost daily check-ins. Yeah, no.

I arrived first, since my school was closest to Faust's.

"Hey, Cecily," I said when I reached the counter.

Cecily was a bast and had worked at Faust's for as long as I could remember. I still wasn't sure if she liked me or not. Her tail always seemed to flick in what I thought was irritation, but she was nice, so I guessed it was okay.

"Hey," she said. "What can I get you?"

"Cider and two donuts, pretty please?" I asked, putting as much charm in as I could, and giving my most amazing smile.

She paused and her ears swiveled. "You look tired."

I deflated. "Yeah, thanks."

Her whiskers twitched as she suppressed a smile. Oh well, at least she thought I was amusing.

I looked behind me to see if any of my friends had arrived—they hadn't—and to scope out a potential spot. There was a couch in the corner with a table in front, and it looked like people were leaving. I could always stand really close and make them uncomfortable until they left faster. That usually worked.

When I turned back to the counter, Cecily was back, a mug of cider on the counter and a plate with not only my two donuts but a third for good measure.

"Aww," I said. "You do like me!"

"Maybe I just feel bad for you," she said, raising one furry eyebrow.

"I'll take it," I said, smiling cheekily. I passed over the coins I owed and an extra for a tip.

Eiael, the angel of luck, must have been on my side, because by the time I got to the couch, the group that had been sitting there were leaving, folding up newspapers and placing mirrors back into briefcases. As soon as I had enough space, I slipped through the gap and laid claim to the entire couch in the most obnoxious way possible.

Thankfully, Lilith strolled through the door before adults could make me move. She searched the room, and I raised my hand and waved to get her attention. She saw me, lit up as always, because I am amazing, and nodded so I knew she'd seen me. I relaxed my couch-guarding position as Lilith took her place in line, and before she had ordered, Aleister had bounced into the café, followed shortly after by Crowley, who entered with a much more casual saunter.

"Scoot," Lilith said, sitting down on the couch and pushing me over with her hip.

I had been distracted by a group of teens who looked like they were going to try to challenge me for the couch, but my attention immediately snapped to the feeling of her hip against mine as she sat down, and the sudden scent of something sweet and light. It was probably from her hair. I leaned in a bit to check, before she looked at me with a *What are you thinking, you pathetic boy?* look, and I immediately turned my head away, only realizing how obvious that was after I did it.

I shoved a donut into my mouth, but when I glanced subtly back, Lilith looked way too amused. She dropped a straw into her soda with a flourish of victory. Ever since we had gotten back from Salem, Lilith seemed to relish it anytime I acted like a lovesick puppy. I mean, she had always liked torturing me. That was just natural. But ever since Salem, she seemed to be keeping track.

"An interesting turn of events," Crowley announced dramatically, before sitting on the edge of the table. Faust would yell at him, but I hadn't seen Faust yet, so maybe Crowley was in luck. From the awesome smells coming from the kitchen, I was betting Faust was back there. Staying solid enough to cook was something Faust had to work at.

"What? Your butt on that table where my food is supposed to be?" I asked. "Not enough carbonation in your soda?"

"Simon and Scarlett breakup?" asked Aleister as he sat next to Lilith and shoved both of us over, resulting in multiple grumbles from me and Lilith both.

"Will you give that up?" Crowley admonished. "Even when it happens, which it will, because he's an idiot, she's not going to be interested in you."

"It could happen," Aleister said. "You don't know."

"I know you're ridiculous," Crowley said.

"What happened, Crowley?" Lilith asked, rustling her wings to fit more comfortably. Her feathers brushed mine, and I felt my cheeks heat in a matching flare to the blue flames that were still doing their best on my wings.

"With very little notice, our teachers completely upended

the syllabi for each class, and now we're studying the effects of different dimensions on our magic." Crowley frowned. "Probably would have been helpful to know before Samhain, but I may have a leg up. I mean, I already figured out how to do it on Earth. Eventually."

"Why is that big news?" Aleister asked. "My curriculum changes all the time."

"Different dimensions," I said. A Cheshire cat grin spread across my face. "Does that mean the mixer is happening?"

We all turned to Lilith.

"I'm not sure," Lilith drawled, but the glint of mischief was obvious.

"Awesome," Aleister said. "Where are they going to do it?"

"I didn't say anything," Lilith said.

"Yeah, yeah, yeah," I said, and waved my hand vaguely over her. "You're absolved. I grant you full plausible deniability."

"Yeah," Crowley said. "Spill."

"Okay," Lilith said, and leaned forward as much as she could with Crowley taking up the table. "It looks like it's happening. They're just in the middle of a pissing contest on lots of stupid stuff, but yeah, it's going to happen. I will say, though, I heard some grumbling that they want it to just be the elders, meaning we would stay here."

The groaning and protests from us were enough to draw

the attention of some people sitting near us, but before we were able to fully work ourselves up to the injustice of it all, Lilith interrupted.

"BUT . . . ," she said, then waited until we stopped grumbling. "That idea was dismissed. Wanna know why?"

"Why?" I asked.

"So, I mean we all remember our little adventure," Lilith said.

"Some of us," Aleister whined. He still hadn't forgiven us for going without him, though we had all pointed out that he could have followed us into the unknown.

"If someone had been loyal to their squad . . . ," Crowley said in a singsong voice.

"Hey!" Aleister protested, clearly about to work himself into another fit.

"Yeah, yeah, yeah," I said. "We've been through that. Aleister is devoted, blah, blah, blah."

"Guys," Lilith said. "You know I *do* have homework to do. Anyway, the fact that Heaven treated us like the bad guys went to show that there is too much propaganda between our dimensions, and apparently other stuff has happened in other ones too. They figure the only way to really solve the problem is to make sure the younger generations get off to a good start before we all get set in our ways. Old dogs and new tricks, you know? And if anything, Mal's little visitor over Yule is only going to make it more urgent."

"I can't believe you didn't call me," muttered Aleister.

"So, we're going," I said, ignoring Aleister.

"We're going," Lilith agreed. "But first we're crashing the negotiations."

# SIXTEEN

"Crashing the negotiations" was kind of an overstatement, since our ultimate plan was just to sort of eavesdrop on the negotiations, which were conveniently being held here. Well, "here" as in Hades, not at Faust's.

As we plotted our unofficial intelligence gathering, Faust emerged to stock cupcakes. This was always a tricky time because if you distracted him in the moment, there was a very real possibility the treats would fall through incorporeal hands. Faust had to focus in order to hold his form solid, and we were not always helpful in that endeavor. But the cupcakes looked amazing, and that was not something I was going to interfere with.

"Hey!" shouted Faust anyway. His chest went slightly transparent, but his arms remained solid as he gestured with his head and booted Crowley off the table. "What is wrong with you? Hindquarters off the table."

We stayed for only a few minutes longer before leaving, after suitably teasing Faust and then convincing him of our undying devotion. We all had homework, although as far as I could tell, Aleister's just involved lifting heavy things.

It ended up requiring a chart to figure out alibis to give our parents. The weekend arrived, and while I hated to lie to them, sometimes a little white lie was the price you paid. If you could even call it a lie. I told my parents I was going to Crowley's, and I was.

"Ready?" I asked.

"Yes," Crowley said, hiking his bag up over one shoulder. He turned to look behind him and yelled, "I told you I already did that!"

There was shouting back from Simon, which I didn't understand, but that was apparently because I didn't speak Older Brother, because Crowley seemed to understand him just fine.

"Do your own laundry!" Crowley shouted back.

". . . could have just thrown it in. Oh hey, Malachi," Simon said as he came into view.

"Hey, Simon," I said.

His jeans were ripped, but it wasn't the stylish kind of rips that Dorian charged extra for. These were just rips. Simon was nearly the opposite of Crowley in every way. Where Crowley was stocky and sleek, Simon was lean and messy. While Crowley was firmly a magic user, with all the study and meticulousness required, Simon had started his Enforcer track three years ago, with all the blunt force trauma required. "Dude, don't you have a spell for laundry?"

"It's not hard," Crowley drawled. "It's already magic. No one's telling you to do it by hand, but by all means, go ahead and do it that way."

"Whatever," Simon said. "Don't need to have an attitude."

"I don't—" Crowley pinched the bridge of his nose. "I'm going."

"Mom and Dad already know?" Simon asked.

Crowley rolled his eyes. "Obviously."

I stifled a laugh. Crowley was the only one of my friends who had a sibling, and I found Crowley's constant irritation at everything Simon said to be epically hilarious.

"See ya later, Simon!" I said, deciding it was best to move this along.

Simon waved vaguely and pulled out his pocket mirror before kicking the door shut in our faces.

"Idiot," Crowley said.

"He's not that bad," I said, already knowing the response that would get.

"He's a doofus," Crowley said.

"But a lovable doofus like—oof."

"Yes!" Aleister said, crashing between us, one arm over each of our shoulders. Crowley and I staggered under the weight of stopping Aleister's forward momentum.

"Why must you do that?" Crowley said.

"Boys' night out!" Aleister crowed, ignoring Crowley's protests.

"Excuse me?" Lilith asked, touching down lightly.

"Squad night out!" Aleister corrected without missing a beat.

"Let's hope this goes better than the last time we snuck off into the woods," Lilith said. I couldn't agree more.

We quickly veered off the sidewalk between two houses and followed a dirt path into the welcoming skeletal arms of the forest. It wasn't an official park, but people did go there to hike or walk their pets, so there were well-beaten paths between the large trees, which were crawling with leaves and other beings. The reds, yellows, and oranges of the stationary leaves swayed gently and lent color to the otherwise black branches and trunks. Glowing eyes blinked out here and there as we walked; it was impossible to feel alone in the woods, but these were the safe kind of eyes. None of the beings here would be revealing any secrets.

The conversation was light and teasing on the walk to our favorite clearing. The farther in we got the darker it became, the light from the flames struggling to reach through the branches above as we headed down paths far less traveled. A faint glow from bioluminescent mosses and plants and the lights from fireflies lit our way.

When we reached the clearing, we tossed our bags onto the ground and Crowley and Lilith started removing every bit of debris. I sat on a fallen log, and Aleister immediately started climbing a tree. Long ago we had learned that it was best to leave the spellcasting to the people who knew what they were doing.

A crunch from outside our circle caught my attention, but when I looked up, I didn't see any reason to worry. We had been coming here for years, and no one had ever followed.

The circular clearing had always been perfect to build a fort in and later to camp in. Once Crowley was able to start using some real magic, we quickly learned that the clearing was a clearing for a reason. Power ran and converged under this spot, which not only kept it clear of overgrowth but also gave us an excellent boost when some serious magic was needed.

Lilith backed away and took a seat on a rock opposite me, leaving Crowley to focus on what he was doing. My knee bounced.

"Can we talk about stuff now?" I asked. "Because seriously, big news, and I've been keeping it in all week."

"Do I need to come down?" Aleister called.

I looked at the tree he had gone up, and if it wasn't for the branches swaying ominously, I wouldn't have even known where he had gone. The trees were so tight here that you couldn't fly to the top. He wouldn't be able to fly down either, which was probably going to be a problem. Wings really only folded in one direction, and unless he wanted to climb down headfirst, he'd need space. I'd like to think he'd kept that in mind for the way down, but knowing Aleister's impulsive "act first, think later" nature, I doubted it.

"Not yet," Lilith said. "The meeting is going to start. We have priorities."

I groaned.

"Were you talking to me or him?" Aleister yelled.

"I'm trying to work," Crowley snapped. "A little quiet, please?"

"What?" Aleister called. "I can't hear you. Let me know when I have to come down."

"Will do," I said. "C'mon, Crowley, you got this."

151

"Let me work," groused Crowley, waving his hand and sending white chalk moving in tiny rivulets.

"Come on, magic man," said Lilith. "We don't want to be late."

Crowley muttered something unflattering, but only a few minutes more had him standing up and brushing dirt off his hands and pants. Our clearing was now decorated extensively with runes and ancient symbols made of poured chalk manipulated by magic.

"C'mon down, Al," Lilith yelled.

The branches rustled and a swarm of leaves ran frantically down the trunk to avoid Aleister's lumbering.

"I swear on all that is unholy, if you mess up this casting . . . ," Crowley said.

"I got it. I got it," Aleister called down. "Ow!"

"Crowley?" Lilith prompted.

"Give him a second," I said, clearly having more faith in Aleister than Lilith did.

"Ow! What the—where is the—argh."

There was always a chance that my faith was misplaced.

"I was rooting for you," I said, already knowing what was going to happen.

Crowley raised a hand. His smile stretched wide. His eyes flared with internal flame, and a red mist swirled up his arm. He always enjoyed this way too much.

An elaborate gesture of his hand sent all the branches arching down, and with a scream, a rustle of feathers, and a thump, Aleister hit the ground.

"Ow," he repeated emphatically while staring daggers at Crowley.

"Dude," I said. "How many times have I told you to leave a way down for your wings?"

The branches creaked and groaned as they righted themselves, completely undamaged by Crowley's interference.

"All right," Aleister said. "Is it actually time? Or did you just want to kill me?"

"If I wanted to kill you, I wouldn't use *falling* as a method." Crowley rolled his eyes.

"It's past time," Lilith said, ignoring the death threat.

We sat around the outside of where Crowley had drawn his runes and watched in nervous anticipation as he completed the surveillance spell. Red swirls of flickering magic rose from the runes until they combined and spread, moving wider and faster until the entire circle was a cylinder of red magic. Crowley continued muttering while his fingers moved in ways I didn't think were normal. Not for the first time I wondered if magicians were double-jointed.

Crowley's last word was said with dramatic finality, and

with it the red haze disappeared until we were looking at somewhere else entirely. Crowley had gotten better at surveillance spells. There was a time when all we could do was hear things in our own houses. Now we were looking into a room completely on the other side of Hades. Although . . .

"Why is the angle so weird?" I asked, cocking my head to the side. We were looking into the room from the viewpoint of something perched in the corner of the room close to the ceiling—if that thing were very bad at perching in the corner of a room close to the ceiling.

"Yeah, seriously," Aleister said. "This is going to ruin my neck."

"Shh," Lilith hissed.

The meeting was in a standard-looking boardroom, with a dozen powers sitting in black chairs surrounding a glass table that swirled with colors. In front of each person was a sheaf of papers. Some of those attending the meeting held quills in their hands to take notes or mugs to sip from. There was a small platter of snacks that looked untouched in the center of the table.

"Are we really humoring this?" asked a man with a pinched face, holding up an invitation very similar to the one my parents had received. His black feathers puffed in irritation.

"Party time," sang Aleister. "C'mon, give us the deets!"

I shoved Aleister with my wing. "Shh."

"We can focus on more than one thing at a time," chastised a younger-looking woman.

"Of course, but a party? In Heaven? Which, by the way, I disagree with immensely. Why, in all that is unholy, would we put our people into their clutches? And make no mistake, it's not as if they've invited all the residents of Hell. They've only invited the angels, as far as we can tell."

"Okay, that's part of the problem," said another woman we could only see from the back. Her curly red hair was the only thing visible that distinguished her from the others beside her. "It's not us versus them, even though, admittedly, it has felt that way for a very long time."

"I'm not sending our people to Heaven," Pinched-Face Man sneered. "There's no telling what will happen."

"What will happen," said Lilith's mom, "is that there will be an awkward mixer where we attempt to get along, and probably stare at each other a lot. It won't be any worse than any other delegate meeting we've had."

"Except they want our kids," said the man. "I can't believe you'd support that after that mess your child was involved in."

I couldn't have stopped the chill of fear if I had tried. Did they know Cassandra had tried to kidnap us? We had sworn to leave certain things out of our stories. Not just to protect Cassandra but to make sure we were not viewed as compromised, or somehow blamed for not only going into the mortal realm, which was bad enough, but also into another great hereafter.

"Heaven," said Lilith's mom with steel in her voice, "was there for the soul. They're not trying to get our kids. And we've already discussed this. It's best for the younger people to go as well if we have any hope of things improving."

I exhaled.

"I can't believe they talk about us like that," grumbled Lilith, her voice slightly shaky in what I was sure was relief.

"But they don't seem to know the extra details," Crowley said, staring at Hell's angelic delegates with a frown.

"Of course not," scoffed Aleister.

We fist-bumped. It was good to know we had all kept our mouths shut. Our parents would probably be even less in favor of this plan if they knew about Cassandra and her kidnapping attempt. As it was, the adults were paranoid enough.

"Besides," Lilith's mom continued, "they'll have their kids too. It's a family invitation. If you don't want to bring your kids, don't."

"Does that mean I can exercise that same option and stay here?" the man scoffed.

"No," came from not just Lilith's mom but at least four others.

Crowley opened a bag of snacks. Aleister rummaged in his bag for drinks.

"Can we at least pretend to be stealthy badasses?" Lilith asked. "Are those flaming choco-melts? Gimme some."

"I think it's a bit much to pretend we're badasses," I said. "We're only eavesdropping about a party."

". . . propose it at least," said a different man. "It makes the most sense; it's neutral territory."

"Wait, what is?" asked Aleister.

"If you shut up, we could find out," I said, taking one of the flaming choco-melts from the bag and popping it into my mouth. The spicy outside immediately gave way to melty chocolatey goodness on the inside.

". . . never go for it."

"Maybe we could ask the fae to set up a pocket dimension?"

"We could have them host?"

"And come back here to find out ten thousand years have passed? I don't think so."

"Are we really discussing this? Have you all lost your minds?" snarled Pinched-Face Man. He stood up so aggressively, his chair fell behind him with a crash. "We have bigger concerns than a blasted party. The escaped soul was just the start. The destabilization here and in the mortal realm, the unease in the Pit. Our very ground shakes beneath our feet."

"And yet we can—"

"Chaos is rising!" he shouted.

What the what now? I exchanged shocked glances with my friends. Lilith looked as stunned as the rest of us.

I was forcibly reminded of Rachel, my would-be bully, who I had passed off as unhinged, with her ridiculous suggestion that I was working to help Chaos. Rumors at school were one thing. Gossip among my uptight track mates was a given. But for someone at this level to be saying the same? That shook me.

"We don't know that," said Lilith's mom. She said it quietly but firmly.

Now, lying is an art form. Like painting or dancing or skateboarding, it takes skill. I was pretty good at it. Only for the best of reasons, of course. Never to be mean. Like when Aleister asked if his new jersey made him look more mature, I was completely successful at telling him with no hint of a lie that he was absolutely a paragon of sophistication. My parents were even better. Lilith's mom was amazing. Kind of a necessity for her job, really.

So, it was shocking for me to realize that she was lying right now.

I don't know what it was. The tightness by her eyes? Some

weird inflection of her voice? A seventh sense? I wasn't sure how I knew, but Lilith's mom was lying.

The man went silent, but he clenched his jaw so tight that I thought something would pop. I couldn't see from the weird angle we were watching the room from, but I would bet his eyes were drowning in flames. The feathers that I could see were trembling, and I was sure he was fighting to keep his wings from spreading. Lilith's mom was still sitting, but from her posture I could tell she was just daring him to say more.

"And if it was," continued Lilith's mom, "that would make ensuring we are one with our brethren a top priority. As ridiculous as this *party* suggestion is, I can't deny the importance of ending this . . . tension."

"Maybe if you could explain why you're so firm in your belief, we would all feel better about focusing on a social event," a man with tousled black hair said much more diplomatically.

Lilith's mom sighed, tapped a quill against her knee, and opened her mouth to speak. We all leaned forward, heads cocked to the side to deal with the weird angle.

"Wait!" said a woman I hadn't noticed, barely visible from our spying point of view. "This meeting isn't private. We're being watched." She started swiveling her head, red magic began to coalesce around her, and we jumped into action.

# SEVENTEEN

Crowley muttered in Enochian while the rest of us dove forward through the image to scrub out the runes decorating the ground. The image turned to a glowing magic haze and then fell in a rush like water that had suddenly been let free. For a few seconds bright sparks of magic covered the ground, before the light faded out and disappeared, merging into the dirt.

"That was close," said Aleister.

"Understatement," I said. My heart was thundering in my chest, and I had the vague feeling that I should vomit.

"Can they track us?" Lilith asked.

"They shouldn't be able to," Crowley said.

"How much trouble will we be in if they can?" asked Aleister.

"None," Lilith said, settling down again in her seat and rummaging through her bag for a snack, which I took to be a good sign. She wouldn't have been snacking if we were going to be sent to the Pit. "The meeting wasn't top secret. It was seriously low-grade—I mean, comparatively—and if they were going to talk about anything important, they should have secured the room better. If anyone gets in trouble, it will be someone in that room, not us."

"Well, that's a relief," I said, before thinking about where that meeting had diverted to. "So . . . uh . . . do we think Chaos is rising?"

When we had planned this night out, it had been just with the hopes of being the first to know where and when we could go to an interdimensional, once in an eternity, raging party. Instead we spent the evening wondering if our entire existence was in peril. We decided it probably wasn't. I mean, what were the odds?

Chaos was practically a fairy tale. It had been subdued at the beginning of creation, when the original beings made order from madness and entire worlds and dimensions took form. There was a balance that kept the system stable, between making and unmaking, and, more relevant to us, between good and evil—specifically that of human soul energy. Since then, so many checks and balances had been put in place that even when we'd faced the threat of Samuel Parris altering the balance of good and evil in Salem, the reality was that Heaven would have destroyed the town or Hell would have sent people to intercede before the balance could have been altered enough to let Chaos rise.

And it wasn't like Chaos had any help. Sure, there were events and people who threatened the balance, but that was just an outcome of their actions, not their goal. I mean, who would want to undo creation? No one in their right mind would ever want everything to go back to nothing. It wasn't even a matter of living or dying. After all, dying was just a transition, not ceasing to be. It wasn't anything like . . . unmaking.

By the time Aleister was nodding off, the scuttling of creatures in the trees had gone nearly silent. There were far fewer glowing eyes, but the ones that were still around were bigger.

"All right," I said, stretching my arms over my head, and my wings out wide. "Let's call it."

"Huh? Wha? I'm up," Aleister said.

"Good," Crowley said, "because I am not putting you to bed."

We stood and stepped back, letting Crowley work one more time tonight. I yawned. My bag hung from my fingers and my wings drooped. Crowley waved vaguely, causing the trees to glow faintly. The glowing limbs creaked as they arched over our clearing, the smaller branches intertwining to form a basketlike netting. We had never been afraid of sleeping out in the open, not really, but before Crowley had been able to manipulate the trees, we used to hang blankets from their branches. This was better.

Once the creaking had stopped, we spread out the blankets and pillows we had brought underneath the shelter formed by the spelled tree limbs. Aleister was snoring even before we were all settled. I curled on my side, my wings and blanket providing plenty of warmth. The trees were so thick here, I could barely see the flames, but I kept them in sight until my eyes closed.

The trembling of the ground underneath me was probably just a dream.

# EIGHTEEN

I groaned, days later, thudding my head down on the lunch table as soon as I took my seat. "Think my parents would notice if I ran away and joined the circus?"

"Probably," Azael said.

We had started having lunch together regularly, and I felt like we had become friends.

Well, at least school friends. I tried not to overthink it.

For a moment I daydreamed of a future performing stunts in dramatic costumes, never having completed Professor Ruth's blessed group project, and never hearing what Uriel thought about anything. Ahh, bliss.

Lately my mind had been a mess of racing theories and

worries, and schoolwork was an annoying nuisance that really needed to go.

"What about locking my group in the dungeon and finishing the project solo?" I asked.

"Pretty sure Professor Ruth would have mentioned if that was acceptable," Azael said.

"Okay, but maybe she'd only mark me down, like, one grade," I said, lifting the top bun on my lunch tray. "What is this?"

"New punishment."

"What?" I asked, not sure I had heard him correctly.

"Oh yeah, didn't you hear?" asked Azael, casually dunking a purple carrot into dip. "Second circle was overrun. Way too many self-centered people, so, therefore, new punishment."

I stared at Azael. He stared back.

"Really?" I asked, looking back at my mystery meat. Was this . . .

Azael leaned forward; our eyes met. He looked from side to side, and then, "Yup."

"Is this . . . ," I whispered.

"People," said Azael.

My jaw dropped, and for half a second I thought we were testing out a new food-source opportunity, but then Azael busted out laughing.

"Nah," he said. "I'm just messing with you. I think they did something with yesterday's lunch."

My jaw stayed dropped. That had been evil. I'd had no idea Azael had it in him.

Azael's laugh faded, and he started to look a little uncomfortable. The curtain was coming down, and oh no, that was not going to happen.

"You wound me," I said, placing my hand over my chest. "I can't believe I never came up with that myself."

I grinned and Azael returned it. He went back to his lunch, and I took another glance at mine, feeling more at home in my new school than I had yet.

"Okay, I know you were joking, but . . . You know what? It's probably fine," I said. Azael snorted in amusement as I reassembled the whatever it was and took a bite.

Azael's mirror chirped an alert, and he pulled it out of his pocket. He glanced at it, smiled, and then gestured rapidly above it before putting it away.

"Sidney?" I asked, swallowing hard. While the school food was typically good, the cafeteria's experiments didn't always succeed. Today was one of those days.

If it was actually people, that would explain a lot.

"Yeah," Azael said. "She has study hall right now."

"Ooh," I taunted.

"Ugh, don't," Azael said. "She's just a friend."

"Sorry, I know," I said. "My bad."

"Don't worry about it," Azael said. Then he hesitated like he wanted to say something. I waited. I had learned that if I interrupted the moment, he would just let whatever it was he was going to say go. "My parents and her parents. I don't know. They have plans."

"Like what?" I asked. "Arranged marriage?"

I laughed at my obviously ridiculous suggestion. Azael didn't.

"Dude, seriously?" I asked.

"No," he said, shaking his head. "I don't know. They just seem to assume that when we're all adultish, we'll like . . . join the families or whatever."

"That seems . . . way early," I said.

"Yeah, never happening," said Azael, his eyes lighting just a bit from within as he locked eyes with me. "With anyone. Ever."

"Oh," I said, blinking stupidly. This was not something I related to. This was in fact the exact opposite of what I related to. "That's okay."

Azael laughed. "I know! It's aces. . . . Wow, that was a *terrible* joke. Never mind. Can we pretend I didn't say that?"

"Say what?" I asked with a wink.

When I got home, I really did try to do homework, but as soon as I sat down, my mind started racing. Surprise visitors, souls in the wrong place, ground quakes? Chaos?! Why were people not stressed about this? Nope, studying wasn't going to work. I thought about just abandoning my books and going to skateboard to get some energy out, but if Dad saw my books, he'd ask what I was working on, and then he'd want to see it, and oh, unholy night, he'd probably want to help.

No, thank you. I shoved everything into my bag and flew up the stairs to drop it in my room. But when I got there, there was no mistaking the glow from my desk. Sean had responded.

I was suddenly singularly focused.

I thought about maybe ignoring it or just throwing the entire box out the window, but morbid curiosity sent me toward it, wondering what Sean would say about my pathetic babbling. But I mean, he probably thought about it for a while before responding, right? It had been days, so if he was responding, he'd probably be nice about it. Or maybe it was just: *I don't think we should write anymore.*

I groaned, and then, with just the tip of my finger, I flipped the lid up . . . which didn't actually help since I couldn't see inside the box from where I was.

Okay, this was like ripping off a finger. Best to do it fast.

I leaned over the open box, still faintly glowing, but where

I expected to see a rolled-up parchment, I saw a blurred image that flickered and swirled. I stood closer and leaned over. I squinted. This was new. The question was, what was *this*?

I reached out to touch it, but then thought back to falling face-first into a new dimension, and pulled my hand back. I grabbed a quill on my desk and touched the surface of the image. It flickered even more, but then I heard a sound that almost sounded like a word. It seemed to be coming from the box.

"Hello?" I asked.

"Mal." At least I thought that was what it was, but maybe I was just being narcissistic. It was echoey and drawn-out. The distortion could have made lots of things sounds like "Mal."

"Hello?" I repeated, and was just about to touch the surface when the image cleared completely. Suddenly I was seeing Sean's profile in high definition. I'd forgotten how nice it was to look at him.

"Sean?" I blurted. He turned to face me for just a second, but then I was looking at his profile again as he turned back to whatever had his attention. I'd have been offended, but the smudges of dirt—and was that blood at his temple?—had concern overpowering any ding to my ego. "What's going on? How are you doing this?" I asked.

"Mal," he said, clearly this time, but then his head jerked to the side again in response to something I couldn't see or hear. Sean cursed. And then he was gone. The box was completely empty. Not only were Sean and the light gone, but there was nothing left to explain. No note, just emptiness.

What had just happened? And why did I suddenly feel so lonely?

It must have been real, but just because I was seeing it now didn't mean it was happening now. And how had he done that? It was beyond my abilities, but Crowley might know. What if Sean was in danger? Was there any way I could help even though I was a dimension away?

Through our brief in-person friendship and our letters, I had learned that Sean wasn't unfamiliar with dangerous situations, and he was good at getting out of them. Not to mention, his mom was a powerful magic user with a strong coven of her own, and his dad was in some secret organization with ties to Heaven that I wasn't all that clear on. He had human allies as well. I was sure he was okay. He had to be okay.

I pulled out another sheet of paper and wrote a quick note to Sean, asking what he had done and if everything was all right. If he didn't respond by tomorrow night, I'd talk to Crowley and see if there was a better way to check in on him.

If the worst happened, checking in on Sean would have been easier. He wouldn't end up here, of course. Sean's soul had clearly been marked for upstairs, but it sounded like we were going to get that mixer after all. Maybe I'd be taking a trip upstairs myself.

I was still shaken, and now permanently concerned, but I felt better with a plan, and this overshadowed my worry about having sent the wrong letter. Maybe Sean had never gotten it anyway. And even if he had gotten it, he clearly had other things to worry about. I knew from Sean's letters that he often helped with supernatural problems in the mortal realm. He was probably chasing a poltergeist or something.

I lit the flame and said the incantation. The letter, the correct and only one, burst into green flames until there was nothing between my fingers at all.

I could only hope that wherever he was and whatever he was doing, the letter found him safe.

I was still staring at the box when Mom yelled that dinner was ready.

# NINETEEN

**P**urple hair and wings that left glitter in their wake was my look of the moment. My parents hated the glitter all over the house, but it faded after a couple of hours, so I didn't know what they were complaining about. Besides, they always said they wanted me to leave a mark on the world. Ha!

It *did* make it a little harder to sneak around, though, so I didn't think this was going to be a keeper. I had skateboarded my way to school the day after Morgan had declared me *très* chic, and when I'd turned to pick up my board, I'd been slightly dismayed to see my entire route reflecting orange and red light.

As a bonus, Zachariah and Uriel were so distracted by my

new style that I was able to add some of the stuff I wanted to the group project without the normal arguments.

By the time Professor Ruth told us to wrap up our group work, I had already added an entire section on Baron Samedi, the *loa* of the dead, while Uriel had tried to rid his book of fallen glitter, and Zachariah had watched in disgust from a chair length away. Our other group member, Melek, whose name I'd only recently learned, had still tried to argue, but with Uriel and Zachariah staying out of it, Melek had only put up token resistance and had eventually grudgingly admitted that my idea wasn't terrible. I made a mental note to do something even more distracting next time I wanted to get my way.

Unfortunately, Rachel and her goons had realized they could find me anywhere, and while they weren't a threat, the constant glares, mumbled comments, and knowledge that they were watching my every move were getting old fast.

I slid into my next class just before the bell to find an already impatient professor tapping his desk with a ruler that existed in this classroom for seemingly only this purpose. We settled quickly, and Professor Jophiel began speaking without even an introduction.

"The chains that bind Chaos are a web that comes from many directions," he lectured, even though I was pretty sure we were supposed to be talking about treaties. "From Baron

Samedi to Anubis, Heaven, Hell, Faerie, and the various underworlds and overworlds, each maintains a line of control against Chaos."

I wasn't even surprised when he met my eyes and held them.

I did, however, jump in surprise when we were interrupted by a booming voice.

"All students will report to the amphitheater after sixth period. That is all."

The disembodied voice thundered through the class. My professor frowned, and I didn't think it was because he had been interrupted. Well, at least not *just* because he'd been interrupted. That was interesting. Not only were we having an assembly out of the blue, but apparently it was a surprise to the teachers as well as the students.

As one could only expect, sixth period was an undisciplined mess of whispers and nudges and notes being passed. No one pulled out their pocket mirrors, but only because of the magic that prevented us from using them during class times.

After Professor Evangeline raised her voice to repeat a question she had apparently already asked several times, if her annoyance was any indication, she threw up her hands and said, "Fine, we'll just sit here, then."

I guess our clueless expressions were just too much for her

sanity, but this was the only assembly us first years had ever had at this school, and there was no obvious boring academic reason for it. I mean, sure, there were lots of reasons it *might* be happening, and those were all worthy of discussion. Much more worthy than whatever it was Evangeline was trying to teach us in Strategy and Treachery.

"It's gotta be about the invitations," whispered Azael.

We had started sitting together once we'd realized which classes we had together, and I was grateful he was in this one. I still hadn't made any connections with anyone else in my new school yet, and it would have driven me crazy to have no one to talk to after that announcement.

"You got one too?" I asked.

"Of course."

"You never mentioned it."

"Sorry," said Azael sheepishly, "but neither did you."

"Well, yeah," I said. "But I'm supposed to be mysterious."

He laughed and threw a pen at my head.

I debated telling him what we had overheard at that meeting and about Chaos potentially but probably not rising, or about the soul that had somehow managed to end up in the wrong hereafter even though Anubis absolutely never made mistakes, but I wasn't sure I should let any of that slip. Azael seemed cool, but it wasn't like I really knew him. Besides, even if I could completely trust Azael, here and now was definitely not the right time or place.

Then I wondered if he had information he was hiding from *me*. I must have narrowed my eyes, because he suddenly narrowed his.

"What."

"Nothing," I said. "Practicing."

"Practicing what?" he asked, eyes still glared in suspicion.

"My smolder," I said. Azael laughed, and I shook off my mood and forced my eyes to release the glare. I didn't want to ruin the one friend I had here with needless suspicion, and at the moment that was all any of this was. Thankfully, Azael seemed to buy my excuse, because I was that good.

Maybe Mom was right and people looked for patterns even when there weren't any. The ground quakes, trespassing souls, surprise visits from baby angels, and whatever was going on with Sean were just random events that I was trying to find connections between, and now I was adding in an assembly that was probably just boring school stuff.

The adults in that meeting we'd magically seen had been doing the same thing, except instead of my disrupted communication with Sean, they'd been adding in the idea of Heaven plotting. I wasn't worried about Heaven. After all, I'd already known that Cassandra wanted to plan a mixer. It wasn't some weird conspiracy. Cassandra just wanted to make friends.

That gave me pause.

If the Heaven invitations had a reasonable explanation, then maybe everything else did too. And that was probably the case. Just because we'd had an adventure at Samhain didn't mean we were due another one just because we had hit Yule.

"Could be about the ground quakes," Azael said, interrupting my musings.

"You think?" I asked.

"Maybe," he said. "Have you ever been to Zagros Mountain? There's a nesting ground for rocs. You know, the giant birds?"

Azael's theory for the ground quakes was an interesting one, and it got the attention of a few of our classmates. Before I knew it, we were taking full advantage of Professor Evangeline's surrender of the class, and got into a full-blown group conversation about whether a flock of rocs had taken up residency nearby, causing the ground quakes.

Our teacher ignored us completely, which I appreciated.

A girl from our class, Parisa, who had joined in our speculating, walked with us when we were called to the assembly. Our teacher tried to line us up single file, and it almost worked, but just as before, she gave up quickly, and while much of the class stayed in their line, Parisa, Azael, and I more or less walked together in a group.

The amphitheater was for exhibitions, assemblies, and theoretically for school plays. I hadn't seen any conversation about a school play yet, and I was skeptical about what that would look like in this school. I seemed to be the only one with a flair for the dramatic, and my confidence that the rest of my classmates could pull off a heartfelt rendition of "Orpheus and Eurydice" was low.

I had only ever seen the amphitheater empty, except for the random groupings of upper-class students who sometimes took their free periods out here. The amphitheater was outside behind the school, with nine rows of moss-covered stone—in reference to the Pit—that circled a central wooden stage at the bottom. The flames on the horizon provided most of the light, but torches around the steps made the interior rings brighter.

I expected to have to sit in the front. In my old school the younger students always had to sit in the front, closer to the teachers, while anyone with any seniority got to hide out in the back. I figured since I was a first year, I'd be stuck front and center, where I'd have to be on my best behavior. But of course that wasn't the case in this school.

All the older students had crowded to the lower levels, and as more students came in, the younger ones were displaced farther and farther into the upper rings.

"Ugh, try-hards," I muttered, shaking my head in disgust. They were all so desperate to be in charge.

"At least we get to sit in the back," Azael said, rolling his eyes.

"Works for me," Parisa said, and the thought crossed my mind that maybe there were more people in this school that were okay.

Everyone settled quickly, but even though all our teachers were on the stage, no one said anything just yet. The rings formed a full circle around the stage, but we were all sitting on one side, creating a semicircle, with the teachers onstage facing our general direction, leaving the rings behind the teachers empty of students.

The muttering quieted as more and more time went by without the teachers saying anything. Why were we having an assembly if no one was going to say anything?

Eventually it was so quiet, I could hear the wails from the Pit, which sometimes carried on the breeze, familiar and meaningless background noise that we all ignored.

I looked over at Azael. He was leaning back on the palms of his hands. I had noticed that the more we hung out the more comfortable he seemed. Were we friends now? Like, real friends, not school friends? Should I invite him to hang out?

I had had school friends before. You know, the people you

talk to in class because you're both stuck there and it's better than being alone, but most of the time you never actually hang out with outside of class? The only people I talked to and hung out with outside of school were my squad, and we had known each other forever. But now Aleister was meeting up with people from his new school, and Lilith probably was too. Crowley had always done his own thing.

And maybe Parisa had school-friend potential, or at least school-acquaintance potential, too. She was sitting straight up at attention like Zachariah always did, but the book she had pulled out of her bag was not a schoolbook. I recognized the cover of the latest Stine book. I hadn't had a chance to read it yet, but it was on my list, and the important thing was that it was fun and interesting and not at all school required.

A bright shift of light brought my attention back to the stage below me. A veil of magic curled up and out so that even though I was near the top row of the amphitheater, farthest from the stage, the screen of magical energy was still eye level to me. The magic cleared, and almost like with Crowley's eavesdropping spell, we were looking into other schools. The screen split, and soon there were views into each track. The Magician, Intelligence, and Enforcer students were similarly arranged at their schools.

The differences in our separate schools were immediately obvious.

The Magicians looked like they were in a dungeon, black walls and glowing runes. Torches lined the walls behind them, casting mysterious shadows across their faces. Seriously, the dramatics were a little over-the-top.

Intelligence students sat in a stark white hall, at tables with bookshelf fronts and sides. There were lights on top of the tables, with even more books scattered across the surfaces, portable mirrors in easy reach.

The Enforcer students were the most chaotically organized, spread haphazardly across a field with training equipment in the background. I saw Aleister immediately, right in the front, shoving a kid next to him and laughing.

Crowley was also easy, front and center. He wasn't interacting with anyone, and I could tell by the cast of his eyes that he was subtly reading a comic he had hidden from sight. But even as I watched, I saw the girl sitting next to him elbow his side. He glanced over and quirked a smile at the eye roll she gave him, before looking back at his comic. Huh. Crowley was making friends too.

Only my school and Intelligence had the older students taking front-row seats. Everyone else with seniority stuck to the back tiers, so I probably wouldn't have found Lilith at all if I hadn't spent years cataloging her every feature. Good for me that I had and I was able to spot her, even though she was small and far away.

She was seated in the back, holding herself stiffly and looking generally uncomfortable. That was an easily solved mystery once I noticed who was sitting next to her: Dina, her nemesis. I wondered how that had happened, but I couldn't help smirking just a little. There was going to be some angry venting later.

In the center of our stage a pillar of fire burst to life immediately, drawing our attention. The roar of flame overrode every other sound, and the wind and heat pushed my hair off my forehead. The flames changed to blinding white, and I shielded my eyes.

I cautiously dropped my arm when the flames died down. A shadow of a figure stood in the middle, somehow facing all directions at once. There was the impression of a tall, broad-shouldered shape, large wings that arched and draped to the ground. My heart was already racing before I noticed the golden gleam to the impression of feathers.

I couldn't see any details. I wasn't even sure if "seeing" was what I was doing, because I knew somehow that this person was appearing not only to the schools of Hades but also to the schools in the larger cities of Dagon and Thoth. And I knew that the feathers were gold, which left very few people that this person could be.

Only archangels had golden wings, and there was only one archangel in all of Hell.

Lucifer.

# TWENTY

I sat up straighter. Azael got off his palms and leaned his elbows onto his knees. In fact, everyone here and in the other schools had either leaned forward expectantly or straightened their spines completely.

"Thank you for your attention."

I had never heard Lucifer speak. I wasn't sure if what I was hearing was his real voice or only an impression because of the simultaneous appearance, but the sound sent chills up my spine. My feathers lifted, and glitter from Morgan's glamour fell to the stone row I was sitting in. I wasn't alone, though. Wings all around me were twitching and shuddering. I knew right then that I never wanted to hear Lucifer angry.

The power was obvious even with just this small greeting.

"I've asked you to attend this assembly regarding recent events. I have been alerted to a potential breach into our dimension."

Everyone near me turned to look at me. Seriously? I mean, okay, yes. I knew about a breach, but it was hardly my fault, and no one else should have known about it. Dad hadn't even let me take a selfie with Not-Aria.

Rachel's glare cut through them all, and with way more hostility.

"I didn't do anything," I hissed. If the shifting at the other schools was any indication, my friends were facing the same accusing glances. Even Jophiel was leveling a suspicious look from the stage.

I blushed. I hadn't thought *that* many people knew about our misadventure. Well, okay, maybe I had, but I hadn't thought they had *suspicions* about it. I'd assumed that everyone had seen it as the badass adventure it was. You know, grudging respect, a little jealousy, that kind of thing. I mean, no one could think we were in league with Parris or, even more ridiculous, with agents of Chaos.

"This breach may be related to . . . outside . . . imbalances. I am providing this information to you as future guardians so that you may be attentive and aware. If you discover anything you believe might be relevant, please alert your teachers. Do *not* take matters into your own hands."

Okay, I knew I couldn't actually "see" his eyes since he was looking in all directions at once, but I certainly got the impression that if I had a soul, it was being stared at right now. I swallowed with an audible gulp. A beat of silence passed.

Wait, what did he mean by "imbalances"?

"There is nothing to be concerned about. These things happen from time to time, and there are systems in place for when they do."

After Parris's successful escape through multiple levels of security, I wasn't 100 percent sure that this was a reassuring statement, but then again, maybe I wasn't thinking clearly, with my face flushing in embarrassment, because people were *still* staring at me.

"I would also caution that rumors and gossip help no one. Indeed, such actions can put everyone at risk. I will not have our world corrupted by those too simpleminded or lazy to verify a source. Having said that, I expect credible information to be reported immediately."

There was some muttering, but for the first time it was not from anyone around me. Lucifer cocked his head, or at least gave the impression of doing that. It was all very strange.

"Oh, yes," Lucifer said. "There will also be a party of

sorts, to foster cooperation and goodwill between . . . well, everyone. More information will be provided. Your instructors are available for questions. I expect everyone to represent us well. That is all."

Lucifer disappeared from the stage in a burst of flame that took me by surprise, and so I was momentarily blinded when the views into the other schools began to invert and disappear, leaving a haze of magic on the stage before everything returned to normal.

I blinked hard, trying to force the dots away. By the time I readjusted to the light, or absence thereof, the other schools were gone. Several of our teachers stood on the stage, some still muttering among themselves, but no one was telling us to leave, so we kept our seats.

*Outside imbalances*, Lucifer had said. Did that have to do with the soul Mom had been talking about? Had it happened more than once? Did that mean it had happened in Heaven, too? We would have heard, right? I thought the soul ending up here was a glitch, but what if it wasn't? What if the imbalances Lucifer mentioned were something else?

I kept going back to what we had overheard when we'd eavesdropped on the meeting. *Chaos is rising*, the man had said. That couldn't be happening. He was obviously overreacting, right?

Lucifer had said everything was fine, but then again, wasn't that a big ol' red flag in itself? We'd had a school assembly with Lucifer himself! That had to mean something. Or was it just because of the mixer with Heaven?

But if the assembly had been about the mixer, Lucifer wouldn't have had to be reminded to talk about it. That would have been the first thing he talked about. Wouldn't he have had that at the forefront of his mind, instead of having to be nudged to mention it?

Well, then. There was only one conclusion.

The adults were hiding things.

Professor Jophiel stepped forward and we waited.

"Attention," Jophiel said, even though it was so quiet that I could hear the crackle of flames and the screams of the imprisoned. "All of the schools in Hades, Dagon, and Thoth are being advised simultaneously. I expect you all to keep clear heads. There have been breaches before, and there will be breaches again. Most are completely harmless, a lost shade or brownie skipping between worlds. These things are being monitored. All we ask is that if you find abnormalities, bring them to our attention so that we can keep the correct people aware. Are there any questions?"

Uh, yeah. I had a million questions. What imbalances was Lucifer talking about? Was Not-Aria the only breach, or had there been others? How did the quakes come into play? Or the weird colors in the sky? Was Chaos actually rising?!

So yeah, I had questions, but no one else had their hands up.

At my old school I wouldn't have thought twice about bringing the spotlight onto myself. Attention was something I hadn't ever feared before, but here in this place . . . Okay, landing a superhero pose with glamoured flames trailing from my wings in a crowd of students two minutes before class was one thing. But demanding answers now, when everyone was silent, and Jophiel was still standing there all intimidating and Lucifer had just looked through me?

Nope. I didn't ask any questions.

"As for the interdimensional mixer," Jophiel continued, "Professor Mariangela will address that. If you please?"

"Yes," said Professor Mariangela, a teacher I had seen around but who didn't teach the first years. I had only ever seen her at a distance. "Over the next four weeks, studies will shift to a curriculum focused on the roles of various dimensions in keeping balance. For the older students some of this will be review, while for our younger students this may be all new information. It is imperative that you are fully informed. We will be sending a scroll home that will recommend that those of you not reaching excellence be kept home. Of course, your parents may choose that you remain home anyway, and that will also be permitted."

There was some muttering at that, and I felt a little better, with that small sign of rebellion from other students. I hadn't felt too much camaraderie with my classmates so far. They all just seemed so . . . complacent, but no one liked the idea of being kept away from the action. Especially with something like this. A meeting between dimensions that hadn't happened since . . . well, probably since shortly after the descent, when Lucifer had flown with his squad to help cage evil away and create balance in the universe. Back all the way in the beginning. At least, the beginning of anything that could be called existence.

Until that moment, Chaos had constantly fought to regain control over creation, but once the balance was established, Chaos was truly made powerless. Nearly so, anyway. And without Chaos as a universal enemy and the constant threat of devastating imbalances, people turned their attention inward, and lines had been drawn. We had lost any unity that had existed, and the sense that we were all in this together was gone.

Technically speaking, either good or evil could screw everything up. After my trip to Salem, I thought there might actually be a 60 percent chance that "good" would send us spiraling, but that might have been my bias speaking, especially since it wasn't just the two of our dimensions holding everything together, and who knew what was going on in the others?

"The location of the mixer is still to be determined, though it will likely be in neutral territory. In the meantime, we will be readying you all in both history and protocol so that we minimize any . . . cultural misunderstandings. If this is a disaster, it will not be due to us, and in case that was not perfectly clear, it will not be due to *you*."

So, no pressure.

True to Professor Mariangela's word, our coursework immediately changed, and my head was spinning with history that I was pretty sure I should have had the next few years to learn. As a bonus, Professor Ruth decided we could scrap our group project entirely, promising we'd get back to it after this once-in-an-eon event had taken place. I was going to do everything in my power to make sure we never revisited this group project idea again.

"Watch it," snarled an upperclassman as a wing thumped into my back.

I didn't need to turn around to know it was one of Rachel's minions or that he had followed me, because there was no reason for him to be in this hall.

"Oh man," I said in mock surprise. "Should I call a healer? You mean you couldn't see me standing here? Really?"

"We're always watching," he said.

"Good," I said. "Maybe you'll learn something."

With a departing glare, Rachel's minion stormed off, no doubt heading to where he should have been all along.

This look had to go!

# TWENTY-ONE

When I arrived at Glamourie after school, Morgan was outside with a bucket and sponge, looking at the wall, disgruntled.

"What happened?" I asked.

Morgan turned. Today their skin was a golden bronze, with gold tattoos framing their bright green eyes. Golden earrings lined their pointed ears. A frown marred the look.

"Oh, just some graffiti," Morgan said.

"Graffiti? Who would do that?" I asked.

I stood next to Morgan and surveyed the symbol, which I didn't recognize. It was a swirl of lines that somehow managed to form different images depending on which lines you focused on: an animal head, a leaf, scattered arrows. Why would someone graffiti Glamourie?

"Have you tried to magic it away?" I asked. "A magician should be able to get rid of it."

"I may call in someone," Morgan said. "Since I seem to be having no luck getting rid of it with my own magic or the old-fashioned way either."

Morgan tossed the sponge into the pail of water.

"But for the time being," they said. They waved their hands in patterns that I knew went along with their casting, and as I watched, the symbol faded from view.

"What does it mean?" I asked.

Morgan sighed. "Just some old nonsense."

We stood in silence for a moment before Morgan turned, put their hands on their hips, and studied me for a beat. "It's not your appointment."

"I know," I said. "Can you pretty please sneak me in?"

"Not liking the new look?" Morgan asked lightly.

"The glitter gives me away," I said. "Seriously, everyone knows where I'm going. My parents realized I snuck down and took the last piece of pie, which apparently my dad wanted, but if he wanted it, he should have eaten it. I mean, really."

"Okay," Morgan said, still looking far too knowing, like I wasn't just here to get a new style.

I squinted my eyes. "What."

"Nothing," they said. "You want to change a look, no big deal. It's what I'm here for. C'mon, let's go inside."

"What," I said again, following them into Glamourie, the bells chiming over our heads.

Morgan sighed and turned back to face me. "How's school?"

"Ugh," I groaned. "School is fine. It's school. Whatever. All my classmates just love everything about it. Some people are jerks intent on making my life miserable. You know, school stuff. I mean, who cares if one of my teachers thinks I'm an agent of Chaos and I'm pretty sure Lucifer looked through my soul or whatever there is? And now we're all expected to be doing a crazy amount of work—"

"Whoa," Morgan interrupted. "Agent of Chaos? Lucifer?"

I sighed.

"Have a seat," Morgan said. "Tea? Cider?"

"Cider, please?" I asked pathetically, throwing myself into my favorite spinny chair and letting it fly. Glitter formed a circle on the floor around the chair.

Morgan stopped the chair with their foot and held out a mug filled with steaming cider. They waved vaguely, and a throne-like chair appeared next to me. They sat down and held their own teacup balanced between the fingers of both hands. The steam swirled in a direction that was not at all natural, forming spirals and shapes up and around Morgan's bright green eyes. Morgan crossed one leg over their knee and leaned back. "Now, start again."

So I did. Sort of. It wasn't the word-vomit of the letter I had accidentally sent to Sean, but it was a decent summary of my school frustrations.

"Are you going to this thing?" I asked.

"The mixer?" they asked. "No. I left Faerie specifically to get out of politics. Besides, the invitations brought here were only for angels. If Heaven wanted me, they would have gone to Faerie, where they think I still live, and you can see how that might cause issues."

"Don't you want to go?" I asked. "If other people in Faerie were invited?"

"Well, we don't know for sure that people in Faerie were invited," Morgan pointed out, before acknowledging, "I would wager that some members of both the Seelie and Unseelie Courts were. If what is happening is truly what I think it is."

"What do you think is happening?" I asked.

"Now, by all means, this may just be an angelic reunion," they said, pausing to blow across the delicate teacup and sending the steam into the shape of a cat, which curled and twisted around the cup until it disappeared with a tail flick. They took a sip. "In which case, it will be you and your lot standing around awkwardly with a bunch of white-winged doves. But . . . with all the talk of late, I would imagine we're really discussing a get-together beyond just the great hereafters. But we'll see."

"What have you heard?" I asked, frowning.

Morgan stared at me, took another sip of their cider, and then set the cup out to the side, where it sat stationary, as if there was a table beneath it. It rested there for just a moment before disappearing completely.

"What are the angels saying?" Morgan asked.

"Nothing, ever," I said.

"I'm sure not nothing," Morgan said. "But what I mean specifically is . . . You know what? Never mind."

"Wait, no," I said. "What were you going to say?"

"Something that would be better suited to someone else," Morgan said.

"C'mon, I told you stuff," I said, fully aware that I was whining and that I was normally much better than that.

"I was going to ask what they're telling you about . . . chaos," Morgan said, letting their voice go airy and light on the last word, making it sound like they were talking about lowercase chaos, when they were clearly asking about uppercase Chaos.

"You guys talk about Chaos too?" I asked.

"We're all about *chaos* in the Unseelie Court," they said,

with a swirling hypnotic twinkle in their eye. They studied me for just a moment longer and then winked.

I glared.

"I worry about your education," they said. "You know that you angels aren't the be-all and end-all of keeping Chaos at bay, correct?"

"Yeah," I said, rolling my eyes. "The reason the mission is successful is that multiple dimensions all play their part, so even if the enemy goes after one, the others can maintain their hold. Heaven and Hell keep the balance of human soul energy."

"And the other dimensions?" Morgan asked.

"Well," I said. "I mean, I know others do their thing."

"Uh-huh," Morgan said. "They just do their 'thing'? There is more to the universal balance than just human soul energy. Faerie plays its part as well, and if one dimension falls, it's more likely that others will too."

"But you're here," I said, and immediately regretted it.

"I am," Morgan said. "And I can easily return to Faerie if need be. I'm very old, Malachi. I've earned my break."

"I didn't mean—"

"I know. Don't worry about it." Morgan rose. "And I think that's enough serious conversation for one day. What are we thinking instead of glitter?"

# TWENTY-TWO

By the time I met up with my friends at Burn This Book, I had a new look—bright red hair and a gargoyle tattoo that curled around my neck. Dad was going to hate it. My friends didn't even blink as they caught my arrival through the stacks of the fantasy section.

I threw myself onto the couch in the nook they had settled in, which wasn't nearly as comfy as the velvet one at Glamourie. The low coffee table was covered in books. I stretched out with a loud groan.

"Hey, wait a minute," I said. I never had this much room on the couch. "Where's Aleister?"

"He had plans," said Lilith. "Some kid in his track. Did

you guys get all this work on the restructuring of the first ring and its corresponding effect on Heaven, or is that just me?"

She looked at my hair and squinted.

"What?" I asked.

"What's wrong with your regular hair?" she asked.

"Nothing," I said. "I just wanted something different."

"You just want to stand out, you mean," said Crowley. "I get it. You're stuck with stiffs."

"Gee, it's nice to see you guys too," I grumbled.

"Don't get huffy," Crowley said, scribbling one last phrase in Enochian before snapping his journal shut. Huh. He really was using the Nephilim journal for school. "And no, Lilith, we are not studying that. Remember how I said we were studying the effect of other dimensions on our magic? Well, that seems to be the theme. We're doubling down on it. Not just theory. We're supposed to practice under real conditions. I have no idea how they're going to do that."

"What about the breach? Do you think it was more than our visitor?" I asked, kicking my feet onto the worn table now that both Lilith and Crowley had closed their books and put them away.

"What, like the one they talked about at the assembly?" Lilith asked. "Mom said there may have been something else, but probably something not sentient or barely sentient. Maybe something unusual enough to cause a rumble, but nothing concerning."

"They think the ground shakes were because of the breach?" I asked.

"It's one theory, anyway," Lilith said.

"Did they say the soul has anything to do with it?" I asked.

"What soul?" asked Crowley. Lilith also looked puzzled.

"The one that ended up here, instead of in Heaven," I said.

Oh, unholy night. Had I not actually told them?

Crowley and Lilith made faces like they had no idea what I was talking about. I dropped my feet from the table and leaned forward. I thought for sure Lilith would have heard.

"Mom got a call, and it was legit, a soul ended up in the wrong spot. It was supposed to go to Heaven but ended up here."

"No way," Crowley said.

"That can't be right," Lilith said.

"Would I lie to you?" I asked, regret rushing through my veins again. "I'm serious. Mom thought it was nonsense, but she checked it out. She had to deal with Heaven and everything. Your mom must know."

"She doesn't tell me everything," Lilith said. "Why wouldn't they say that at the assembly?"

"That's what I wondered," I said. "Mom didn't even believe

it when the call came in, but when she admitted it was real, she acted like it was no big. But we'd just finished having an entire section in school on why Anubis never makes mistakes, so . . ."

"Theoretically he doesn't," Crowley said.

"Where else could there be a problem?" I asked. "If Anubis never makes mistakes, how does a soul end up in the wrong hereafter?"

"And why didn't they tell us?" Crowley asked.

"They don't tell us anything," Lilith said with an adorable scowl. *Not the time, brain.*

"We just had an assembly," I said. "Lucifer spoke to all of us, in the middle of a school day."

"Yeah, because we have that party coming up," Lilith said. "That's history in the making."

"True, and that would be reason enough, but if that was why we had the assembly, why wasn't it the first thing he talked about?" I asked. "Lucifer had to be *reminded*. He talked about the breach first, which by everyone's reasoning is supposedly a trivial little situation where some brownie or shade wandered in or maybe a gremlin wandered out. But a soul ends up here when it was supposed to be in Heaven, and no one says anything?"

"We all know about the mixer," Lilith said. "But they don't announce work stuff to us."

"True," Crowley said. "Maybe the soul *was* the breach,

and they just didn't want to give us details? I mean, besides Mal's pet baby angel."

"That could be it," I acknowledged. "And she's not my pet!"

"But if that were true, why would they ask us to report any information?" Lilith asked, her fingers tapping out a rhythm on the surface of her book. Not the rhythm that meant anxiety was swallowing everything, but the one that meant she was puzzling something out.

"Maybe they think it will happen again?" I suggested.

"Or maybe they're just not telling us everything," Crowley said.

"See, this is why we need to get our own info," I pointed out. "It's got to be related, right—all this stuff and all that talk about Chaos with a big *C*?"

"The only one I've heard Chaos talk from was the guy we listened in on, and he seemed unstable," Crowley said. "I would hardly qualify that as 'all that talk.'"

Wait, what? It seemed to be the only thing I heard lately!

But I supposed what Crowley said was true. Technically that was the only time it had come up with all of us together. I hadn't told my friends about the drama and suspicion I was experiencing at school. It should have been funny that my classmates thought I was secretly an evil agent for Chaos, but for some reason it wasn't. It was embarrassing. My friends already knew I went to school with people I wasn't meshing with, but I'd rather them have the impression that I was coolly aloof than isolated.

Whatever, I didn't care if the people in my track liked me anyway.

"Actually," Lilith said, "*we're* talking about Chaos at school."

"You are?" asked Crowley, surprised.

"I mean, a little," Lilith said. "But it came out of nowhere."

"What do you mean?" I asked.

"I mean, until the invites, we were following a syllabus, and now . . . we're not," said Lilith. "Well, I should say we're following a new syllabus. It does include some randomness about Chaos, though. Mostly about people or groups who have followed Chaos in the past."

"Followed?" I asked.

"Yeah," Lilith said. Her eyes lit up the way they always did when she was passionate about something. "Ever since Chaos was locked away, there have been people who've wanted to let it out."

"Why would anyone want that?" Crowley asked in disbelief.

"Some people have thought that the rules and order that maintain the balance are restrictive, that true freedom has no constraints at all, and that if Chaos were free, everything would be as it was meant to be."

"That's ridiculous," I scoffed. "That isn't freedom, that's destruction."

"And those are the other followers," Lilith added. "You have the true believers, who think being free is in the constant making and unmaking of everything, and then you have those that just want it all to end."

"Why would anyone want it all to end?" I asked.

"Eternity is a long time," Lilith said pointedly.

"Crazies," I said. "All of them."

"Definitely," Crowley said. "Maybe the crazies are trying to cause problems. Or Heaven. You know, same thing."

I thought about Cassandra's letters and Sean's random appearance in the box and wondered if they were related to the things happening now.

"One of my teachers seems obsessed," I said. "And Morgan mentioned something, but then they changed the subject."

"Fairies are tricky," Crowley said.

"That's a stereotype," I said.

"A stereotype for a reason," Crowley said. He frowned. "You haven't been accepting food from them, have you?"

"That's racist," said Lilith. "Besides, the food thing only works on mortals who happen to end up in Faerie. Neither of which applies to us, but that is interesting."

"It was one cup of hot cider!" I said.

"Not that," Lilith said. "Of course you're not going to be stuck in Faerie forever, especially since you're not in Faerie right now. I was talking about the other thing. It is possible the adults are trying to sweep something under the rug. I mean, Lucifer spoke to us. Lucifer! An archangel spoke to all the angelic students in Hell. That must mean something, right? Beyond just what our teachers said. Or I suppose it could be that they're genuinely freaking out about the mixer."

"Freaking out?" I said skeptically.

"Not everyone has been to Heaven," Lilith whispered. "Or even met another angel who wasn't a power. And when they have, I get the impression that the interactions haven't even gone as well as ours did."

"Ours worked out," I said. "Eventually."

Crowley snorted.

"It did," I said, feeling defensive of both Cassandra and Morgan, and a little irritated that I was defending the former. "Why is Aleister not here?"

"You already asked that," Crowley said. "Maybe the glamours are ruining your brain."

"I know what you said, but he should be here. This is something we should be discussing as a squad," I grumbled.

"You're in a mood," said Lilith, which definitely put me in a mood. It was rare that I got irritated with Lilith, because she was usually amazing and perfect and made my stomach all tingly, but right now I was irritated. Maybe I *was* in a mood.

"But it's possible we all are in a mood," Lilith continued. "Meet up tomorrow?"

Lilith stood up and packed her bag. She slung it over her shoulder, and we did the same.

"Hey, wait," I said, remembering my promise to myself, Aleister's absence solidifying my determination. "Remember Azael? What do you think about letting him come sometimes? I've been hanging out with him and he's cool."

"You've been hanging out with him?" asked Lilith. "Like, a lot?"

"Obviously not," I said, "Since I'm always with you guys. Just at school, but I think he would be fun outside of school. I mean, if it's a problem—"

"I don't see why it would be a problem," said Crowley, an evil grin forming on his face. "Do you, Lilith?"

"No," said Lilith. "Of course not. Whatever. You're allowed to like whoever you like."

"Not everyone is my type," I said, rolling my eyes. "Contrary to popular belief. Besides, he's ace, but whatever, he's cool."

And apparently *the mood* had taken full hold, because normally the hint that Lilith was jealous would have been all I needed to float for the rest of the night.

"I'll see you tomorrow."

I was out of Burn This Book before anyone answered, and even though I felt my pocket mirror activate, I ignored it. I really wanted to write another long letter to Sean. Not that I had gotten a response to the last one. Unless you counted that weird appearance, but there had been nothing since then. Maybe I should try again. Even if the worst had happened and he had made his way to Heaven, my letter should still have found him. And knowing one way or another would feel a lot better than wondering.

I ignored my mirror completely the rest of the night. Dad hated the tattoo. He didn't say anything, probably because of my *mood*, but I could tell. After dinner I went up to my room and was beyond disappointed that the box was dark. I wrote another letter anyway. Nothing long or venting like I wanted to. Just a check-in to see if everything was okay. I did the ritual so carefully, it easily took twice as long, but I knew my letter would find him. It had to.

I couldn't sleep. It was probably too early anyway. I didn't want to read or listen to music. Nothing sounded like fun. I thought about grabbing my skateboard and hitting the roof, but Mom would say it was too late for that. Or worse yet, she'd think something was wrong and want to talk. Blech.

After a bit of tossing and turning and staring, I decided

I'd do something new. It was a gamble. If we weren't actually friends, this could come across as very cringe. Because what I should have been doing was reaching out by mirror, but, well, we hadn't actually swapped handles yet. I scribbled out a quick note before I could think twice.

> *You up?*
> *—Mal*

I tossed it up and watched it disappear with a brief flash of flame.

It took a few minutes, but before I could completely work myself into a panic about school friends not actually equaling real friends, a piece of parchment fell from the sky onto my stomach.

> *Yeah. What's up?*
> *—Az*

Maybe I was capable of making friends on my own. Who knew?

# TWENTY-THREE

It turned out that trying to cram an eternity's worth of history into a couple of weeks' worth of classes was a nearly impossible task. A task that only Lilith's and my tracks were focusing on, so much so that I was seeing less and less of Lilith as she crammed at home.

The magicians were working practical magic under unusual conditions, and who knew what Aleister's track was doing. He had missed more and more of our daily check-ins as well, but unlike Lilith and me, it didn't seem to be so he could cram schoolwork. It was so he could hang out with his new friends, who were clearly more important than us.

Crowley was a "natural" at his new assignments, though

we all knew it was only because he'd had a head start. He had already learned how to use his magic in the mortal realm, and under much higher pressure.

I was also starting to have a sneaking suspicion that he had spoken to Charity, even after we'd returned home. There were moments when he'd let something slip that sounded an awful lot like it had come from one very chatty witch. As the silence grew between me and Sean, the urge to talk to Crowley about that suspicion grew larger. I would remember at night after I fell into bed, then would forget immediately when morning came. Then it would happen all over again.

The frantic—and, let's be honest, ridiculous—amount of work greatly reduced our snooping, as well as our squad hangouts. I hadn't seen Lilith's basement in weeks. On the other hand, Azael started coming over to study, and my parents were ecstatic.

By the time my regular appointment at Glamourie rolled around, I was so tired, I fell asleep in Morgan's chair. I hadn't even told them what I wanted, but when I woke up, my hair was back to its natural color, with silver highlights that sparkled in the light of the flames. My wings were almost natural but *more*. All the blue, purple, and green highlights that were normally there when I caught the light just right were emphasized so that the colors were always there, even without being directly under the light.

"It's perfect," I said.

"Of course it is," they said.

And then Morgan packed me a bag of tea from Faerie that was supposed to give me energy and focus for study but smelled like perfume. I brought it home and tossed it on the counter, just as Azael knocked on the door for yet another study session.

I took one look at Azael's tired face and decided to throw caution to the wind and brewed a couple of cups, which were currently sitting on the coffee table beside us. It didn't actually taste like perfume, and while it did seem to perk us up, it didn't make the work any less boring,

"Why are we doing this?" Azael said, dropping his head through the hologram hovering over the coffee table. He'd been reviewing the text for his essay. "It's just a party."

"Apparently, it's a very extremely important diplomatic mission," I said.

"How bad could Heaven's people possibly be?" Azael asked, lifting his head and clearing the hologram. He hadn't gotten permission to go to Glamourie, but he had started being more creative with his fade, and it now featured shaved flames on the side of his head. "I mean, do the adults think this party idea is a trap? Or, like, we're going to violate some hundred-thousand-year agreement?"

"Not a clue," I said. "How many words was this essay supposed to be?"

"Two thousand," Azael said. "Skip the contractions and add a bunch of adjectives."

"Ugh." I set my head on the table.

"What do you think it's like?" Azael asked.

"What what's like?" I asked. "Being so stuck in your ways that you're afraid of a party?"

"No," Azael said. "I've met my parents; I already know what that's like. Heaven. I know we're probably not going there, but wouldn't it be cool? Maybe if this goes well, we can set up a student exchange program. Unholy night, wouldn't that be great? To go somewhere else for the whole year?"

I must have stared at him for too long, because Azael shifted, and his expression closed off like it used to before we started being actual friends instead of two people stuck in the same track together by Fate.

"Not that I want to go there," he said, getting ready to reactivate his hologram. His spine was stiff, and his wings were closed tight to his back.

"No," I interrupted. "Trust me. I'm the last one to say that you should only want to be here doing this. I've been."

"Been what?" Azael asked, tentatively making eye contact again.

"Been . . ." I hesitated. My squad had sworn secrecy. I should ask them if this was okay. "To Heaven."

Or I could just blurt it out.

"What do you mean?" he asked slowly.

I could totally say I was kidding.

"You can't tell anyone," I said.

Or I could double down.

Azael leaned forward, and there was that hellish mischief on his face. I looked over my shoulder. My parents were still at work, but you never did know, and this was news that could not get out.

"When we were in Salem," I said. "That's the city in the mortal realm we went to. There was this seraph named Cassandra. She . . . ended up being okay after she stopped trying to kidnap us—"

"Kidnap!"

"Shh! Yes, it all ended up okay. Anyway, we were working together, and there was this moment when we were using mortal and celestial magic—"

"What?!"

"Shh! Do you want to hear or not?" I admonished.

"Okay, okay," he said. His wings were practically trembling in excitement, and if my parents came in now, they would know we were up to no good. "I won't ask about the potential world-ending mixture of magic."

"Yeah, then Crowley got his to work too," I said. "So it was mortal, celestial, and infernal."

Azael laughed. "Universe-ending!"

"Anyway," I said. "There was this moment, and all of a sudden, we were there. In Heaven."

"No way. What was it like?"

"I mean, we weren't there long. Only a couple of minutes, tops. It was weird?"

And so, I filled Azael in on our adventure. It was a story I hadn't really told before. Not by myself anyway. When we'd gotten back, we'd of course filled Aleister in, but when I'd been interviewed by the Powers That Be and my parents? Let's just say we'd all decided to leave some details out. But with Azael I didn't leave anything out.

I mean, okay, part of my brain was dinging wildly, like maybe I was sharing too much and this was going to bite me in the butt, but I ignored that part.

By the time my parents got home from work, we had pushed our work aside and were in the middle of a game of *Soul Vengeance*. I vaguely remembered that I hadn't picked up the free games from Alighieri's, but I really didn't have time or energy to deal with Tony. Normally my parents would have grilled me on whether my work was done, but they were so happy that I was making friends with someone in Command that they just invited Azael for dinner and that was that. It was exactly the break I needed.

"Oh, brimstone," said Azael just as he was getting his things together to go home. "I think I left that book Professor Jophiel let me borrow in your room."

"Yeah," I said. "C'mon."

He followed me up the stairs, and I threw my door open. "I think it's on my desk."

I shuffled things around. The book had to be on top. We'd just been in there. Scroll. T-shirt. Ooh, graphic novel I'd meant to read but had forgotten about. Boxer shorts—oops, hide those. Ah, there it was: *Introduction to the Great Divide and Other Cataclysms*.

"Here it—" I turned and immediately lost all train of thought when I caught sight of my bedroom mirror. My mouth dropped open, and I frantically turned to my still-open bedroom door.

"Uh," Azael said. "What is that on your mirror? Are they—"

"Quiet," I snapped, and raced to the door to close it as softly as possible.

"Is this a . . . story?" asked Azael. "Where are their wings?"

"You can't tell anyone about any of this," I said quickly,

before turning back to my mirror. "Sean? Charity?"

Because yeah, even though it was very much impossible, Sean and Charity were on my bedroom mirror. WHY WERE THEY ON MY MIRROR?!

"Is this working?" asked Sean, but he wasn't talking to me. He looked to Charity.

"I don't know," Charity said, shaking her head. I was glad not to see any blood.

"Sean," I hissed, careful not to be too loud.

"What are they?" Azael asked. "Wait, didn't you say—"

"Yeah, I did. They're humans," I said. "Charity, can you hear me?" I touched the mirror. Charity froze. My heart raced.

"What?" demanded Sean, but he wasn't looking at me. He glanced over his shoulder at Charity and then immediately back to something I couldn't see.

"I don't know," Charity said. And then she moved her head and looked directly into my eyes. "Crowley?"

I gasped. I think Azael might have too, but I couldn't concentrate on that right now.

Before I could say anything, the mirror went blank. I touched the surface again, but it just swirled, waiting for my command like a normal mirror.

I stepped back and sat heavily on my bed. Crowley.

Charity had said "Crowley." They *had* been in communication. I knew it! My first reaction was anger at being kept out of the loop, but I quickly squashed that down because, let's be honest, that was more than a little bit hypocritical.

Azael cleared his throat. I jumped.

"So . . . ," he said. "Does this happen a lot?"

"No," I said. I lay back on my bed. I rubbed my face with my hands. "Sean—the boy human—and I have been pen pals, sort of? But this is the first time whatever that was happened." I waved vaguely toward my mirror, before abruptly sitting up.

"Actually, it's not," I said, realizing. "Normally I have a box spelled as a landing spot for the letters, just a simple homing signal with breadcrumb stone, you know? Anyway, it gives me a notification glow when new letters show up, but the other day I got the alert, and it wasn't a piece of paper."

"What was in the box?" Azael asked in a whisper.

"It was his head," I whispered back.

"His head?!" Azael shrieked.

"Shhh!"

"Sorry, sorry," he apologized, lowering his voice and tilting his head, apparently to hear if my parents had noticed.

"Not his head-head. Like, a hologram head," I explained.

"I sent another letter, but I haven't gotten one back. I don't know why things changed."

"When did they change?" he asked, sitting down next to me.

I tried to think back. Ever since our manic studying had begun, the days had blurred together.

"It was after the Nephilim concert," I said. "I think. He asked if anything here was strange."

"The Nephilim concert," Azael muttered. "The night the ground shook for the first time? The magic didn't work after that?"

"I don't know," I said. "I mean, yes, the timing is right, but my letters go through just fine. Or at least it seems fine from this end."

"I wonder . . . ," Azael said. But then he reached into his pocket and pulled out his mirror, gesturing to send a message. "Oh, brimstone. I've got to go."

"Yeah," I said, still feeling off-kilter. Was this pseudo-visitation going to happen again? Had Sean been getting my letters and just not been able to send any back for some reason? Were he and Charity in trouble?

Charity had looked tired.

"I have to talk to Crowley."

"Sounds like," Azael agreed, distracted, but then he paused. "Hey, the mortal realm, does it always look like that?"

"Look like what?" I asked. I hadn't noticed anything besides Sean's and Charity's faces. Had there been something strange in the background? Maybe Azael had seen the blue sky on Earth. That could be shocking.

"Azael! Do you need company home?" called Mom from the bottom of the stairs.

"No, thank you," he called back. "I've got to go. I don't know. Ignore me. I've never seen the mortal realm; maybe that's what normal is. Talk to Crowley."

"Yeah," I said. "I think it's time we talked. And, Azael?"

"Yeah?"

"You can't say anything. About any of this."

"I know." Azael rolled his eyes, but then he smiled softly and said more seriously, "I know."

# TWENTY-FOUR

As soon as Azael left, I sent Crowley a flare saying we needed to talk, not relying on my pocket mirror because this was definitely a conversation I didn't want a record of. I paced my room and focused on the remaining adrenaline and worry to keep myself awake. Something was going on, and it wasn't just the adults who were hiding information. Not for the first time I wondered if I had lost more of my friends than I'd thought.

My head was bobbing with near sleep by the time the knock came at my window. My wings flared in surprise, and I stumbled on feet that were barely keeping me upright.

"Shut up," I muttered as Crowley laughed outside my

window. I pushed it open and shoved past him as I flew out of my yard. I touched down on the opposite side of the fence. He dropped down next to me, still snickering.

"Past your bedtime?" he mocked, keeping his voice low.

"Some of us have been working our butts off," I grumbled.

The woods behind my house were an excellent place for privacy. The tree branches hung low, and it only took a few steps to be in the dim light, surrounded by the scent of cinnamon and dead leaves. The scuttling of leaves and other things in the trees reminded me that we weren't alone, in the comforting way that the presence of Damien did. Crowley and I didn't exchange another word as we stepped farther in, to a place with a fallen tree that made an excellent spot for sitting. The moss added a cushy layer that made it ideal. I yawned as I sat, and shook off the last wave of exhaustion with a rustle of my feathers.

"A flare is typically urgent or secret," Crowley said, still standing. "And yet you're barely awake."

"I'm awake," I said. "Besides, you're here."

"Yup," he said, and then he narrowed his eyes. "Why?"

I looked at Crowley. He looked suspicious, but then again Crowley almost always looked suspicious. It was right up there with disdain as his number-two look. I debated trying to ask the right questions to get Crowley to admit on his own whatever he was doing, but he was right. I was tired. And frustrated. And I didn't really care.

"You've kept in touch with Charity, right?" I asked.

Whatever he'd thought I was going to ask, this wasn't it, because Crowley's face paled, his mouth dropped open, and his eyes bulged. I smirked. I wasn't proud, but getting the upper hand with Crowley was amazing. And I had been feeling a step behind ever since school had started. So this felt pretty awesome.

"You might wanna . . ." I gestured to my own face and then to his still-open mouth.

He snapped to attention and shook himself. His mouth abruptly shut, and he cleared his throat. I laughed, and a weight lifted.

Crowley scowled in response, and for a minute I thought he was going to come up with a denial or some other attempt at wiggling his way out of admitting anything, but then he seemed to stop running through excuses in his mind, and instead huffed like I was putting him out. He leaned against a tree, his wings spreading enough so that they were free of the tree trunk against his back. He crossed his arms across his chest and then narrowed his eyes at me.

"So, what if I did?" he asked. "Are you really going to tell me that if you had the magic, you wouldn't have kept in touch with that human you were making eyes at?"

Hmm. Interesting. Crowley didn't know I had kept in touch with Sean. How inept did he think I was that I couldn't manage a simple interdimensional communication? Dude, that was offensive. I debated what I should say and raised an eyebrow in the meantime.

"Okay, fine," said Crowley. "I should have offered to help, but seriously, there's no future there. He is a mortal, and of course there's Lilith."

"Lilith's a friend," I said automatically, even though I still felt my cheeks grow hot. First insinuating that I didn't have the magic of a fledgling, then bringing up my not-so-secret crush? Rude.

"Yeah, yeah," Crowley said, waving away my response. "We've heard it all before. But I admit, I still should have made the offer to get you two in touch. . . . Sorry."

I rolled my eyes.

"That's not the human I'm talking about, and I'm not talking about hypotheticals," I said. "Why did you stay in contact with Charity?"

"Purely educational," he said, in that way that meant it was definitely a lie. "We did work well together at the end, after all. The real question is, How do you know that?"

"I'm just that good," I said. "Plus, I kept in touch with Sean."

"Impressive. Have you heard from him recently?" Crowley asked, having the decency to look at least somewhat respectful, but the question was clearly loaded.

"What's going on?" I asked.

Crowley sighed, and then slumped to the ground. He wrapped his arms around his knees, and I moved from the log to sit down and join him, cross-legged on the cold ground.

"I don't know," he said. "When we got back home, I sent a message to Charity, mostly to see if I could do it or maybe to see if *she* could do it. She can, by the way. Anyway, we've been meeting up once a week or so. It's made school much easier, especially now that we're studying interdimensional effects on magic. Although, we haven't met up since the switch. . . . Anyway, once you know how the mortal realm affects our magic, it's not a leap to figure it out for other dimensions. Well, except for how it would work in Faerie, obviously."

I nodded. I didn't know a lot about magic, but it was universally understood that Faerie had its own rules, which were less actual rules and more . . . guidelines. I always thought I'd like Faerie.

But wait a minute—

"Wait, what do you mean 'meeting up'?"

"It's not *really* meeting up," Crowley said. "We just open the veil enough for a visual."

"Open the veil?" I said. "You can do that? Also, dude, that can't be good! Are you sure it closed? Did you just leave openings?!"

I mean, hello? Didn't we just have an assembly on interdimensional breaches! Was that how Not-Aria "jumped" here?

"Calm down. It's more like scrying than anything else," Crowley said, waving off my concern. "And it takes both of us to keep it open. We're not leaving openings anywhere. How have you been talking to the mortal?"

"Letters," I said, "like a reasonable person who does not want to face endless grounding again."

"No, it's good," Crowley said. "I'm surprised you managed it."

"Dude!" I objected.

"What? It's still impressive," Crowley said. "Don't be offended; you're not a magician. Anyway, we were meeting up regularly, until a couple of weeks ago."

"Until the night of the concert," I guessed.

"Yes," Crowley said. "I suppose. But . . ."

"But what?"

"She seemed . . . distracted? Uneasy? The last time we met up, she seemed stressed. I assumed it was some mortal nonsense."

While he might have been dismissive about "mortal nonsense," I could see the clear worry. Somewhere along the line, despite his over-the-top complaints, Crowley had not only started caring about a human, and not just as a learning opportunity, but considered her a friend. Maybe even more than that.

"Maybe she just changed her mind," Crowley said, but his voice was smaller than it normally was. "It's not like we were real friends anyway. Just interdimensional . . . acquaintances."

I was reminded of my internal debate about whether Azael was a school friend or a real friend. Were we making this friends thing overly complicated? Maybe it wasn't really this hard.

"I think something's wrong," I said. I explained Sean's vague question about weirdness, and the lack of a written response but the surprise visitations of bodiless heads and candid peeks into whatever the heck it was that I saw when Charity asked for Crowley in my mirror. And oh yeah, you'd better believe I mentioned that, too.

"You didn't mention you were in touch," I grumbled.

Crowley justifiably glared at me.

"All right, full disclosure," I said. "I talked to Cassandra a few times too."

"That was not smart," he said.

"We're all on the same side," I said.

We both rolled our eyes.

"Anyway, we need to do more digging," I said.

"Yeah," said Crowley. "If something is really happening in the mortal realm, it could have to do with the imbalances Lucifer mentioned."

I had considered that, and I had really been hoping that Crowley would have a better idea of what was happening, that Charity had told him something, or that his magic made him more intuitive to unseen things.

What I had really, really been hoping was that Crowley would immediately know what was up and it would be something completely trivial. Like Charity and Sean were in some weird magic-free zone or something. Unfortunately, that left the not-so-good explanation that something was wrong.

"Maybe Chaos really is returning," I said, and immediately felt like ice had taken residency in my stomach. Wasn't that a terrifying thought?

Ever since I was little, Chaos had been the perpetual threat, the boogeyman under the bed, kept locked away only as long as the balance was maintained. We were part of keeping that balance, and that was why when Salem had started going off the deep end, Heaven had been willing to destroy everyone on Earth, to preserve the balance. Now, I don't think Parris was an agent of Chaos; more like an agent of chaos, lowercase.

Sometimes that happened.

Sometimes people just couldn't help themselves, but they didn't necessarily know what they were doing. Most mortals didn't even know that Chaos with a capital *C* existed. But me and my friends? Those white-winged littles upstairs? We all got the same warnings. If the balance fell, if Chaos rose, it would be The End.

As was true of most childhood spooky stories, the fear instilled back then kind of went away as we got older. Nothing had happened. No one had seen Chaos or any actual agents of Chaos in forever. If they ever had.

I mean, okay, yeah, we all learned about various uprisings and battles, but once creation happened, once life and existence burst forth and stabilized into fully formed concepts, Chaos had never taken back control. I had always assumed that the adults were overreacting to keep us in line. Tell a spooky story about *consequences*, and we'd all do what we were told. But I admit, I was starting to wonder if maybe I should be a tiny bit more concerned.

"Chaos is *not* returning," Crowley said dismissively. "But maybe we should start trying to find some answers to what *is* happening, because clearly something's going on, and while I'm not into conspiracy theories, the reality is that our communications with the humans got weird when everything went strange. And they don't seem to be able to fix it themselves."

"Agreed," I said, feeling better than I had in a long time. Crowley nodded like it was no big thing, but the smile he tried to hide was more relieved than I'd expected.

# TWENTY-FIVE

E at something before school," Mom said as I flew into the kitchen. She put a plate of smoked meat and an oatmeal muffin down on the table and pointed at a chair. I sat.

"Where's Dad?" I asked. "Eww, raisins."

"Just pick them out," said Mom. "Already gone. He's got a briefing this morning."

"Did you know raisins are just dead versions of a fruit that is way better?"

"Yes, I did."

"Do you think Chaos is rising?"

Mom choked on her tea, spluttering droplets over the table. She coughed while I picked out raisins and waited patiently.

There was a good chance she was going to try to come up with a non-answer, but I had already decided I wasn't going to accept a non-answer.

"Do you?" I repeated once she was quiet.

Mom sighed and leaned back in her chair. She took another sip of her tea, more cautious this time, and stared at me over her mug. Mom was almost always embarrassingly squishy with me, but occasionally I was reminded that even though Dad might be the gung-ho leadership responsibility guy, Mom had been placed in the same track and ultimately had outranked him. It was intimidating, but then again, I had been placed in Command as well. And quite honestly, after pseudo-Lucifer staring into my pseudo-soul, I felt better equipped to handle a Mom glare.

"I think," Mom said carefully, placing her teacup on to the table in front of her, "that every once in a while Chaos makes some noise, but I also think that the balance is held in such a way that Chaos can't ever really get a good hold. You have to remember that every dimension plays its part in maintaining the balance, right? So even if there is a fumble in, say, the mortal coil, the balance is still being held by the others. Heaven, Hell, Purgatory, Faerie, they all have a major grasp."

"Yeah," I said, trying to ignore the discomfort of her choice to highlight the mortal coil. "But the balance is delicate, right? Shift one way, and it's gone."

"True," she said. "But it takes a lot to make it shift."

"Lucifer spoke to us at school."

"I know," Mom said. "We were told."

"He said there were imbalances."

"That happens sometimes," Mom said, picking up her tea again and leaning back in her chair, looking much more comfortable now. "And things have been fixed. The wrong soul was sent back to where they belonged; your little friend was taken home safely. Lucifer was just warning you all as a precaution in case the imbalances are still happening. The quicker we can correct things the better. The actual thing you should be focused on is this mixer, which you were so excited about."

"I still am!" I said. "I just don't understand why we're studying so much! It's just a party!"

"It's a diplomatic mission," Mom corrected. "Hopefully it will be . . . fun, but we also don't want any cultural misunderstandings. The last thing we need is a diplomatic nightmare. Then Chaos really would have a hold."

"Not that I needed any pressure or anything," I said.

She waved me off. "I'm exaggerating. Everything is going to be fine. The real worry is going to be how boring this so-called party will be."

I laughed. "Probably," I said, thinking about Cassandra

and what her idea of fun could possibly be. "But seriously, trusted guardian Mom to beloved son: We don't need to worry about big-picture stuff?"

"The party *is* big-picture stuff. We all have to work together, and interdimensional cooperation has definitely been neglected for far too long, but no, you don't need to worry about anything like that." Mom leaned forward. "Sweetie, even if the worst was to happen, and Chaos somehow started taking steps, it wouldn't be yours to worry about. You know that, right?"

"I know," I said. But I wasn't sure either of us really believed it.

By the time I got to school, my conversation with Mom had made me feel better about pretty much everything. Why was it that late-night dreads never seemed like anything significant in the day? What had I been thinking? Of course, I *could* worry about our human friends, but there were angels with literally millennia of experience on both sides. Lucifer had been part of the forces to lock Chaos away, and I was sure there were others in Heaven, Purgatory, and Faerie who had been there as well.

It was most certainly not up to me and Crowley, and Crowley was sure all the random stuff that had been happening had nothing to do with Chaos anyway.

By first period my main worry was the enormous stack

of reading we had on heavenly customs and traditions. The books unceremoniously dropped onto our desks were ancient. The pages were brittle and yellow, and the covers had obviously not been cared for. I wondered where the teachers had even found them. I raised my hand.

"Yes?" asked Professor Sauriel, my history teacher.

"These look really old," I said.

"Heaven is really old," said Sauriel, looking decidedly unimpressed. Someone snickered in the back of the class. Probably Raphael. He had the honor of being my least-favorite person in this class. Rachel might have been a third year and not in my classes, but she had admirers, and Raphael was one of them.

"Yes," I said. "But don't customs change over time? I mean, aren't these out of date?"

"Unlikely," said Sauriel. "Those in Heaven are known for being set in their ways. This will be fine. Now, I expect from each of you a two-thousand-word essay on the proper greetings to each angelic class by occasion and phase of moon. Begin."

I flipped the cover open with an ominous cracking sound. I swore that if they blamed me for breaking the spine, I was going to flip. Thankfully, I heard similar sounds from the desks around me, so if I was going down, we were all going down.

The script was old, and the language was practically in code. When I finished the first sentence, I had no idea what

I had just read. I furtively looked around at my classmates. Some were resolutely staring at the page, like if they glared hard enough, it would become clear. Others were glancing around like I was, including Azael, who made a face when I caught his eye. I grinned and stifled a laugh.

"Excuse me, sir."

And it was the last person I'd expected.

"Raphael?" Even Sauriel sounded surprised that Mr. Perfect would question an assignment.

"It's just . . . could you explain what . . . um, all of it means?"

"Oh, unholy darkness," said Sauriel. "It's all right there."

He strode up to Raphael's desk and ripped the book off it. A page fluttered to the floor. "It's very clear! It's not even in the original Enochian." Professor Sauriel opened the book. "As you can clearly read . . ." He frowned, and the room filled with a gleeful sense of justice. It was the first time I had felt that sense of oneness in my new school, and for the moment I was going to enjoy it. I grinned and turned my head enough to see Azael, who was grinning right back at me from the next desk.

It was as clear as the water of the River Lethe that Sauriel was realizing that Raphael—and, let's face it, the rest of the class—was right. This book was indecipherable.

"I suppose it's been a while since it was last translated,"

admitted Sauriel. He rustled his wings and snapped his spine straight. "Sit silently while I update the translation. Raphael, collect the books."

We sat silently.

Until he left the room.

Immediately the room rustled into movement, and while most of my classmates began working on other assignments, I decided to seize the opportunity to take a break. I slouched in my seat and spread my wings as wide as I could without bashing my classmates. I didn't need to start a fight; I just needed a moment to breathe. I lazily dropped my head to the side, only to see Azael facedown on his desk. I would have been disappointed to see him working but had kinda hoped to chat.

Oh well, there was always lunchtime. I needed to fill him in on my talk with Crowley, and I was still uneasy about whatever it was he had noticed in the mirror and I hadn't. Of course, he had never been to the mortal world, so it wasn't like he knew what it was supposed to look like, but still, what if he had noticed something that could help answer some questions?

I dropped my head back and stared sightlessly at the gray stone ceiling. I had a list of things to do for school. I still had to meet up with Crowley to figure out how to reach out to our human friends, and that meant confessing to Lilith that I had kept in contact with Sean, which felt weird and uncomfortable, like I'd been doing something wrong, when I absolutely hadn't been. Probably hadn't been . . . maybe.

Okay, to-do list:

1. Come clean to Lilith. (Oh, and probably Aleister, too.)
2. Make sure the humans are okay.
3. Get my ridiculous stack of work done.
4. Get awesome new outfit for the mixer.

I wondered if I should reach out to Cassandra again and ask what she was going to wear. I smiled, just imagining what kind of monstrosity she would pick out. Or would it just be a white gown? It was going to be interesting, that was for sure.

I opened my eyes, which I hadn't realized I had closed, only to be blinded by a flare of orange-and-red flame. There were cries of distress, one of them mine, and I felt something hit my face as I jerked my head down to get away from the light. My wings retracted, tangling in Azael's feathers as they pulled back, and I blinked my eyes rapidly, trying to regain my vision.

I tried to look around for danger, and was already rising without conscious effort, my training kicking in even though

I couldn't see a thing. Everywhere I looked was covered in red-and-white dots, and I blinked frantically as I held on to my desk. It was disorienting, and I swayed on my feet. My wings jerked out to help my balance.

"Are you okay?" asked Azael.

I rubbed my eyes again; the dots were fading but my vision was still blurry. The classroom had quieted. though, changed from distressed sounds of surprise to confused muttering. "Yeah," I said. "Just blinded a little."

The door slammed open, hitting the wall.

"I said to sit silently!" Sauriel roared. His wings rose and spread far larger than any of our own, while his eyes blazed with flickering flames. Our wings collapsed against our sides simultaneously in an embarrassing automatic response.

"We were," I said. Sauriel swung his gaze my way, as did everyone else in my class. I tried not to shrink in on myself, and instead forced myself to stand a little straighter. "Something happened. Didn't it happen everywhere?"

My classmates all swung their gazes back to Sauriel. He seemed knocked off-kilter by the attention, at least for a second. "What do you mean 'something happened'?"

Even though I had literally been staring at the ceiling while whatever it was happened, I wasn't really sure what it was, especially considering I'd been almost instantly blinded.

"There was—" Raphael started, but then looked around for help. I was surprised he'd said anything. I'd assumed he would say the opposite of whatever I said, just on principle.

"The ceiling ignited," said Parisa. "Like, I don't know, the outside came in?"

Sauriel looked at the ceiling. I cautiously did as well, but apparently, I didn't have to be so cautious. The ceiling was normal gray stone.

"There were flames in the room?" he asked, frowning.

We nodded. All of us.

Go, us.

"We'll have class outside," he said. "Grab your things and take a book. Quickly."

I turned back to my desk. Most of my stuff was in my locker, so I only had a few items to grab, but what I hadn't noticed while I'd been frantically trying to regain my sight was that my desk, along with a few others nearby, was covered in debris, scraps of paper, torn and charred. But right there in the center of my desk was a feather, as white as snow.

I stared, frozen, my heart racing in my chest. That feather didn't belong here, but somehow, I knew that it was meant for me. Yup, possibly my ego again, going and thinking everything was about me, but in fairness, when trouble emerged, it was typically meant for me. And that feather right there, that was trouble.

I grabbed the feather and put it into my pocket. I desperately wanted to bring it to my nose to see if it smelled like vanilla, but it would have been obvious, and people already thought I was weird. Although, no one was actually looking right then—they were all busy collecting their belongings.

"Mal," said Azael. "Come on."

"I'm coming," I said, gathering my things to my chest. As I turned to leave, my eyes caught on a scrap of paper. They weren't all blank. There was writing. Snippets of words, letters, a symbol here and there. I couldn't even tell what language it was in; there wasn't enough text. I thought the writing looked familiar, but I wasn't even sure about that.

"Malachi, Azael," snapped Sauriel. "Clear the room."

"Yes, sir," we said. I swept the scraps I could reach into my hand and right into my pocket. The burnt scraps were going to be a pain to get out, but I wanted to take a closer look, and I couldn't do that in the classroom.

Azael and I were the last students left in our classroom, but other people had already come into the room. Professor Sauriel must have summoned help to take a closer look.

There was Professor Jophiel and another teacher I recognized from the older levels. I didn't have her yet, but that was because she only taught fieldwork—something we'd do as we got closer to graduating. She was already studying the ceiling with another woman who had come into the room. I didn't recognize her at all, but when the red swirls sparked at her fingertips, I knew why. If she was a teacher, she wasn't one for the Command track.

"Excuse me," I said, making my way carefully between the debris and the adults and out the door.

I felt eyes on my every move, and when I made it into the hall, I couldn't resist taking a quick glance behind me. Professor Jophiel watched me the entire way.

# TWENTY-SIX

My squad hadn't had plans to meet in days, and I had never brought Azael, but I figured he was part of whatever it was that was happening now. Plus, he seemed to be a friend-friend at this point, and it felt weird to leave him out, even if he wasn't technically in my squad.

Our normal hangouts were all public places, which were great for snacks and comfort, not so great for privacy, which was why, as soon as I had access to my pocket mirror, I messaged for a meet-up at Pandemonium Park.

When I arrived, Lilith was sprawled out on the moss with a stack of books. Crowley lazily tossed spells between his hands. Aleister was tugging a rope that was currently being held tightly in Damien's jaws. My school was the farthest away, so it wasn't a huge surprise that everyone else had gotten there first.

"Mal brought a friend," announced Crowley, twisting purple glowing runes between his fingers so that they seemed to almost be dancing. Lilith jerked her head up from her book, her expression unreadable.

"Hi," said Azael, lifting a hand and waving awkwardly.

"This is Azael," I said. "I mentioned him before."

"Yo!" called Aleister in greeting, which was quickly followed by "Whoa!" as Damien jerked him forward so he could make his own greeting. And even though Aleister could have just let go of the rope, I knew he wouldn't . . . and he didn't. "Ow! Damien, stop."

Damien's claws churned up the moss under his feet as he dragged Aleister with him in his overeager quest to greet Azael. His glowing eyes were wide open, and wisps of flames streamed past his head as he made his way forward, the rope still clenched between drooling fangs.

Azael suppressed a laugh, clearly unsure whether he could or should laugh at Aleister's obvious distress.

"Oh, for—" Crowley scowled, made a complicated hand motion, and snapped out a word in Enochian I didn't understand, before whipping his hand forward. A bolt of red spark raced forward and sliced the rope in two.

"Dude!" yelled Aleister. "You could have hit my dog!"

"Oof," said Azael as Damien plowed into him, aided by the added boost of not dragging Aleister anymore. Azael spread his wings, shifted his stance, and somehow managed to keep his feet. "Hello, big guy."

"It wasn't going to hit him," Crowley said dismissively, lifting his chin in defiance. "I've been practicing."

Aleister brushed his pants clean and grumbled, "You owe me a new rope."

"Give it," Crowley demanded, and held his palm out imperiously.

Aleister slapped the rope end into Crowley's palm.

"New kid," Crowley said to Azael, even though I had *just* introduced him. "May I have the other piece?"

"Oh," said Azael. "Yeah, sure."

Azael playfully pushed Damien to the ground to find the end of the other piece of rope. Instead of just pulling the end that wasn't lodged in the hellhound's teeth, he distracted Damien with his free hand so that when he finally reached down to twist the rope out of his teeth, Damien didn't even notice. He handed Crowley the rope, while he kept Damien at bay with ear scratches. Smart.

Crowley took the two ends in hand. His magic sparked up, sending red fog up and around the rope until the cut ends grew and twisted, weaving themselves back into one piece. His magic faded and he held one end in each hand. He held the rope up in front of Aleister's eyes, raised an eyebrow, and yanked the rope hard. It held. He tossed it to Aleister with a smirk that was pushing down an enormous and very uncool smile.

"Well," I said, taking a seat on the soft moss beneath us. "Maybe that can lead into why we're here."

"I certainly don't know what you mean," said Crowley.

"What's up?" asked Lilith, closing her book and placing it back into her bag. "I get that this isn't just us hanging out, but I feel like I'm out of the loop here." Her eyes flicked to Azael and away.

I felt guilty for a minute, but just as before, when I was feeling all squirmy about telling her I had kept in touch with Sean, I knew that I wasn't doing anything wrong.

Everyone else had friends in their new schools. Aleister had even missed get-togethers to hang out with his new friends. Why couldn't I have new friends? My squad mates were the ones pushing me to accept destiny and just go with the program like everyone else. Lilith couldn't get mad if I was finally doing what she wanted, right?

Damien put his drooling head in my lap, and Azael tried to pretend he was comfortable. Slight twitches in his feathers told me he still wasn't sure this was a good idea, and I was reminded that until very recently Azael hadn't really looked comfortable anywhere.

"Okay, so *Crowley* and I have a confession," I said. Crowley, the loser, didn't pipe up at all, and I narrowed my eyes at him as he pretended to study his fingernails. "Look, when we got back home, I . . . got a letter from Cassandra."

"The seraph!" blurted out Aleister, like he knew the answer on a game show and was up for the grand prize.

"SHHH!" Lilith, Crowley, and I hissed.

Damien huffed at the outburst, but when I looked around, no one in the park was paying any attention to us. There were kids running and playing with a gargoyle kite that flapped its wings and growled as they ran. There were a few adults enjoying the weather and peace of the park compared to the bustle of the streets. A fountain gurgled loudly enough near us to (hopefully) disguise our exact words from people farther away.

"Anyway," I continued. "It wasn't much. Cassandra just wanted to see if we were okay. She said she had gotten permission . . . to set up a mixer."

"You knew!" said Lilith. "Before we got the invitation."

"I didn't know-know," I protested. "Cassandra says lots of things. It's not like she's in charge of Heaven, so just because she says she wants to do something doesn't mean that it is actually going to happen."

"'Says,'" Lilith repeated. "Like, present tense."

"I mean," I said, "we still talk, and she still exists."

"You kept in touch?" Lilith hissed. Her eyes took on a dangerous gleam, not quite flaming but oh so close. It was kinda hot.

"Just once in a while," I said.

"I can't believe you did that!" Lilith snapped.

"So what?" I snarled back. "I'm allowed to have friends."

Lilith looked like I had slapped her. "That's not what I meant."

"We're getting off topic," said Crowley.

"Yeah," agreed Aleister. "Besides, you said you *both* had a confession."

"I haven't been in touch with Heaven," Crowley said. And I glared so hard, I would have burst his head into flames if I could. "Okay, fine. But I *did* keep in touch with the human."

"Sean?" asked Lilith.

"Charity," he said. "Mal kept in touch with Sean."

I internally groaned and tried to ignore Lilith's gaze on me.

"Okay," said Lilith slowly. "Let me get this straight. Mal has been talking to *Heaven*, and you both have been talking to humans this whole time, without telling any of us. Even though you *know* that any fallout would have affected the whole squad."

At our confused looks Lilith threw her hands up in frustration. "We all paid the price for going to the mortal realm," she said. She held up a finger to Aleister, who was already opening his mouth to object. "Yes, I know you didn't go, Al, but you still got grounded, didn't you? We do not have permission for interdimensional communication, and yeah, I know, we've never cared about that before, but after Salem? We really have to be more careful."

"Going to the veil wasn't my idea," I hissed back, and Lilith at least had the decency to blush. "And it was only letters. At least on my end."

"Glorified scrying," Crowley said glibly. "It's not like we were seeing each other in person."

"So why are you guys telling us now?" asked Aleister. "And no offense, dude, but why is he here? This seems like top secret and he's not squad. No offense, New Dude."

"I trust him," I said. "And, well . . . he was there when Sean and Charity showed up."

"What?!" exclaimed Lilith and Aleister.

Between Crowley, Azael, and myself we explained everything as well as we could. Including what had happened in our classroom, which I wasn't convinced was related. I talked about how Sean and I had chatted through letters, just keeping up with each other and answering random questions about our worlds. Nothing top secret, and for all of Lilith's freaking out, I knew that even if the Powers That Be read the letters Sean and I had exchanged, they wouldn't find me guilty of anything.

Who cared what kind of flowers grew in perpetual twilight or what it was like to walk through a forest where the leaves climbed your legs, or dragonflies tried to burn your eyebrows off when you got in the way of their dinner? That wasn't top secret. That was just . . . normal.

I explained that after the night of the concert, and the initial rumbling, the letters from Sean stopped appearing and his face started to. Crowley talked about how Charity had missed one of their chat sessions, how they had been talking magic since we'd gotten home, and although he didn't say it outright, how they had become good friends. Crowley's magic had obviously taken a boost, and while I'm sure his professors would have loved to take the credit, I was betting there was a human witch element at play there.

I mentioned Sean's question about weirdness. Crowley said that Charity had seemed tense the last time she'd showed up. I mentioned the blood I had seen on Sean's skin. Crowley mentioned waking one night to the feeling of a scry, but nothing being there when he looked around. We mentioned the timing. How the weirdness in our world correlated with the weirdness in our mortal communication.

I talked about the flames across the ceiling in class, the scraps of paper falling. Azael filled in the details I had missed when I had been momentarily blinded. How the flames had roiled and changed to green across the ceiling, which sounded an awful lot like what I had seen in the sky the night of the concert. How shadows had seemed to move in the flames' depths and how as quickly as they had come, they had disappeared.

"And then there was this," I said. I pulled the white feather from my pocket. I let it brush my nose, but if it had ever smelled like vanilla, it didn't now. It smelled like home, cinnamon and dead leaves, with a just a hint of the body spray I had put on before I'd left my house.

Everyone's eyes tracked the movement, and I placed it on the moss between us, our bodies keeping it hidden from anyone around us. The white glowed where it lay against the blue-and-green moss, and whereas our feathers took on sheens of blue, purple, and green under the flickering skies, the white feather reflected the orange, reds, and yellows. It was obvious it didn't belong here.

"Heaven?" asked Azael. "The messenger had white wings."

"He did," said Crowley. "But Cassandra's didn't quite look like that."

"Our wings are different from each other," pointed out Aleister. "Maybe theirs are too." That was true but . . .

"It came through the ceiling," I said. "Those flames were not heavenly."

"It has to all be related," said Lilith. "The human issues, the quakes, the breach into Hell, the mistaken soul, the problems in your classroom . . . and then there was what we heard that time in the woods."

Lilith gave a significant look that clearly said we shouldn't go into that eavesdropping session with Azael here, but I was sick of keeping secrets. I was sick of feeling like I had to be only loyal to my squad even if they were all finding their own way. I had to find my own way too.

Azael already knew things he shouldn't have, and he hadn't ratted us out. Sure, I supposed he could have had a long-term plan to sabotage us, but pretending to be friends just to backstab us would be seriously corrupt. Azael might not have fit the mold in our track any more than I did, but he wasn't a traitor. I would have heard about it by now. Reputations were KNOWN here.

"Some of the adults seem to think Chaos might be making moves," I said. Azael's head jerked up. I took the feather back from where it lay on the ground and hid it away.

"Except we don't actually know if they're right," Lilith said. "I haven't heard anything like that from Mom."

"Your mom is good at keeping secrets, Lil," I said. "Especially when it's something big. Although, my mom seems to think potential universe-ending is not something we should worry about."

"Which is true," Crowley said. "Excellent! So . . . Faust's?"

"Wait," Lilith said, leaning forward. "We shouldn't worry about it because nothing is happening, or because she thinks we're kids?"

"We are kids, Lilith," said Aleister, leaning heavily on Damien, who lay panting puffs of steam over his dangling tongue. His tail thumped lazily on the moss.

"You know what I mean," Lilith said.

"Well, what should we do?" asked Aleister. "That's why we're here, right? It's not just to fill us in. You think we should do something. Isn't that right, Damien? Yes, he thinks we should do something and get grounded again. Yes, he does."

"Stop that," I said, nudging Al with my wing and nearly losing a feather to Damien's mouth in the process. "Besides, you didn't get grounded as badly as we did anyway. Look, adults lack imagination. It's just the way it is. They're not going to think about Chaos, because they trust the way things have always been, but let's face it, they're freaking out about the mixer because they haven't left Hell in forever, but we have! We have contacts in Heaven and the mortal plane, and weird things are happening everywhere. They have to be related."

"Weird things are happening in Heaven?" asked Lilith.

"Well . . . okay, I'm not sure about that, but probably," I said. "I mean, a toddler apparently jumped here. And at the very least they're happening in Purgatory, or we wouldn't have ended up with a soul that wasn't ours."

Lilith frowned and bit the side of her thumb. Her other hand was tapping out her stress rhythm: one-two-three-four, one, one-two-three, one-two-three-four.

"And what happened in our class was strange," Azael said.

"Yes, it was," I said. "Sauriel called in help, and there was definitely a magician looking at the ceiling with Jophiel."

"It was Winifred," Azael said. "She's in my mom's squad. She teaches potions in the Magician track."

"She's good," said Crowley, and he sounded impressed. "She teaches the higher grades, but they call her in for any disasters. But if Chaos is actually rising, I'll give you fifty denarius. There's just no way."

"Right," Aleister said. "So, they've got this, and Lucifer obviously knows about whatever the imbalances were, and I'm sure your mom reported the soul."

"Yes," said Crowley. "But they're going to keep that information internal."

"Mom did talk to Heaven, when they put the soul back where it belonged," I pointed out.

"Did she bring one back here?" Lilith asked. "Did she bring a soul back to Hell?"

"I'm not sure," I said. How had I not thought to ask?

"Whoa," Aleister said, sitting straight up and whacking Damien in the face in the process. The hound huffed an excited bark before leaping to his feet. "You think one of ours ended up there?"

"Well, it would make sense, wouldn't it?" Azael asked. "The balance and everything."

"Not necessarily," Crowley said. "It's not like the judging is done in pairs."

"True," Azael said. "But if something went wrong with the transfer, then it would make sense that the glitch would affect both hereafters."

"If that's what happened," Crowley said, with a dark edge to his voice.

"What else would it be?" I asked. It had to be just a doorway mess-up, right?

"Maybe something's wrong with the Jackal," Crowley said.

"You think he judged them wrong?" I asked, in my most derisive voice. "Or maybe he just let them pick their own doors. I bet that's totally what happened."

Crowley stared at me, completely unimpressed.

"Just a suggestion," Crowley said lightly. "You don't have to be sarcastic about it."

"It's impossible," Lilith said. "There's no way there was a mistake at that point."

"But there was a breach, too," I said. "And don't you think this is a lot of random occurrences to be a coincidence?"

"Maybe," Lilith said. "Or maybe not. Not everything is a plot."

"Around here?" Crowley asked. "Everything is a plot. Regardless, finding out what happened to our humans—"

"They've tried reaching out," I said. "I'm sure of it. So, it's not that they want to ghost us. Can you do a location scry, like you did for Al?"

"Only if you have something of Sean's," he said. "I haven't been able to do it for Charity."

Everyone was looking at me.

"I don't," I said. "I mean, I have letters he touched, but I don't know if that counts."

"I could try," Crowley said, but he didn't sound very convinced. As much as Crowley pretended like nothing bothered him, I knew he was worried about Charity. He would have tried everything he knew to find her, and if that hadn't worked, why would this?

"Okay," Lilith said. "Game plan?"

"I'll get Crowley a letter that Sean has touched," I said. "Lilith, find out what you can about Chaos. I know, I know—" I held up a hand when she opened her mouth to object that all this random stuff was most certainly nothing and there was no point wasting time looking into Chaos. "It might be nothing. Just, can you check into it? If the old people are just overreacting, then we'll know, but maybe find out what has happened in the past? In case there are signs to look for now?" She nodded reluctantly. "Aleister, can you investigate the imbalances Lucifer was talking about? And see if there were any other breaches besides the one we know about? Your school might know more about it."

"You got it," he said. "What are you going to do?"

"I'm going to see what I can find out about this feather," I said, already thinking of the letter I would write Cassandra when I got home.

"Um."

All eyes shifted to Azael, and he looked uncomfortable for a moment before straightening. "I could help, if you want. My friend Sidney is in the Enforcer track too, and my mom is friends with Winifred. I could do some snooping. If you want." He shrugged.

"Sidney is cool," said Aleister when no one else said anything.

"Okay," I said. "Yeah, that would be helpful."

"Great," Azael said.

"All right," interrupted Lilith. "Is there anything else I need to know? From any of you?"

"I'm thinking of wearing a green coat to the mixer," I said.

Crowley groaned, and the conversation relaxed into lighter topics. I was pleased that Azael seemed to fit in. Damien loving on him certainly seemed to help, at least with Aleister, who immediately liked anyone Damien approved of.

Soon, though, we all had to admit that beyond our self-assigned investigations, we also had a pile of homework to do, since our teachers were still doing their best to ensure that we never, ever embarrassed them in the slightest. Or maybe they just wanted to make sure we were too exhausted to make trouble.

It was a toss-up, really.

# TWENTY-SEVEN

I reread every letter Sean had sent me and decided to give Crowley the last one I got. It was closest to when everything went wrong, and as a bonus, there was nothing embarrassing in it, but rereading the letters made me miss Sean even more. I had been so busy with schoolwork, and while it was nice to be making my own friends, I missed having someone outside of all this. Outside of tracks and destiny. Outside of daily life, a friend where I didn't need to worry about who would say what to whom. And separate from what everyone else accepted as set in stone.

Because as much as Azael seemed different from the other people I went to school with, in all the times we had hung out, he had never complained about being tracked the way we were, or even that we were tracked at all. I had softened my resistance to letting the Fates choose my eternal destiny, but every once in a while I still rebelled with every bit of my being. And no one seemed to get it. Except for Sean, who was going through the same thing in the mortal coil.

Or at least he had been. We still didn't know what was happening with the humans, because as much as Crowley tried, so far everything had either outright failed or blown up in his face.

Literally.

There was smoke and ash everywhere.

I knew Crowley had said it was an educational exchange between him and Charity, but as his attempts to get a connection or at least find the humans continued to lead nowhere, he was becoming snippier and more tense.

I reached out to Cassandra immediately, but even as I did, I felt like I was making the wrong leap. Something about the feather, even as white as it was, just didn't make me think *Heaven*, especially after my visit from Not-Aria. The problem was, I didn't know what it *did* say.

And no matter what I did with the scraps of paper I'd managed to save and reshuffle, I couldn't make any sense of them, either. They weren't in a language I understood, which was weird, because language barriers weren't usually a thing when you were from one of the great hereafters. The language must have been very old or secret, and maybe if I had heard it spoken, it would have been different, but even still, the writing seemed so familiar. If only I could figure out why.

Cassandra's letter came back with a denial that Sean and Charity were in Heaven, and then five paragraphs asking me for opinions about punch, cookies, and decorations, including whether devil's food cake was offensive and if harpsichords were considered cool. I didn't even know what a harpsichord was, but it seemed like a no-brainer that they were not, in fact, cool.

Sidney came around the next time Azael did, and it was fine. I liked her, and the three of us melded well. I don't know what I was expecting, or what I was afraid of, but when Azael asked if she could come by too, my immediate response was dread. I covered it up with a massive amount of bravado, as was my way. But I guess my stressing was for nothing, and soon enough she was, if not an actual friend™, at least friend-adjacent.

In the meantime, we had gotten used to the ground shaking every once in a while, but my classroom ceilings were staying flame-free, and I was slowly catching up on the mountain of work my professors kept throwing at me.

I was 95 percent sure that my assignment on customs and etiquette was complete garbage. Not the essay. The essay was fine, assuming anything I had read was remotely accurate, which I was skeptical of. While I wasn't an expert on Heaven or its residents, I guaranteed I knew more than whoever had written the book.

And worse yet, with the pile of schoolwork we all had to do, our own snooping was taking a hit. I hadn't figured anything out about the feather and the writing except for the fact that it wasn't celestial, and it certainly hadn't come from here. Unless there was another newcomer like Morgan lurking around somewhere, which I used to think was unlikely but was starting to wonder about. After all, Morgan had been speaking to someone in that dressing room, and it wasn't anyone from here.

Cassandra's letters came more frequently, with frantic questions and ominous statements that she absolutely was not worried AT ALL, and all the planning was going GREAT. I had a feeling that Cassandra was as out of the loop as we were, because suddenly a date was announced.

And nothing else. It was enough to drive anyone crazy.

Obviously this was unacceptable, and we were totally going to figure out more, except Lilith was buried in essays, Crowley was obsessively trying new spells, Aleister was doing whatever it is enforcers do when school assigns work, and I was barely keeping up with the days. At night I studied the scraps of paper and the feather, I wrote letters to Sean that I knew wouldn't be answered, and I promised that I would do more the next day.

"It's about time you stopped all that ridiculous stuff," said Uriel one day at school while I was distractedly scribbling the last answer on my history assignment, two minutes before class.

"What are you talking about?" I asked, barely sparing a fraction of brainpower to wonder why Uriel was even talking to me.

"You know, the hair, the skin, the clothes," he said, making vague gestures.

"What?" I repeated. Why was he wasting my time with nonsense?

"You look normal," said Uriel. "I mean, you need a haircut, but still."

And that was when I pulled away from my assignment and actually paid attention. I turned to look at Uriel, crew cut, boring black clothes that looked like they were trying way too hard to be a field uniform. And then I dropped my gaze to my own clothes.

Oh, unholy darkness!

Black pants, black hoodie. There were no tattoos. And

even though I couldn't see my hair, I knew. Oh, brimstone, I knew. It was my natural color. Dear Lucifer, how had I let it get this bad?

My mouth dropped open, but Uriel had already shaken his head and moved on. How had I come to school like this? How long had I been doing this?

I flipped my hoodie up to cover my naked hair. There were three more hours of school. I was of a select angelic line tasked with keeping the forces of evil locked away. I had been specially trained my entire life to be brave, decisive, and true. I was one of the elite.

I could make it to the end of the day.

# TWENTY-EIGHT

The gasp was louder than the bells as I slunk into Glamourie. Morgan raised an eyebrow, which was green today, and I cringed but didn't make excuses, not wanting to interrupt them when they were with a client.

"Have a seat, darling," they said. "It's going to be a bit."

There was already someone sitting in the chair I normally waited in, so I took a seat on the purple velvet settee in the corner. It was even softer than it looked, which was impressive because it looked pretty soft. I missed being able to spin, like in my normal chair, but the chandeliers did send rainbows across my skin, which was nice.

Morgan was charming their client into a giggling mess

while they worked their magic, which was subtle. I wasn't sure what the bast had looked like when she'd come in, but as I watched, more and more highlights appeared in her dark brown fur, until finally gold threaded its way through, catching the light and sparkling.

Unlike when Crowley used his magic, Morgan's wasn't accompanied by a red haze. I watched and tried to see it happen, but the fae's magic was more subtle. I could feel it in the air, though. Something like drinking hot chocolate while wrapped in a cozy blanket on a cold night, but doing it somewhere exciting. It was an odd sensation but nothing visible. The shop smelled like perfumes and spices, so it was hard to tell if there was a scent of ozone, like some magic gave off.

"Voilà," Morgan announced with a flourish, and I startled in my comfy seat, where I had been close to dozing. "What do you think?"

"I love it!" At least that's what I thought she said.

The purring was so loud, it overwhelmed her voice. Morgan gave her care instructions, and she gushed about what a beautiful job they had done, and after a few more minutes the door closed behind the bast with a chime and a thud.

"What are you wearing?" demanded Morgan. "I mean, I knew you missed your appointment, but are you feeling all right?" They held the back of their hand to my forehead, which was still beneath my hood. "I mean, really, Malachi, this is just shocking. I expect more from my favorite client."

"Ha, ha," I said.

Morgan smirked. "Everyone has off days," they said lightly. "I mean, not me, but other people."

"Morgan," I said. "This is an emergency!"

"Absolutely," they said. "Have a seat."

I sat.

"No spinning?" they asked. "You really are off."

They had no idea. "Morgan," I whined. I did. There was no other way to describe it, but everything was wrong, including myself. "Help me."

"As much as it pains me to say, a fashion emergency is not actually an emergency," Morgan said. At my expression, they continued quickly. "Obviously, how we present ourselves to the world matters, and it matters that it reflects who we are, even if it's only who we are in that moment. But the situation is easy to remedy."

They winked, and I immediately relaxed.

"How do we want to make this better?"

"Can you just do your thing?" I asked.

Although I certainly wasn't the only one trying out Morgan's glamours, most people didn't want a look as out there as the styles I had been playing with. My adventurous spirit was why

267

I was one of Morgan's favorite customers. They said I let them stretch their creative muscles.

The real reason the shop was so popular was because Morgan could look into what made a person who they were and bring that identity to the outside. I didn't know if it was a fae ability or if it was just Morgan, but it was certainly a special ability in Hell. I didn't often take advantage of that skill, since I preferred something more dramatic, something that reflected maybe more who I wanted to be, rather than who I actually was on the inside.

Even as I said the words, I wondered if I should take it back. Did I want to see what Morgan thought I was on the inside? Did I want to show that to the world?

Morgan didn't say anything for a moment, and neither did I. Maybe they would decide to give me a wild look that I hadn't explored yet. I mean, I was creative, but most of my life had been spent in Hell, and Morgan was from Faerie and had been around a lot longer. A part of me wondered what Morgan saw for me; another part wasn't sure I wanted to know.

After a moment they nodded and patted my shoulder. "Relax, kid. I've got this."

And then they turned my chair away from the mirror.

When Morgan had first arrived in Hell, I had spent my entire appointment peppering them with questions on how this all worked. Morgan said that glamouring oneself was nearly instantaneous. Those best at the art simply knew who they were and had a clear picture of what they wanted. Foggy minds led to foggy illusions.

Glamouring others was almost as fast, as long as you only wanted to hold the illusion while the person was with you. Applying a glamour that would stay when you left their presence took longer, and according to Morgan, not just any fae could do it. Morgan said they were the best, and I believed them.

Mom and Dad insisted it was a waste of power.

Mom and Dad didn't remember what it was like to be a kid.

Now that my chair was turned away from the mirror, I let my eyes wander around a side of the shop I didn't normally have in my line of sight. There were odd crystals that glowed with inner light, a strange weblike ornament that I couldn't determine the purpose of, and art that seemed to move as I stared at it. In fact, I wasn't sure if I *should* stare it.

I blinked furiously and turned my gaze away, afraid to move my head in case I screwed up whatever Morgan was doing. Wait a minute . . .

"Morgan," I said, returning my eyes to the artwork, but this time not to the art itself but to the matting around it. "What language is that?"

"Hmm?" Morgan asked vaguely, and then turned to look.

"Ah, that's Elvish. An old form still in use in both the Seelie and Unseelie Courts, though usually only among the very old or very sneaky. Why do you ask? Looking for a secret language?"

"I've seen it before," I said. Where had I seen it before?

"I find that unlikely unless you've been to Faerie," said Morgan. "Have you had more adventures that I don't know about?"

"No," I said.

Was it in one of my textbooks? The scrolls they had been forcing us to read? We had a book on Faerie. Had Elvish been in that? Definitely not in the translation about Heaven. Ugh, if school hadn't been torturing me, I'd have been able to figure it out. Where had I seen Elvish before?

And then I knew. The scraps of paper that had fallen from the flames in my classroom. The white feather. For a moment I was disappointed. I had been hoping that the scraps of paper were somehow tied to Sean, but if the writing on those scraps was Elvish, and I was almost certain that it was, then it was a separate mystery altogether.

Now things were all coming together, because I remembered something else. The symbol that had been on the scraps of paper. It had looked familiar, but now that I was here, I remembered where I'd seen it. Someone had painted it across the wall of Glamourie.

"Are there feathered creatures in Faerie?" I asked.

"Many," they said, though there was suspicion in their voice.

"With white feathers?" I asked.

"Is there something you want to tell me?" they asked.

I didn't answer for a second, wondering what I should say. School was already investigating the flames-on-the-ceiling incident, and although I had taken the only feather, there had been more scraps of paper with writing on them left behind.

Probably.

Someone had painted the symbol on Morgan's wall without permission, which meant that Morgan didn't agree with whatever it was, or at least didn't want to be publicly associated with it, but I trusted Morgan. So, I told them what had happened, and that I had been trying to decipher the mystery with what little brainpower I had left.

It turned out that while there weren't any residents of Faerie with bright white feathers, there were creatures with white feathers that were often used as decoration.

"Do you have the feather with you?" Morgan asked.

"Yeah," I said, retrieving it from the interior pocket of my hoodie. I followed the feather with my eyes as I pulled it out, which was why I was looking directly at Morgan when they got their first glimpse. Whatever Morgan had been expecting, this wasn't it.

"Can I see it?" Morgan asked, holding out their hand. I hesitated for only a fraction of a second before handing it over.

"Do you know where it came from?" I asked. "Is it from Faerie?"

"No," they said. "It's from a very rare creature. You should hang on to it, though. The feathers are considered lucky."

They handed the feather back and returned to spellcasting with a pensive look on their face.

"Can I ask you another question?" I asked.

"It's not like you to ask permission first," Morgan said with false lightness.

"The symbol that someone painted outside," I said. "I've seen it in other places. What does it mean?"

"Where have you seen it?" Morgan asked, their voice blank.

"Written on paper," I said.

Morgan sighed deeply, and their hands stilled for a moment. The feel of magic in the air shifted for a moment to where it felt like the hot chocolate was scalding and the blanket was itchy, before shifting back into the soothing, exciting feel I was used to.

"That symbol," Morgan said, "is the symbol used for the Order of Puck. It's an old society that believes the natural state of existence is that of chaos."

A chill went up my spine, and it felt like a block of ice had dropped into my stomach.

"Over the years it has ranged wildly on what that means," Morgan said. "Sometimes they are devout followers of Chaos itself, seeking to free it from its bonds. Other times, the order is a social society embracing chaotic behavior and living on impulse. Sometimes the order disappears for a long time, before it reemerges. Like Puck, the society is unpredictable."

"What is it now?" I asked. "If sometimes it's a social club and sometimes it wants to destroy creation, what is it now?"

"Unfortunately," Morgan said with a wry smile, "that's a question that can only be answered in retrospect."

They stepped back, nodded once, and then turned the chair to face the mirror. "What do you think?"

Normally when I had a new look, it was wild, dramatic, a flurry of colors and gimmicks, so at first I wasn't sure what Morgan had done. I looked . . . good.

I dropped down from the chair and stepped closer to the mirror. My hair was mostly my natural color, but it was perfectly styled and there were glints of color—bronze, red, orange, at the tips of my normally dark hair. My eyes sparkled, and as I leaned closer to the mirror, I saw that there were actual glints of light, not like the flames that got going when my temper rose but like tiny shards of metallic gold and silver. My wings looked the way they did when the feathers caught the light from the eternal flames. I spread them just a bit to see the purples, greens, and blues, and each feather was perfect. None were misaligned or disheveled. I stepped back and straightened my shoulders. I looked . . . like me, but better. Stronger. More confident. Proud.

I found Morgan's eyes in the mirror, and the expression they wore was nothing short of smug. They gestured to my arm, and at first I was confused, but then I rolled up my sleeve. Underneath my bland hoodie was an intricate design of silver shining from my skin.

"What is it?" I asked, studying the swirls that were almost but not completely contained within a circle.

"Just an old symbol from home," Morgan said. "It protects from magical attack. If you believe that sort of thing."

"Thanks, Morgan," I said. "I love it."

"It's you," they said. "Now, by the Lady's grace, go change those terrible clothes. I do not do my best work to have you ruin it with lack of effort."

"I will," I said. "Thanks, Morgan, for everything."

"Of course," they said.

I was just reaching for the doorknob when Morgan called out. "Mal!"

"Yeah?" I asked, turning.

"Keep that feather on you, from now on," they said. Morgan locked eyes with me, a serious expression on their face. "For luck."

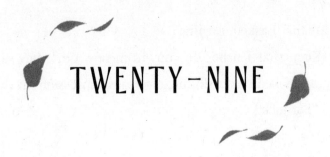

# TWENTY-NINE

As the day of the mixer drew closer, Crowley figured out a location spell that he swore had worked but had also indicated that Charity and Sean were not in the mortal realm. But if they weren't in the mortal realm, where were they?

I already knew they wouldn't be in the Pit if they had passed over. Their souls had been far too bright for their destinies to have changed that quickly. And I had already messaged Cassandra to see if they had turned up in Heaven. She had replied in the negative and then followed up with even more questions: Did living in Hell make us more sensitive to cold temperatures? Should Heaven provide sweaters? Was our eyesight worse? Did it make more sense to turn the lights way up high or to dim the lights entirely? But then if they dimmed the lights too low, the heavenly angels would need more sensitive glasses, and were night-vision glasses really necessary?

I didn't even know what to say to any of that, so I simply thanked her for her help and said I was looking forward to seeing her soon. Hopefully.

I told the squad about the Order of Puck, and Lilith attempted to get more information about them from her school library, but the sources on Faerie were limited and she couldn't ask for interdimensional book loans without causing suspicion. Lilith was snippy when she was frustrated, as we all were, and our recent conversations had not been great.

The next morning at school, the classroom was abuzz with chatter about the big event.

". . . you're going, right . . ."

"My mother said . . ."

". . . black with, like, silver . . ."

"QUIET!" boomed Professor Jophiel. "I know you're all excited, but that is no excuse for a lack of discipline, and I swear on all that is unholy, if you lot turn this into a diplomatic nightmare, I will make your very immortality a nightmare of its own."

Jophiel glared at me like my ultimate plan was to single-handedly start another Great War.

What had he been hearing?

The class did get quiet at that, but it was the same scenario throughout the day. Once the date had been set, the mixer was all anyone could talk about. What was the point in focusing on great wars of the past when we were going to see our counterparts in reality in the near future?

The conversations immediately picked up at the end of Strategy and Treachery class, just like it had at the end of every other class, while I packed my notebook in my bag with a sigh of relief, very eager to be done with the day. And that would have been all well and perfect, except for what was waiting by my locker.

I sighed.

"I suppose you're going," sneered Rachel.

"Yup," I said, rolling my eyes. "Just like everyone else."

"Don't even think about doing anything," Rachel said. "I have eyes everywhere."

Dramatic much? I leaned closer, and she seemed taken aback. My go-to move had been to ignore her and her friends as much as possible, but I was done.

"Do you really think I'd work alone?" I asked, putting as much devilish mischief into my smirk as possible, and forcing the flames to flicker in my glamoured eyes.

Rachel paled and stepped back. Her wings clung to her back, and I smiled fully. She tried to recover her dignity, but it was too late. I laughed as her friends pulled her away, and I closed my locker door with a gleeful slam.

Huh, turned out the day did end well!

# THIRTY

N o," I said. "You are not!"

"What is wrong with my field uniform?" Dad asked.

One of the unforeseen outcomes of it having been millennia since the dimensions had gotten together was the absolutely hysterical problem of the adults not knowing what to wear.

"My parents are dressing up," Azael offered. "You'll see when they get here."

Azael had already changed and even had a new smattering of stars shaved onto the side of his head for the occasion. Even though he had been coming over more often, it was still weird to have someone besides my squad at my house getting ready for an event, but everyone had been so busy, and our tempers had been short.

But at least I had an ally. And thankfully, for the sake of fun and fashion, so did Mom. Meg had decided to leave for the mixer with us.

"We shouldn't even be going," Dad said. "The soul mix-ups, the unexpected visitors, the ground quakes, we haven't resolved anything."

"And yet," Mom said, "all of that is being investigated, and if anything, the instability makes this diplomatic mission crucial. Other people will keep working while we're gone. It will be fine, dear."

"Exactly, don't be so uptight!" Meg said. "I agree with the kids. You can't wear that."

Dad grumbled, but when it was all said and done, while Dad's new outfit wasn't what I would have chosen, it was far better than it could have been, and it was definitely not a field uniform.

The logistics of how this mixer was happening with most of the angels of Heaven and Hell and potentially representatives from other dimensions as well was beyond me. There were literally hundreds of thousands of us, and yet somehow we were all meeting up at once. At least the ones that were going.

There were people staying behind to guard the Pit, and I

assumed the same would be true for Heaven. After all, leaving either dimension completely alone would just be asking for trouble. Even though my classmates were idiots for thinking I was in league with Chaos, it didn't mean that no one was.

True, the Order of Puck graffiti could have been a prank, but then again, we had seen the same symbol on the papers that had fallen in my classroom. Maybe the group existed and they were just into harmlessly acting out?

But what if they weren't? Morgan had said we wouldn't know until it was too late, and that wasn't very encouraging.

I was looking forward to seeing Cassandra but also dreading the possibility—let's be honest, the inevitability—that the seraph would say something incriminating in front of my parents. My recent grounding was still fresh in my mind, and that had happened without my parents knowing I had gone to Heaven.

"C'mon," I said. "Let's go!"

"Maybe I should stay—" Dad started.

"NO," Mom, Meg, and I all shouted before he could finish.

We met at the assigned portal location, where a steady stream of powers all headed in the same direction. There were a few curious glances, and some suspicious ones, from the locals who hadn't been invited. I saw my squad and felt nerves hit my stomach. Things had felt weird lately between us, and I was walking over with Azael and his parents, which also felt weird.

And it wasn't just my squad waiting. All the parents were there, plus Crowley's brother, Simon, who looked a little irritated to be stuck with us and not off with his own friends.

Lilith was wearing a shimmering lavender dress over black pants or leggings or whatever they were, but unholy darkness, she looked amazing, and my heart was doing bad things in my chest. If I died tonight, I thought I'd be okay with it.

"H-hey, guys," I said, and cleared my throat in an attempt to regain my composure.

Azael waved awkwardly, but Aleister greeted him like he was oblivious to any tension.

"You look good," I said to Lilith, who immediately smirked. "I mean, everyone looks good. You look good too, Crowley."

Crowley smiled mockingly, but it was fine, because he hadn't been smiling much lately, and at least his mocking was familiar.

"I can take this off when we get inside, though, right?" Aleister whined, tugging hard at his formfitting jacket. It was a hard turn from his normal clothing choices, but it was a definite improvement, even if it was a little boring.

"Dude," I said. "One night. You're fine."

"Listen to Malachi," said Aleister's dads simultaneously,

and I grinned broadly. Aleister rolled his eyes, but then smiled, and shoved me with a wing.

"Oh, so it's like that," I said, relieved that the short tempers we had all been exhibiting lately were gone. "I get it. Not everyone can look this good."

I smoothed my hand down my new favorite green jacket from Dorian's. Crowley rolled his eyes, but Lilith smiled, and just like that, everything felt normal again.

The adults chatted about whatever adult boring things they were planning to do tonight, and we teased each other over the extra efforts we had put in to look good. The waiting line was filled with nervous energy, obvious in everyone my age, and even in the adults, who tried to hide it.

Admittedly the energy on our end was more like waiting for our favorite band to take the stage, while the energy on our parents' end was more like waiting to be ambushed.

Fingers danced a little too close to razor-sharp halos that had been peace bonded for the occasion with leather straps and decorative buckles to prevent them from being used, or at least make them harder to pull out on impulse. Unfortunately, I knew there was still a large portion of the parents who believed this was a trap, and I had no real way of explaining that Cassandra was definitely—probably—not plotting against us, and she really did just want us all to be buddies.

Of course, she had repeatedly tried to kidnap us when she'd thought it was the right thing to do, so there was that.

At least we didn't have to be worried about being separated this time or trapped in another dimension. This trip was completely by the book. We all had our invitations, and our RSVPs had been properly logged and spelled. Supposedly nobody was getting through without one.

Even though we were going to the same place, through technically the same dimensional opening, there were check-in gates all over Hell, which was why it wasn't overly crowded at our portal. Lilith said it was like all the tollbooths were just making the door extra wide, so we didn't bottleneck like Aleister and I tended to do whenever we went down the narrow staircase at Faust's.

I wondered if crossing would feel different from how it had when we'd crossed into Salem, but I didn't bring that up to the parents. No need to remind them what we had done, especially since I was pretty sure there were going to be reminders everywhere tonight.

The line moved quickly. Our times of departure were all staggered in five-minute increments, and soon I could see the booth, and a very familiar imp.

I nudged Crowley and gestured. His attention drew Lilith's, and they both grimaced.

"What?" asked Aleister, still fidgeting with his formal jacket. "I'm starting, like, ten points behind here. You guys owe me explanations. Yes, in fact, that's the rule. Anytime there's an inside joke or you recognize someone, or something has to do with anything you did when you abandoned me, you have to tell me."

"We didn't abandon you," Crowley said.

"And I swear on all that is unholy," continued Aleister, "if you guys run out on me again—"

"Okay," Lilith said. "For one thing, you need to learn to be discreet. For another, we didn't abandon you, it was an accident, and although I'm glad you made the mature decision, you could have followed. We would have found you. And yes, we will tell you stuff. You can relax."

"Easy for you to say," grumbled Aleister.

"I'm right there with you," Azael said to Aleister. "If it makes you feel better."

"Dude," said Aleister, placing one hand on Azael's shoulder and the other over his heart. "That means a lot."

We laughed and the sound was echoed by our parents. Azael's mom and dad were fitting in just fine, and more important, if the parents were having fun, they wouldn't be watching our every move.

# THIRTY-ONE

Thankfully, as our group approached the booth, our parents took the lead, and Terrence, the imp we had taken to bribing when we were in Salem, was distracted by checking the invitations he was responsible for, and our parents were back in their own conversations.

"Didn't you get punished for taking bribes?" I asked.

Terrence jerked his head up, and immediately narrowed his lime-green eyes into angry slits. "You."

"Yup," I agreed. "We're doing it the right way this time."

"Hmph." He stamped an invitation, which hissed and sent smoke into the air.

"Come on, Terrence," said Lilith, looking carefully at

our parents to make sure they were still distracted. "Last time we saw you, you had a giant babysitter. Are you out of trouble?"

Terrence stamped another invite; another sizzle and a puff of smoke. He looked up at us and sighed.

"I'm guarding internal transports only," he said. "Ten times the work, and nothing good to eat. It's awful."

"Sorry," I said, feeling only a tiny bit bad. After all, Terrence had already been accepting bribes before we had offered him one. No one had made him take it. But considering we had all been punished on our return, I did have a little empathy. "How long until they let you go topside?"

"A hundred years," he said. He stamped another scroll. The smoke it released was scented vaguely like Heaven, not that the adults knew that.

"That's not bad," Crowley said.

"Wait, what happened?" Aleister said. "You're already breaking your promise."

"Come on, gang," called Aleister's dad Cael. "It's our turn."

"I'm sure the time will go by quickly, Terrence," I said. He grumbled something I couldn't quite make out, and I then stepped forward through the wavering veil.

When I'd crossed into Salem, there'd been the icy coldness of nothing, and then I'd landed face-first on the ground. This time I stepped into a place of brightness and movement and a feeling of nothingness.

I felt like my teachers should have prepared me better for this. Was I supposed to keep walking? Was I supposed to wait? Had something gone wrong? But before I could completely panic, the colors around me swirled and rushed by like I was flying through fireworks, and then I was out, standing on a marble floor, surrounded by people, all without the icy coldness or a fall to the ground.

The ballroom we appeared in was enormous, and I seriously considered whether "room" was the correct term. From where I stood, I couldn't see where it ended; it seemed to go on and on forever, not ending in a wall but just fading from my vision.

I was surrounded by black-winged powers dressed to the nines. A quick glance to my right and left let me know that my parents were here, and so were my friends. It was nice to end up in a strange dimension with familiar faces.

I glanced behind me to see if I needed to make room for more people coming through the veil, but the room must have still been growing, because there was plenty of space.

There were streamers and balloons, and white silk cloths draped between ornate columns that went from marble floor to . . . well, whatever was up there. I wondered if I took to the sky if there would be more decorations higher up, wherever the columns ended. There was music playing from stringed instruments, no doubt harps included, although I couldn't actually see where the music was coming from.

There were tables piled with food, and cakes the size of carriages standing on pedestals. There were empty high tables to stand around, and lower tables arranged with chairs to sit. There were large open spaces that looked like they might be dance floors, but if our hosts expected dancing, the music was seriously going to need to change.

"Oh wow," breathed Aleister.

I followed his gaze across the room to see a whole group of other people, white-winged and stiff, like they wouldn't be able to recognize or enjoy a good time. They wore white gowns that were almost indistinguishable from each other, and they were glancing nervously at our side of the room like they were waiting for the attack to come. It was almost exactly like an awkward school dance, if instead of shyness there was the fear of murder.

"Can we look around?" I asked Dad.

"I don't know," Dad said, not even moving his eyes from the other half of the room.

"Come on," I said. "People are still arriving. Nothing is happening, and this is supposed to be a party, not a fight."

"Supposed to be," Dad muttered.

"Do you have your pocket mirror?" asked Mom.

"Yes," I said.

"Just let them go," said Haylel, Lilith's mom, before she turned to my squad and Azael. "Stay together. Don't do anything stupid."

"We would never do anything stupid," said Crowley. "I mean, I wouldn't."

"Hey," objected Simon, who I had completely forgotten about. "I have friends here too. Why do I have to stay with *them*?"

"We never said you had to," said Crowley's dad. "Same rules go for you. Don't be stupid, and make sure you're reachable. They're supposed to announce when the return trip is. Once they do, make sure you're back here in plenty of time."

"Thanks!" And Simon was gone. No doubt looking for Scarlett. I wondered how long he'd be looking or how far this room really went.

"I told Sidney and Parisa I'd meet up with them," said Azael. "I'm sure we'll see you guys later."

My squad mates and I waved goodbye and surveyed the room for our own game plan.

This was going to be a night to remember.

# THIRTY-TWO

ome on," I said, nudging Aleister with my wing.

We broke out from the crowd that was our parents and our fellow powers. One quick glance back showed more than a few hands on halos, and more than a few terrified-looking faces on the other side. I sighed. That was not going to help things.

I rolled my eyes and straightened my shoulders. If there was going to be any sort of understanding between our dimensions, it was going to be up to us. Never leave things to adults when you can have kids handle them.

"We have a lot of work to do," I said, and my squad nodded in unison.

I grabbed a puffy-looking thing off a snack table and popped it into my mouth. My friends stared at my face to watch my reaction. I gave a thumbs-up, and they turned to the table and began piling snacks onto too-small plates. I grabbed several cookies of the melty chocolate variety that I knew had been made especially for us by a certain reformed angelic kidnapper, and some other things I didn't recognize. And speaking of that reformed kidnapper, I wondered where she was.

Once our plates were loaded up, we began to really investigate our make-believe location, because that was where our mixer ended up being. None of the dimensions involved had been willing to give anyone else the home advantage, so a pocket dimension had been created, with representatives from each dimension playing a part in its creation.

For as much studying we had done on Heaven to avoid *cultural misunderstandings*, I couldn't help but think it was more for the sake of following the old "know thy enemy" mantra than trying to build relationships.

"Hey, Lil," I said. "How many dimensions are showing up here?"

"I'm not sure who confirmed," Lilith said after swallowing a bite of something. "All the major players were invited, and most were committed to sending some people. But it was only Heaven and Hell that were quote-unquote *required* to attend. The upper echelons didn't say it, but apparently, we're the weak links."

"What do you mean?" Aleister asked.

"I mean, our *animosity* is a security threat," Lilith said. "Not that there's any question about us each doing our jobs, but I guess our visit to Salem made it clear that we view each other inaccurately? I guess that's not a problem for the other dimensions."

"Really?" Crowley asked, skepticism clear in his voice. "Because I'm pretty sure if this were being held in Faerie, I wouldn't have been allowed to go."

"That's only because adults don't understand Faerie," I said. "Not because they view it as the enemy."

"I don't think they view Heaven as the enemy necessarily," Aleister said.

"Maybe *we* don't," Lilith said. "Anymore."

"Thank Lucifer the adults don't know how close Cassandra came to kidnapping us," I said, looking around to see if I could spot her.

"I still can't believe I missed that," Aleister said. "You guys get all the fun!"

"Arriving from Faerie," announced a voice everywhere and nowhere at once. "Titania and Mab of the Seelie and Unseelie Courts, with entourage."

"Where?" I asked, frantically looking everywhere, but to no avail.

No matter where we looked, and brimstone, did we look, we couldn't find the entrance to the room or where the arrivals were coming in, even though we kept hearing announcements.

"This is so annoying," Aleister grumbled. "What is the point, if we can't see them?"

"I think we're supposed to be making nice with the white-feather folx," I said.

"Yeah," Crowley said. "But where are the ones our age? Are there any?"

"There's supposed to be," said Lilith doubtfully.

"Oh, there are!" gushed a very familiar voice. "There *are* kids your age, and I can't wait for you to meet them!"

"Hey, Cassandra," I said, and was immediately pulled into a tight hug. I got a mouthful of white feathers and attempted not to suffocate while clumsily hugging her back. I moved my head and tried to spit out a feather without being insulting. "Nice to see you, too!"

"Oh, my gracious!" she said, pulling back and squishing my cheeks unpleasantly. "I'm so happy!"

My friends' laughter dragged her attention away from me, and before they knew it, she was tugging them into tight, breathless hugs.

"Oh," Cassandra said, stopping before she hugged Aleister. "I don't know you."

"This is Aleister," I said. "Our friend that stayed behind."

"What, I don't get a hug?" Aleister asked. "I miss out on the adventures and the love? That's not—oof!"

"Of course you get a hug too!" she said as she engulfed Aleister.

We were becoming a spectacle, and between Cassandra's excitement—which was being rapidly amped up by an enthusiastic Aleister—and the shocked stares from those around us, I couldn't help laughing and exchanging grins with Lilith and Crowley. I was so relieved, I could cry.

Just like old times.

"So, Cassandra, what is the plan here?" I asked when there was a lull. "Because I'm a little confused. You kept calling this a mixer, but I don't really see any mixing."

Cassandra pouted and gazed at the room, where there was a distinct division between the forces of Heaven and Hell, both staring awkwardly at each other, and a conspicuous absence of anyone else.

"I know," Cassandra said. "I don't understand why they're not making friends. I mean, you and I became friends right away!"

At which we all exchanged significant looks, until Aleister blurted out, "You did? Because I thought—"

"It took work," interrupted Lilith. "Like any good friendship."

"We did work well together, didn't we?" Cassandra asked wistfully. "Oh well. Never mind that. There are people I want you to meet!"

Cassandra told us that she had thought the adult party might be too boring for us and had advocated for a youth area, which would, in theory, be livelier. And looking around at the room at large and whatever was happening here made me think she had a point. Whatever this was, it was not a party.

Instantly my mood lifted. I couldn't deny that while I had low expectations for what Heaven's kids considered fun, I was still insanely curious, and it absolutely had to be better than this awkwardness.

Cassandra led us past white-winged guests who eyed us suspiciously while she greeted them warmly like she didn't notice the tension at all, and past a delegation from Faerie with iridescent wings and horns, who I really wanted to stop and talk to.

"Wait," I tried to protest, but Crowley just shoved me forward, and apparently, we hadn't wandered far enough, because as we followed Cassandra through the never-ending room, we were finally seeing delegations from various other dimensions as well.

A group with gray cloaks, and shadows that moved independently of their bodies, had Lilith nearly stopping in her tracks. Another group sparkled in green and red. They had pointed ears like Morgan's but smelled like peppermint and sugar, and they giggled freely like they managed to make fun wherever they went.

I had no idea where they were from, or why they weren't in the youth area, because they looked like they were kids, but maybe they weren't? In any case, I didn't have time to check them out, because Cassandra was determined to keep us moving and introduce us to what I assumed was going to be kids our own ages.

Finally, past more tables covered with food that we snagged samples from, we approached an archway that dripped with flowers of every shade and gauzy fabric curtains that swayed in an impossible breeze, an archway that appeared to lead "outside."

# THIRTY-THREE

"Outside" in a pocket dimension is a subjective term, since technically everything is inside the pocket dimension and therefore nothing can be outside. While the ceiling in the ballroom had been hazy and indistinct as it had faded upward, the "outside" had a sky. Or should I say "sky"?

It was flat, more like a ceiling than anything else, with distinct edges. It wasn't the glowing warm sky of home, or the startling blue of the mortal realm, but it wasn't the lavender of Heaven either. It was a navy blue with touches of pinks and purples, white spots that twinkled in and out of view, and glowing yellow orbs. There were swirls of sparkling silver that moved in lazy turns. And for all that glittering movement, the sky was obviously fake.

The ground was spongy and soft, so much so that I almost stumbled when we moved from marble to whatever this was, and my wings flared just a bit to help my balance. It was covered in grass, or what was supposed to be grass, lime green in color. The "outside" didn't have walls but it did have a fence, white picket, that a girl from Heaven older than us was casually leaning against. The outside continued farther, much like the ballroom had, and I had no doubt that the fence continued along every edge.

We were the only powers that had ventured this far, and I didn't know if the other dimensions besides Heaven and Hell had brought kids, but if they had, they weren't here yet. Even still, it wasn't empty. There were plenty of white-winged kids from Heaven here. Some were older than us, others our own age, and some much younger.

Heaven had a larger population of mortal souls than Hell did, which meant they had a much larger population of angels. In Hell it was just us powers, and all the responsibility fell on us. In Heaven there was the seraphim, the cherubim, the thrones, and several more archangels, and they didn't even have to guard souls from escaping, because as Cassandra had pointed out, their souls *wanted* to be there.

"Is this babyproof?" asked Crowley, pressing a finger to the top of the white picket fence, which squished down in response.

"You can have fun without getting hurt!" exclaimed Cassandra.

"No way," breathed Aleister. He threw himself against the fence, which stretched on impact.

"See. Perfectly safe," Cassandra said. "And look, there's food over there, and oh, this is going to be so much fun! We'll never forget tonight, ever, ever, ever! Okay, go make friends and I'll see you soon. I need to figure out why no one is socializing. Not every adult is as cool and modern as I am."

"She's hilarious," Aleister said as soon as Cassandra left the room. "No wonder you had so much fun."

"She thought we were demons," Crowley said pointedly. "She zapped us to an island and was going to send us off to live in Heaven."

"You don't have to rub it in," grumbled Aleister. "I've never been to an island."

And then a very familiar pair of chubby arms were wrapped around my legs. I wasn't sure if Not-Aria was supposed to be here, but somehow I wasn't surprised to see her.

"Well, hello there," I said. "Again."

And then as soon as the hug was over, she ran off. She

definitely looked bigger, but then, didn't adults always say kids grew up fast? Still. I didn't think they grew that fast.

"What happens if we fly over the fence?" asked Crowley.

"Not sure," I said. "Should we try?"

"Yes!" Aleister said, and immediately launched into the air.

"I wouldn't," Lilith said, grabbing his foot and yanking him to the bouncy grass, reminding us why she was our squad's Intelligence.

"Good call," a voice from behind us said.

We turned as one—well, except for Aleister, who was fumbling in the squishy artificial turf—to see a white-winged angel approaching us. She looked a little older than us, but she didn't have a halo, so she couldn't have been that much older. And unlike some of the other heavenly angels who were still staring at our sharp, jet-black wings, she approached us confidently. Her white wings seemed brighter than some of the others, and I wondered if she was a seraph like Cassandra. Her dark curls stood in contrast to the blinding white of her feathers, and she casually tucked a stray curl behind her ear as she leaned against the babyproof fence.

"This is a pocket dimension," she said. "But it doesn't go on forever. If Cassandra and the fae who helped built this place were careful, they would have put protections in place so we couldn't get beyond what was real. If they didn't, though, you're pretty much guaranteed to have your brains dissolve into madness. Your call, though. I'm Zira: seraph."

"Malachi: power, obviously," I said. "But my friends call me Mal. This is Lilith, Crowley, and Aleister."

"Hi," said Zira. "So, what's Hell like?"

"What?" I asked. "Not going to assume we're demons right off the bat?"

"Nah," she said. "I mean, if you are, don't keep it a secret."

Crowley scoffed.

"Definitely not," Lilith said. "What about Heaven? Do you really play harps all day?"

Zira laughed, and that seemed to loosen everyone up, and the angels that had been lurking nearby began to edge closer.

While all of us except Aleister had been to Heaven, we had really only been very briefly in one room in the business district. It turned out that just like Hell wasn't one big torturous pit of torture, Heaven was more than uptight bureaucrats in office buildings. That is, if Zira was to be believed and wasn't just trying to convince us that Heaven was better than it was.

"Yes, we have movies."

"But are they *good* movies?"

"Isn't that kind of subjective? But seriously, do you really have fire everywhere? How does that even work?"

"Are you seriously saying you don't? Even the mortal realm has a ball of fire in the sky."

In no time we were doing exactly what this whole thing was for. More people from home had even arrived. We made introductions when we knew them and even met some people from distant cities in Hell that we didn't know. If the adults were still awkwardly staring at each other, that certainly wasn't the case in what we had fondly named "the day care."

Well, with the exception of Uriel, who still seemed skeptical, and vaguely disapproving.

Somehow the youngest angels had totally overwhelmed Aleister, and the squishy ground was getting a workout. Azael, Sidney, and Parisa had joined us as well, and Sidney threw herself into the chaotic mix of littles right along with Aleister.

"Al, could you maybe not crush the littles," Crowley said.

"They're fine," Zira said dismissively.

But the light in the outside strobed for just a second, and I looked up to see our artificial sky glitch out and disappear.

"What the—" Zira gasped.

Gone were the bright pinpoints of stars, the swirls of galaxies, and the deep purples and blues, and in their place was the void of nothing.

# THIRTY-FOUR

J ust as when I had looked out into the nothing in the memory of what had once been Beadle's Tavern, my brain made a valiant attempt at melting. No one was meant to understand true emptiness, not even angels.

The younger angels screamed, and I tore my gaze away and instantly felt a little better. Aleister and Sidney spread their wings over the littles' heads, and they quieted. Zira ripped her gaze away from the sky. I wouldn't say I had a lot of experience with seraphs, but it didn't take an expert to see her widened eyes, and to see that somehow her dark skin had lost an internal glow that was apparently innate in the burning ones. She shook the fear off quickly and rushed to the little kids, but by the time she'd managed the short distance, the sky was back to normal.

Aleister looked up cautiously and then folded his wings against his back. The background sound I hadn't been aware of until it was gone was back. In no time the voices grew louder, and the concerned murmuring was replaced with laughs and excited conversation. Aleister and Sidney led the younger angels, who had become rapidly obsessed with the enforcers, to the snack table, where they began shoving melty chocolate chip cookies into their mouths, while Azael and Parisa joined the rest of us.

"What was that about?" Azael asked.

"A glitch?" Parisa asked.

"What happens if a pocket dimension glitches out while you're in it?" I asked.

"You don't want to know," Lilith said.

"That won't happen," Zira said. "This thing has been planned to the very last detail."

I couldn't tell if I was jaded or if being blindingly optimistic was a Heaven thing, because I wasn't convinced.

Maybe being trapped in another dimension had given me trauma, but at least getting trapped in the mortal realm had meant that I'd been trapped somewhere real. Everything here was fake, but the pocket dimension was still *something*.

If everything except what was real disappeared, we would be left in the nothingness of the void.

Pocket dimensions were built in the spaces left behind—not even the space between dimensions that the Wild Hunt traveled through, but the ones untouched by a hint of creation. Pocket dimensions needed the voids in order to create space for their own realities. And one of those voids was where we would find ourselves if our pocket dimension failed.

No one wanted that.

"Maybe we should still check in," I said. "And I don't want this to be the only thing I see tonight. Who knows the next time we'll all be together?"

"That's a good point," Zira said, her glow returning. "I heard there were representatives from Faerie here."

"Yes!" Lilith said. "And there were people out there from places I'm not even sure of, and Purgatory is supposed to be here too."

"You don't mind a tagalong, do you?" Zira asked.

"We are supposed to be making friends," I pointed out.

"Wait!" Aleister yelled, untangling himself from the littles, who launched a chorus of protests. "Are you seriously thinking about leaving me behind again? With the parents here this time, giving me the third degree? Nuh-uh. No way."

"Relax," Crowley said. "No one was leaving you."

"I think we're going to stay a little longer," said Azael.

"Yeah," agreed Parisa. "Before all that happened, I was in a really good conversation that's seriously going to give me a leg up on that assignment in Professor Ruth's class."

I cringed, and so did Azael. Who was thinking about school right now?

"Sidney's still here," Azael said, shrugging, and we all glanced over to where Not-Aria had taken to latching on to Sidney's legs. "We'll catch up with you."

Back on the "inside," the party hadn't gotten much better. There were scattered groups of intermingled black and white wings here and there, but the conversations looked awkward, and most of the room was still divided, with people staring suspiciously at each other.

"Okay," Zira said. "The group from Purgatory isn't expected to be very large, so we'll have to keep our eyes open for them, but Anubis himself is supposed to be here."

"No way," I said. "The Jackal is coming? We have to find him."

"You really want to be judged?" Zira asked.

"I— He wouldn't do that, would he?" I asked.

"I'm not sure he turns it on and off," Lilith said. "But we can find out."

"Ha!" Aleister said. "Bring it!"

"Are we not worried about the glitching at all?" Crowley drawled.

"Why would we be worried about that?" asked Zira. "It's an angelic plan, straight from Heaven! There is literally nothing that can go wrong. Have a little faith."

"I have faith that anything that can go wrong, will," Crowley said.

While we hadn't been told not to leave the kiddie area, it still felt vaguely like rule breaking, which was always fun. The thought of flying wasn't even at the forefront of our minds. It was too important to be among the crowd, seeing who was here. There were a good number of fae around, and they weren't congregating in groups like the angels were. They wandered here and there, in colors and shapes and features that were surprising even to me. Morgan had been holding out!

"Now, isn't that interesting," murmured a voice so pure and musical, I knew immediately it would be one of the fae. I had been feeling pretty fancy with my threads from Dorian's and Morgan's glamour, but looking at the fae, I immediately felt like that time Lilith had seen me in my two-day-old boxers.

The fae was tall and slender, and a sparkle of gold covered their skin, complemented by the dribs and drabs of jewels. They wore leggings of shimmering bronze cloth decorated with strips of golden leather, and a white velvet vest embroidered with golden thread, which had a train that flared in the back. The fae held a wineglass of something iridescent.

"What— I mean, excuse me," I stammered. "Sorry, what is interesting?"

I glanced over to my friends, who were taking in the activity of the room and the musicians in the corner. Lilith was locked in an animated conversation with Zira.

"The glamour complementing your wardrobe," they said. "Interesting since you aren't from Faerie. Interesting because I recognize its flavor."

I really didn't know what to say to that. I wasn't sure why Morgan had left Faerie. They always brushed it off with some excuse about boredom or made up some silly reason, but in the moments when they dropped their guard, it seemed there was more to the story than that. If I admitted to knowing them, would it put them in danger? Had I already put them in danger?

"Don't fret," they said. "I may be of the Seelie Court, but we're not all uptight. What's your *name*?"

The way they asked made it sound like something more profound than just wanting to know what I was called, and I was reminded of Crowley's concern about giving our real names. Still, I hadn't hesitated to give my name to Morgan, and this was supposed to be a diplomacy mission.

"Malachi," I said.

"Mine is Rowan," they said. "I'll be sure to remember your name, Malachi. Don't forget mine."

"I won't," I said, and then Rowan winked and wandered away.

I was not going to be winning any awards for charisma. I shook my head and cleared the stunned stupidity that was probably, but not definitely, from my own brain and not faerie magic, just in time for my friends to join me.

"Want some of this?" Aleister asked. "Zira said it's called 'angel food cake.' Can you imagine? Mal, look, it's squishy."

I took the squishy cake, which was really good, and we wandered farther. Even though we didn't see more musicians, the cringe-worthy music remained constant.

"Who picked this music?" I said.

"Isn't it great?" asked Zira. "This song has been trending for weeks."

"Huh," I said.

"Want me to show you the dance?" she asked.

Absolutely not.

"Yes!" Aleister said.

Of course.

"Now arriving," boomed a disembodied voice, "the representatives from Purgatory—oh, what? Are you seri—"

And then there was nothing. Well, nothing but the cheesy song that Aleister and Zira were now grooving to.

"Where would Purgatory be arriving?" Lilith asked.

"Yeah, that was a sketchy announcement," I said, before being stalled in my tracks by the sight of a familiar person. "Hey, wait, Cassandra!"

The seraph faltered midflight before looking over her shoulder. She looked back the way she was heading before looking at us again. I put on my most pathetic *Pretty please* face, and she dropped lightly to the ground.

"Wait." Zira stopped mid-wiggle. "Do you actually know her?"

"She tried to kidnap us," Crowley said. "While we were saving all of creation."

"What—"

"Is there something wrong with the outside?" Cassandra asked, twisting her hands together.

"Is there reason to think there would be?" Crowley asked.

"Where are the reps from Purgatory coming in?" I interrupted. "Can we see? Why did the announcement stop?"

"I'm sure it's fine," she said. "I'm sure everything is fine."

"Okay. Are you heading that way? Can we come with you?" I asked. "Come on, Cassandra. This is supposed to be bonding time, right?"

"No, I'm not going to the fountain. I'm going somewhere

completely different! But you should stay here," she said. "Because everything is fine."

"Great!" I said, smiling broadly. And then after a beat, in my most charming voice, "It's nice to see you."

"Oh." Cassandra blushed. "Oh, of course. We should really have tea and I can tell you all about— Oh! I'm being called. I really do need to go."

"Because everything is fine," Crowley said wryly.

"Yes, of course!" After a moment of dithering, Cassandra took off and resumed her flight.

"We're heading to the fountain, right?" I asked.

"Obviously," Zira said.

"Wait, really?" Lilith asked. "I thought you'd be . . ."

"What? You thought I'd just do what I'm told? A mixer like this may never happen again. I want to see *everyone*!"

"Then we're in agreement," I said.

"Yes," Zira said. "And while we walk, you can explain how you know Cassandra. She's famous!"

Zira was a great addition to our group, except for her horrendous taste in music. We were way outnumbered by our heavenly comrades, and even though Zira didn't know everyone, she did know more than we did, and just having her white wings mingled with our black ones made our heavenly counterparts less wary.

"That's it!" shouted Aleister, lifting on his wings for a second before dropping back down. "Right?"

Zira giggled, and even though we didn't take to the air, we did quicken our steps, walking comically fast and shoving each other with our elbows and wings. My stomach thrilled with nerves and excitement. There was a crowd under an archway whose only purpose seemed to be separating the spaces or making you forget about the fact that there was no ceiling. The milling group included representatives from Faerie, Heaven, and Hell.

I saw Rowan from a distance. Their eyes seemed to find me right away, and although they didn't make an obvious sign, somehow I knew they were waiting for something to happen. And whatever it was, I was here for it!

"Good to see you making friends."

I knew that voice, and just like that, my excitement turned to stone.

"Hello, Professor Jophiel," I said. "Yes, just doing what we're supposed to. As usual."

"Make sure you are," Jophiel said, before nodding to my friends and moving away.

"He's scary," Zira said. She shuddered, and her feathers puffed up. "Who is that?"

"That's my teacher," I said. "Pretty sure he thinks I'm a bad guy."

"What?" asked Lilith.

"Didn't I tell you that?" I asked.

"Uh, no," Crowley said. "Fill us in."

"Yeah, I'm pretty sure he thinks I'm an agent of Chaos," I said. "You know, with the capital letter."

"You're not, are you?" asked Zira. "Don't get me wrong, that would be interesting, and I would have questions, but I would also turn you in immediately."

"I'm not," I said. "Anyway, why are there still no Purgatory people? This is the right place, right?"

"It's got to be," said Crowley.

"Yeah," said Aleister. "She said 'fountain,' and that's definitely a fountain."

The fountain was enormous, a polished marble so bright, it reflected rainbows across the tile floor, while the water danced in the air in gravity-defying leaps. What was more important was what was next to the fountain. A team of two angels, one with white wings and the other with black, each anxiously staring at a clipboard and gesturing wildly behind them, where the wall disappeared into purple darkness.

"Do you see anyone who looks like they're from Purgatory?" asked Aleister.

"No," Lilith said. "And the guards by the portal are looking anxious."

Suddenly there was a commotion as a figure stuck her head partway out of the portal. She looked in both directions, and the angels by the door rushed to where her upper body was leaning out of the swirling purple. A frantic whispered conversation happened, and we tried to move closer without being obvious. Another head, this one transparent, poked through and looked around like they had no idea what was happening. The white-winged angel yelped and shoved the being back into the portal.

"Was that a soul?" Crowley asked, his voice ominously loud at the end.

"Why is it wandering?" I asked.

Alarm bells began ringing in the back of my mind. Did Purgatory have a stray soul? Where was Anubis? Mom had made it sound like the misplaced soul had been a onetime mistake, and that had been disturbing enough, since Anubis wasn't supposed to make mistakes at all, but this was all getting very disconcerting.

"Indeed," said Rowan, appearing out of nowhere and making us all jump. "Systems seem to be breaking down everywhere."

"Everywhere?" I asked, heart still pounding hard in my chest. "In Faerie, too?"

Rowan seemed to consider the question, staring into the

distance before slowly answering, "It's hard to tell in Faerie. If you'd ever been, you would understand. But, yes, I would say there, too."

"What does it mean?" Lilith asked. "And who are you?"

"It may mean nothing," Rowan said. "Or it may mean that a new era rises. We'll just have to wait and see."

Rowan regarded us over the top of their wineglass, and then surveyed the room before continuing absentmindedly, "Sometimes people have been around for so long that they expect things to be a certain way. They don't see the changes as they happen. By the time they notice, it's already too late, change has already occurred, and progress has been made. In many cases this is a good thing. But occasionally the changes are wrong, and it takes fresh eyes to see the problem."

"Are the changes now 'wrong'?" asked Zira.

"Oh, I wouldn't know, dear," Rowan said. "I'm far too old."

Rowan winked and sauntered away like nothing that could ever happen was of any importance.

"Are all fae that weird?" asked Aleister.

"I'm starting to think all *adults* are that weird," I said.

"Okay, who was that?" Lilith asked.

"Their name is Rowan," I said. "And I get the impression they know Morgan."

"Definitely of the Seelie Court," Zira said. "Come on,

people are going to be suspicious if we hang out here. This is supposed to be a party; we're not supposed to hang out by the door."

"Especially not one with problems," I said. "Somehow this will be my fault and I'll end up in the Pit for sure."

"I think you like the reputation," Crowley said, and snorted.

I protested, but it did no good, because my friends were monsters who lived to torture me, and one outside good influence was not going to change that. We circulated to look more natural but kept close to where Purgatory was supposed to arrive, still hoping that we'd see the Jackal up close and personal. Zira ran into some friends from Heaven who she introduced us to, and I saw some of my classmates, who I did *not* introduce to Zira. No one needed to know Rachel. I was doing Zira, and both our dimensions, a favor.

Eventually we were shooed along, and we strayed farther from where the officials were still looking uncomfortable. With nothing else unusual happening, we let down our guard, assuming the unerring Anubis had everything well in hand.

And then one friendly shove sent Aleister falling through a wall and disappearing entirely.

# THIRTY-FIVE

O h, brimstone. Did I just shove him out of the dimension?" Crowley asked, his face pale and sickly.

I stepped up to the wall and ran a hand over the surface, and then deeper when the surface of the wall didn't feel like anything. And then something was grabbing my hand and yanking me forward until my head popped through the wall-that-wasn't, directly into . . . a raging party and Aleister's gleeful face.

"What—"

But before I could finish, I was being yanked back out.

"Ow!" I said.

"We were saving you," said Zira.

"No," I said, smiling devilishly. "We're going in."

I reversed the grip so that instead of Zira holding on to my elbow, I was gripping her forearm. I reached over to Crowley and grabbed the lapel of his black suit jacket. He started sputtering, but before he could really work up a protest, I gave Lilith a *Let's go* head jerk and pulled my hostages through the non-wall.

"What is this?" asked Crowley as Lilith tumbled in after him.

"Isn't it incredible?!" asked Aleister.

The room was filled with fae of all types. Some high-court like Morgan and Rowan but others more humanoid, with fur and four legs and long tails, but eyes that showed shrewd intelligence, and loud voices. Colored lights swirled around the room like at a nightclub, and pillows, cushy chairs, and elaborate thrones filled the room. And it wasn't just the fae, although most of the group was. In this hidden room there were some black- and even occasionally white-feathered wings.

"Is this a pocket dimension inside a pocket dimension?" squeaked Zira.

"That seems unstable," Lilith said.

Unstable or not, it was a real party, jovial and loud, with people extending greetings like they hadn't seen each other in ages. I was sure we were going to be kicked out as soon as the adults noticed that a bunch of kids had invaded, but I was determined to enjoy it as long as we could. The music was *way* better.

"Is this supposed to be music?" asked Zira.

"This is what music should be," Crowley said. "Experience and learn."

Now, this felt like a reunion, and I imagined that if Heaven and Hell hadn't spent eons viewing the other as enemies, this would have been what this mixer was about. But too much time had gone by and too much animosity had built up, and now this reunion was a diplomatic mission going awkward, at least for the angels.

Or at least *most* of the angels.

Who were these angels here who seemed to be besties with the fae? When did that happen and how could I get that job?

"There's no way this is legal," said Zira. "I mean, look at the ceiling, smell the air. This is a separate pocket dimension attached to the one we're supposed to be in. We should leave."

"No way," I said. "Not until we get kicked out. Besides, creating this probably caused a bit of a glitch, right? So that mystery is solved."

"Actually," said Crowley, "that's probably true. Now we just need to wonder what happened to the Purgatory reps."

Having an explanation for the glitch led us to drop our

guard more than we should have. We should have been more worried about why Purgatory hadn't shown up, but we were kids, and if the adults weren't panicked, why should we have been? There were people responsible for this stuff, and it wasn't us.

Besides, it wasn't like Purgatory was required to attend, like Heaven and Hell were. It was completely optional for them, and maybe the mortal world had gone off the rails again and Purgatory had been inundated with souls. It could have happened. It certainly had before, and Sean and Charity were definitely dealing with *something*. Anubis was probably just busy.

". . . wasn't supposed to happen."

". . . stop? Everything will be fine. Just—"

If there was one thing I was attuned to, it was the conversation of trouble, and *that* was conversation about trouble. It didn't even matter that it was in some weird fae language I had never actually heard before. I could tell it had swooping lyrical sounds that blurred and blended even in the harsh tones they were using. But when you're from one of the great hereafters, there's no such thing as a language barrier, and I understood every word.

"How did you think it was going to happen?"

"Obviously there will be collateral damage."

I glanced around, never able to resist gossip, and looked directly into a red pupil set in a black sclera. The red pupil narrowed, slit-like in annoyance. The eyebrow piercing glinted in the party lights, and I jerked my head away, which was stupid because I had already been caught, but maybe whoever owned the eye would agree to pretend that I hadn't been eavesdropping.

"Hey!" said a voice.

I jumped back from the face that was suddenly inches from mine. I was already thinking up excuses before I realized that the irises were purple, and not the ones that had seen me eavesdropping.

"How old are you?"

"Uh," I said. "I mean, I was invited."

I took a step back, but the six-legged fae just shifted from standing on four legs to standing on two and leaned in closer.

"You look too young to be in here," he said, before leaning his serpentine body backward. "But what do I know? You all look the same."

"I think that's offensive," Zira whispered behind me. "Is that offensive?"

"Who cares?" exclaimed Aleister. "Besides, if he can't tell us apart, he can't get us into trouble."

"I don't think we can get in trouble," Crowley said. "I mean, our parents literally brought us here."

"They didn't bring us here-here," I said, scanning the room without being too obvious. I hadn't seen whoever had been speaking to Red Eyes, but there was no one looking at me to make me think that person was still here or had noticed. Brimstone. A flash of black fabric caught my eye, and I turned to see someone striding through the wall.

"You were absolutely right, Angus," said Professor Jophiel to the six-legged fae. "They are much too young to be here." Jophiel turned to us. "I believe Cassandra set up a kids' area, or if you're not happy with that, you can find your parents."

"Ah! No," said Aleister. "Definitely not with our parents."

"Is there a reason why we shouldn't be here?" I asked, deciding to be brave. "I mean, we weren't told anything was off-limits."

"Pretty sure the hidden door was a message," Jophiel deadpanned.

"Oh, our briefing didn't tell us we had to stay in any one zone," Zira piped up. Jophiel looked surprised. "I mean, they didn't brief us on secret rooms, though. . . ."

"Consider this a—"

And then the glitch we had experienced in the kids' zone was seriously outclassed. The walls disappeared, the party lights died, and the dense nothingness of the void pressed in around us. The music changed to screaming and even a few roars.

"Run!" yelled Jophiel.

He shoved me toward the opening. At least I assumed it was him. I was jostled into Lilith, and I steadied her as I frantically looked to make sure our squad plus one was intact. Most people were shoving toward the portal where this room attached to the larger pocket dimension, while others looked like they were trying to stabilize the room. I wasn't going to wait to see if they succeeded.

"C'mon," I yelled, pulling Crowley with me. He had stopped like he was going to try to use his own magic to help. I didn't know if he was capable of it, but I wasn't letting him risk his life in the attempt.

"Brimstone!" he swore. "Fine, let's go."

We moved as well as we could through the crowd, the portal flashing as each person made their way through. The color flashed gold around Lilith's wings, and then I was following through the light, pulling Crowley with me. But people were still rushing around here as well. The larger pocket dimension might have been more stable, but something was happening here, too.

"Come on," I said, catching a glimpse of a black cloak flapping in the breeze.

The area was crowded, so I ran for a few steps before launching into the air. My friends called after me, but I kept flying. I knew I'd seen something suspicious, and I was determined to find out more. My intuition was screaming at me to follow, follow, follow.

So I did.

# THIRTY-SIX

The floor beneath me was a mass of confusion, between those running around attempting to fix whatever was going on, others standing around bemused or assuming other people would deal with it, and of course my black-cloaked target weaving between them and any other obstacles. And now that I was really looking, I was startled to realize that this wasn't just some random black cloak. This cloak was the same one I had seen at home. Over and over again.

I had seen it outside my house when I was checking the mail with my blue-flamed look, it had been at the concert on the stranger talking to Morgan after the world shook and the sky had turned strange, it had been on the stranger that hadn't waved back when I was walking home from Lilith's. I knew, without a doubt, that it had been the same one every time.

I was so focused on giving chase that when I first heard the flap of wings, I assumed it was my friends. When the voice came, I almost dropped from the sky.

"Which one?" asked Professor Jophiel. Was this guy everywhere?

"Um," I said. "I was just—"

"Oh, unholy darkness, Malachi," groaned my teacher. "You're not in trouble. Which one are you following? You heard them plotting. You heard the Order of Puck agent, didn't you?"

"I—I think?" I said, sparing a glance at my professor beside me, who just rolled his eyes. "Black cloak with a hood."

"I don't see . . . Lead the way."

Uh, okay, then. I had barely been keeping an eye on my target, but I had managed to stay on top of the black flap of motion, even if I hadn't gotten a better view of the wearer. I was worried my frantic flying would draw attention, especially with a teacher by my side and my friends following, but nobody seemed to pay me any mind. Maybe being with an adult made it seem like we were doing what we were supposed to.

It was only seconds later that I realized where we were going. The fountain. The portal. It had to be, right? But why?

Were they trying to escape? I didn't even know if they had done anything. I just knew that they were up to something, and that whatever their plotting had intended, it had gone wrong. And I didn't think they'd just been plotting an illicit party.

Then we were there. The fountain was beneath us, and it was an odd combination of us giving chase and casual party-goers. I guess the glitches hadn't affected the whole event. I lost sight of my target as they slipped through a group of black wings and suits, but then they turned, and bloodred pupils in black sclera bored into mine.

My wings must have been on autopilot, because the fact that I didn't drop to the stone was amazing. The glare coming from those eyes was filled with power, but where I might have expected anger or rage, there was just curious calculation and not a small amount of irritation.

In the moment before the figure turned away again, I caught a fuller view of the fae. Sharp pale cheekbones on red skin and small twisted golden horns filled out a feminine face. And there on the shoulder of the cloak was a very familiar symbol: the Order of Puck. Professor Jophiel was right, but what did that mean? Social club, or world-ending danger?

"Stay here," snapped Jophiel, and for once I listened.

Jophiel dove into the crowd, sending others fleeing with shouts of protest. I expected the fae to run, but she didn't, and now that she had stopped moving, I realized how small she was, despite her having a presence that seemed so much more powerful. The fae stood as Jophiel closed the distance, and in the instant before he collided with her, she smiled.

Now I did drop from the sky, as the room burst into a swirl of color and screams. The air filled with sparks as a griffin of flame launched itself into the air, roaring like a dragon. I wasn't sure that was the sound griffins normally made, but it was suitably terrifying, though maybe not as terrifying as the people around me seemed to think. I even saw a few powers scrambling at the peace bonds on their halos.

I stumbled to my feet and saw the fae take advantage of Jophiel's distraction to twist out of his grasp. She slipped through the chaos to head for the portal. I wondered if I should follow, and turned my head to check in with my squad, only to see Crowley igniting his magic, Aleister and Lilith getting into a fighting stance, and Zira slowly backing away, her mouth dropping open in shock. I looked back up at the griffin, which was swooping and diving and roaring and very much not real.

"C'mon," I said. "The fae went to the portal. We should follow."

"What about that?" Lilith asked, pointing at the griffin flapping its wings over our heads.

"It's a glamour," I said. "Why is everyone freaking out?"

"That is real!" shrieked Zira. "Something else must have crossed over."

"No, it isn't," I said, now completely confused. "That's just a glamour, but that fae is getting away!"

"How do you know?" demanded Professor Jophiel. His halo was in hand, and he was still throwing suspicious glances toward the griffin, but he had stopped and was actually listening. To me. "How do you know it's a glamour?"

"Can't you see it?" I asked.

The griffin was loud and majestic. The wings dripped flames, the claws flexed, and the tail swished angrily, but the beast looked like it was a holovid superimposed onto reality—well, as close to reality as a pocket dimension could be.

Why was I the only one who seemed to realize that?

The griffin wasn't here, and given the red-eyed fae's smile right before it appeared, I assumed it was her magic that had conjured it. But then again, I *had* heard an argument at the illegal party, an argument between people who knew about whatever was going on, which meant there were other people involved. Other people who were potentially still with us, terrifying almost everyone with a make-believe monster.

A flare of red magic shot toward the griffin, while a halo sent sparks showering over all of us as it hit the wall opposite whoever had sent it flying. The glamour swooped and dodged, but I didn't understand how no one else had noticed that the halo had gone right through the wing, without doing any damage. There were shouts and arguments breaking out, and the light from the portal flared as a black cloak made it through.

"It looks real to me," Jophiel said. He seemed to argue with himself for a moment, before he turned and looked at me. "Go! Follow them. I'll deal with this."

"But don't you think I'm the bad guy?" I blurted.

"Why would I think that?" he asked, and he was so confused that I wondered if rather than coming to a pocket dimension, I had inadvertently ended up in an alternative timeline. "We need people who can think for themselves, who are fearless and know who they are. We need more people like you, so I expect more from you."

What? His pointed looks and glares were what? Support? Encouragement? Had he not seen me repeatedly changing my look, my distinct inability to fit in? Jophiel thought . . . that I mattered? That more people should be like me? I wasn't actually a colossal screwup at this? Unholy night!

"Now go," he snapped. "This is going to get ugly."

And it was certainly getting ugly. The griffin roared, and the room was filled with smoke and fire. None of these were things griffins could do, but no one seemed to be considering that, because infernal and celestial magic was sparking up everywhere. Where were the rest of the people from Faerie? I didn't know why no one else could see what I did, but I knew that this was a glamour, and I knew that if there was a chance for the illusion to end before everyone destroyed everyone else, we would need a fae to end it.

"Are you sure it's not real?" Zira asked.

"Positive," I said. Red Eyes was getting more and more of a head start. If we were going to stop whatever she was doing, we needed to go now.

But just as I went to follow, I was jerked back and to the floor, and before I could get to my feet, I felt a hand at my throat. When I was able to focus, I saw that it wasn't Red Eyes or an angry adult. No, it was someone even more annoying.

"Call that thing off," snarled Rachel.

I jerked myself out of her grip.

"It's not mine," I said. "And I really don't have time for this."

I turned, but Rachel's friends had separated me from my squad and, maybe even more important, from the way Red Eyes had gone. Brimstone, Rachel was awful! We didn't have time for this, but before I could completely freak out, Rachel was swept off her feet.

"Oops, sorry," said Sidney from on top of Rachel, who was

barely visible, squirming and making zero progress to get out from under the enforcer.

"Don't even think about it," snarled Azael from behind me. I turned. He spread his wings as he advanced on Rachel's friends, and it wasn't just him but Parisa, too.

Azael looked over his shoulder at me. "We've got this. Do what you need to do."

"I owe you one!" I shouted, already moving through the gap. I only hoped that my new friends—yeah, definitely friend-friends—had come to the rescue in time.

"Let's go!" I said as I reached my squad plus one.

"So, we're going through that portal?" Crowley asked.

"Wait, really?" Zira asked, eyes wide.

"We are absolutely going through that portal!" Aleister said, with more enthusiasm than the situation warranted.

"Well, then, let's go," Lilith said. Crowley jerked his head in a sharp nod.

The smoke all around was thick and glittery, but even though others seemed to struggle to see through the haze, I didn't have any trouble at all.

The fountain burbled delicately as we approached. The clipboard-wielding guards were long gone, no doubt throwing themselves into the fight behind us, and to my horror, the portal was closing. In a fraction of a second I debated whether I should follow and chance getting stuck in what was either a space between or Purgatory itself. But I thought back to the chill in my gut as those red eyes had met mine, to the instability in the worlds, to Sean and Charity missing and possibly in danger, to the graffiti on Glamourie's wall, to Rowan's cryptic words, and to my professor apparently thinking not only that this was a problem but that I could do something about it.

And, there was the fact that I was somehow the only one who could see this distraction for what it was, and, yeah, I didn't have much choice but to follow.

"Hurry!" I yelled, and without looking at my friends, I dove through the closing portal and hoped I wouldn't be facing the fae alone.

# THIRTY-SEVEN

The world in front of me was gray. Completely.

I stepped cautiously forward into the fog. The portal flared as each of my friends came through, but the light was quickly swallowed, as if nothing could penetrate the haze.

"Where are we?" asked Zira. Her voice fell flat, like the sound waves couldn't travel any farther than the light could. I was surprised to see her. Go, Zira.

"Purgatory," said Crowley, and I knew without question that he was right.

Crowley's magic still glowed faintly over his arms, but it was muted along with everything else. Even Zira's wings were a dull ivory instead of the glowing white they had been at the party.

"Everyone okay?" I asked.

"The portal closed," Lilith said. "Aleister barely made it through."

"It's true," Aleister said. "I think one of my shoes is still at the mixer."

I looked down, and sure enough, Aleister was only wearing one shoe. His other foot sported a striped athletic sock with the logo of the Dagon Gorgons Dodgeball team, but like everything else, the normal team colors of purple and green were dull, and barely visible through the haze.

We were in a drab world of nothingness, devoid of anything beyond muted light and sound. I stepped farther in and watched fog swirl at my feet. There was no sign of the fae, and even worse, there was no sign of an exit. Back the way we had crossed was just more of the same . . . and an angel having a panic attack.

"Breathe, Zira," I said, and everyone turned to look at the junior seraph, who was rapidly panting. Her wings trembled.

"I'm okay," she said quickly in a high-pitched voice that was very much not okay.

"We'll get out of here," Lilith said. "Mal's professor knows where we are. He'll send help if we don't find the way back on our own, which we will. This has to be Purgatory. Anubis will help us. We just have to find him."

"But first we have to find that fae," I said. "She's up to something big."

"So where should we go?" Crowley asked. "Does anything look different to you? Any traces of a glamour?"

"I saw someone go that way," said a voice. "Perhaps that's who you're looking for?"

I turned and saw an old woman, human by the looks of her, standing in the gray. She was hunched and leaning over a cane.

"Maybe," I said. "Which way?"

The woman pointed a wrinkled, crooked finger to her left.

"Excuse me, ma'am," Lilith said. "Why are you walking around here?"

"I've been walking for a while. I figured I would find something eventually, but I haven't yet."

"There's no one else here?" Crowley asked sharply.

"Oh sure," said the woman. "I've seen lots of people. The bickering was terrible. But I haven't found anyone who knows anything, and there's nothing beyond this terrible fog. But you're different. What are you? You look like angels, but this can't be Heaven. Is this Hell?"

"This is just a holding spot," said Lilith.

"You haven't seen anything like a feather or a scale?" asked Zira. "Or a man with the head of a hound?"

"No dear," said the woman. "Should I keep looking?"

"Yes," said Aleister. "And we will too. This is just temporary, so . . . hang in there!"

The woman laughed as Aleister gave her a thumbs-up.

"I've waited a long time. I can wait longer. But I did see someone run that way. I saw a black cloak, but nothing more."

"We'll look that way, then," Lilith said.

"Why don't you rest?" Zira said to the old woman. "We'll find you help and move you on your way to someplace better."

"Thank you, dear," said the old woman.

"You shouldn't have said that," Crowley told Zira once we were far enough away that the woman wouldn't hear us. Not that we really needed to go far. Sound didn't travel here.

"Said what?" asked Zira.

"That we'd get help or that she'd be on her way to somewhere better," Crowley said. "There is no guarantee we'll find help, and what if she's slated for Hell? No one would be in a rush to move on to that."

"Oh, there's no way," Zira said confidently. "She was far too nice to go there, and we'll just find Anubis, and—"

"Whom she didn't find when she died," I pointed out. "And you absolutely can't tell where people are going, at least not without seeing their aura, which you can only see on the mortal plane. Nice does not equal good, and if she was that good, she would have gone directly to Heaven."

"The fact that she didn't go straight to Anubis, though?" asked Lilith. "That's concerning."

"The Purgatory crew never showed up tonight," Aleister pointed out. "And that fae ran in here like she wasn't worried about getting into trouble."

"C'mon," I said. "This isn't solving anything, and if I don't see some color soon, I'm going to go crazy."

Walking through Purgatory was like walking through a sensory deprivation tank. There were no sounds from our footsteps, and any noise we made was flat and dropped away. The gray of everything made me feel blind. Even the air was scentless, and the temperature was indecipherable. It was enough to make your mind break, and I wondered if that was what happened to souls that stayed too long. Did they crack?

Probably, which was why we really needed to find something. I huffed a breath that went unheard.

"I think I see something," Lilith said.

And finally there was actual motion ahead, and in a few more steps we realized there was way too much motion. There were souls everywhere, most of them looking very confused.

"Is Anubis on break?" asked Aleister. "Unless it's always this crowded. Maybe he hands out numbers or something."

"No," Lilith said. "There's no one from Purgatory here."

As we watched, more souls arrived. Many were old, but not all of them; some were our age or younger. All were a bluish gray and vaguely translucent, but only when you really looked. There was no mistaking them for living people. They were clearly dead, just maybe not dead-dead. Mostly dead?

"Finally! Are you the manager? This wait has been interminable."

I was suddenly face-to-face with a man who looked like he had spent much of his life yelling at employees to get their managers. He really didn't need to wait for Anubis. I already knew where he was going.

"Uh, no," I said. "But we're looking for him."

"Look faster," the man snapped. "I don't have all day."

"You do, actually," I said.

"What?" he said, irritated.

"You have all day," I said. "And the next one. You have literally all of the days."

"Am I dead?" asked a girl behind me.

"I'm so sorry," said Zira, who looked up at me with tears in her eyes.

"Oh man," said another, a teenage boy wearing a backward

baseball cap. "Dude. Jasper was right. That other building was too far away."

"At least he can't say 'I told you so,'" said Aleister.

"Dude!" said the teenager with an enormous smile. "You're so right!" He held out a blue-gray fist, and they fist-bumped. Leave it to Aleister to make friends everywhere.

"We need to keep moving," said Crowley, shaking off a hand from one of the many souls trying to talk to him.

Crowley was right. We had drawn attention, and the wandering dead had taken notice. Anubis was nowhere to be found. There weren't even any Purgatory residents here, not that I thought there were many of those, but the absence of anyone in charge was a cause for concern. Add in the fae who was clearly planning something bad, and this was all looking like existential threatening stuff.

Again.

As often as we promised souls that we'd look into things, and that everything would be fine, and told them that while it was very sad that they'd died, this wasn't actually the end of things, so if they would just be patient and hang out . . . Well, that wasn't really having an impact, and we were still swarmed by the recently deceased.

The old woman had had a point. It was stressful and distracting among all the whining souls, and if we didn't get out of here, we'd never figure out what was going on.

"Brimstone," I gasped, just barely not falling over my feet, but when I looked down, I noticed black soil. It was still covered by fog, but there was something different there. Something beyond the gray nothingness that was everywhere else. I pushed through the dead people with my head down, trying to find the edges of the soil.

"What did you find?" asked Lilith, suddenly by my side amid grumbled protests.

"Look," I said, pointing.

"Oh!" Lilith exclaimed. "Okay, that's different."

"We have to find the edges," I said, still walking. "Maybe it's a road."

If it was a road, it was one that made no sense, because although I found an edge on the left, Aleister insisted his was over even farther, but so did Zira, who was completely on the other side. Crowley said he found an edge as well. Maybe it was just the way souls arrived and it wasn't actually a road that went anywhere. Maybe it was multiple roads. Maybe it was—

"I know what it is," I said. "Zira, find the center of the path where you are. Okay. Crowley? Yeah, you too, Aleister. Lilith?"

"Already there," Lilith said, and from her tone of voice, I knew she had already figured it out.

It was difficult to tell with all the dead swarming around

us, but looking around at where my friends stood, I was positive I was right.

"Okay," I said, "everyone walk toward the middle."

And then, with some gentle nudging of the dead with my wings, I started to walk toward the center. The reason the black soil paths were seemingly scattered everywhere wasn't because they were random, and it wasn't a coincidence that the dead congregated here. These weren't just roads; this was a crossroads.

There in the center where we all met, the roads of black soil converged into a meeting-place square.

And in the center of that square sat a top hat.

# THIRTY-EIGHT

The hat was black with a white velvet band around its base, and decorating the band was a row of sharp teeth. A purple feather stuck out of the velvet band.

I knew that hat. It was iconic.

My heart raced in excitement before I allowed myself to question why a hat belonging to *him* would be lying in a square of soil in the middle of a foggy gray wasteland.

I reached for it with a trembling hand.

The moment I touched the black fabric, I felt a pull in my stomach like someone was yanking me through the sky. The world around me sped past like diving through smoke, and then with a sudden jolt, the feel of movement stopped.

My senses came back in a rush. So much so that I realized how much sensation I'd lost when we'd passed into Purgatory. We had arrived on a hillside at night, all of us in the crossroads transported when I triggered the portal in the hat. The black soil that had made up the crossroads was everywhere now, but even in the nighttime setting, the place we found ourselves in was a riot of color and sensation. The night sky contained shining stars and swirling galaxies, with a backdrop of midnight blue, black, and pink.

The Land of the Dead was beautiful.

I thought this might have been what Cassandra had been going for in the kids' zone, but her imitation was a weak one. This was something that could only exist in a real otherworld.

There were crooked trees that dripped with delicate plants of olive green clinging to their limbs. In places the ground was churned, and the smell of petrichor, rich earth, and spices I couldn't identify filled the air. Whereas sound fell away in Purgatory so that everything felt closed and isolated, here the word felt open and endless. There were the sounds of crickets and the caws of birds and the noises of moving things. There were drumbeats floating across the air that mimicked the sound of hearts beating.

"You're not who I was expecting to return my hat."

A figure sauntered from behind a tree dressed in a suit

that would have made Dorian Gray weep. It was black and fitted with purple lapels. A white cravat with a skull pin in the center was tucked beneath a purple vest. The figure's dark fingers were decorated with sparkling rings, and a shovel dangled from one hand. Meeting his face, there was no mistaking who this was. A white translucent overlay of a skull seemed to be superimposed onto his regal face like an impression. His eyes were golden and filled with power.

"Baron Samedi," I said.

"Yes," he said. "And that's mine."

"Oh, sorry," I said, handing him the hat, which he placed on his head before setting his shovel down against a large gray stone.

"Now," he said. "Why are you the ones returning my hat? Do you bring a message from the Jackal?"

I hadn't heard any adult call Anubis "the Jackal," and if they had, they certainly wouldn't have used it in front of people who they thought might be associated with him. Not that we were, but the Baron didn't know that. In fact, he thought we *were* and yet he wasn't concerned.

Baron Samedi was the epitome of cool.

"No," I said. "We were kind of hoping you'd be able to tell us what's going on."

"I sent my hat to the crossroads of Purgatory," the Baron

said. "How did you come across it without meeting Anubis?"

"There was no one there," said Crowley.

"Yeah," said Aleister. "Nothing but lots and lots of the dead."

"What?!" snapped the Baron, and swirls of flame burst from his eyes, temporarily interrupting the skull facade. "Tell me everything."

So, we did. All of us. Our voices overlapped as we filled in details, and as more details were told, we had to go back further, until the Baron knew even more than my squad and I had known about what was happening in Hell and Heaven, because Zira, of course, had her own stories about Heaven.

". . . and we followed the fae, but by the time we were through, we'd lost her," I finished.

The Baron spit out curses in a language so old that it didn't quite translate properly, but it didn't really need the translation to get the point across.

"I sent a message through because I knew something was wrong," the Baron said. "He missed poker night, and that's just not like him."

Lilith started coughing.

"You guys have poker nights?" asked Aleister. "Don't the bodies pile up?"

The Baron lifted an unimpressed brow, and suddenly we were surrounded by copies and copies of the Baron. "Do you think we do our job as a singular being?" asked all the Barons, so that the question echoed around us. Then the copies merged into each other until he was just himself again. "The Jackal does the same."

"So, poker," prompted Crowley once we recovered our voices.

"Well, poker and this."

The Baron rose and reclaimed his shovel. He selected a spot on the hill and began to dig. I didn't see the problem at first, but then, as I watched the shovel cut through the soil, I started to understand.

"It's filling back in," I said.

"Indeed," he said, setting the shovel aside. "No one can die if I don't dig their grave. You see the problem."

"But how does Anubis affect that?" Zira said.

"He doesn't, necessarily," the Baron said. "But our worlds are closely connected, and most of those I dig graves for go to him in their travels. Besides, he's a friend. I would have sought his counsel regardless. But a problem in Purgatory? Anubis himself missing? This is deeply disturbing and must be connected to my own difficulties."

The land of the dead wasn't a resting place, and there were no souls that spent eternity with the Baron, but it was true that no one could die without the Baron digging their grave.

It was that action that separated the soul from its body. And that was kind of a prerequisite for everything else that needed to happen. If the Baron didn't dig the grave, the person stayed alive . . . no matter what.

"The fae we saw," Lilith said. "They must have something to do with Anubis's disappearance."

"Yes," the Baron said, and then turned to face me. "Give me the feather."

The Baron held out his hand imperiously, and for a moment I wasn't sure what he was talking about, because how could he possibly know about the feather I had found in my classroom? But then I remembered that this was the Baron we were talking about.

"How do you know I have it?" I asked, retrieving the pure white feather from my interior pocket. I had taken Morgan's word to heart and kept the feather on me *for luck*.

The Baron gave me a look, and I handed the feather over without another word.

He held the feather up and studied it. He ran it over his face, disrupting the skull visage again, and smelled it, and then he laid the feather flat in his palm and ran a finger up its shaft. The feather responded to his touch, glowing slightly, and then shuddered in his hand. He passed it back.

"You'll need that," he said. "But you'll also need these."

And then there were more of the exact same feathers in his hand, perfect replicas of the one Morgan had told me to keep; apparently, it wasn't just himself that the Baron could replicate.

"I suspect the fae you were following is involved with Anubis's capture, and you'll need those to get where they are."

"Capture?" Zira asked. "Maybe he's just sick?"

We all looked at Zira.

"Or captured," she said. "That's totally reasonable. I deal with nefarious plots all the time. This is completely no big deal, so yeah, where are we going?"

"I assure you this is a *very* big deal," said the Baron. "And one that should not be left to children."

My squad made sounds like they wanted to protest but were holding themselves back, possibly by biting their tongues, which was what I was doing. The Baron sighed.

"Though, I suppose I don't have much of a choice. I'm limited in my travels. There are certain crossroads, and of course I can be summoned—in some circumstances, anyway—but I can't go where you'll need to go. Do you know what that feather is?"

"Morgan—this fae that I know—said that it belonged to a rare creature," I said. "And that I should hold on to it for luck."

"Luck," muttered the Baron. "Those of Faerie do love their secrets. This feather belongs to a sylph."

Lilith gasped, and we all turned to face her.

"What?" Lilith asked, blushing. "I've studied them. They're fascinating. I just can't believe I didn't put it together."

"I can," said the Baron. "They're extremely rare, so it's no surprise that you didn't suspect them, and they primarily live in the space between worlds. Given all you've told me, I'm certain that's where Anubis will be. The feathers will let you pass back and forth. Return here when you've accomplished the mission, and I will send you back where you all belong."

"How do we get to the space between?" I asked. "We went through portals before, and by accident found the crossroads that brought us here."

"I can show you a door," he said. "But I can't open it. You'll have to do that yourselves. I can't tell you if all the conspirators are from Faerie, or if there will be others. What I can tell you is that whatever is keeping Anubis away will be something he can't overcome himself, and that the space between is the closest to where Chaos still has any sort of power."

"Chaos? Maybe we need an adult," Zira said anxiously.

"Child," the Baron replied, "we are running out of time."

"We've got this," I said. I hoped.

The Baron led us between hill-like mounds of grass and dark churned soil, past gray stones and moss-covered trees.

"Ah," he said. "Here we are."

The gray metal door was set into a mound of earth. There was no obvious way to open it, but that didn't stop the Baron from doing so. Well, sort of. He opened the door, but it just revealed another identical door underneath.

"You'll need to move quickly," the Baron said. "Anubis would be here if he were able to free himself. With any luck his jailers will be few and you'll only be dealing with a mystical block."

"What about the fae we followed into Purgatory?" asked Aleister.

"No one has come through my world," said the Baron. "Though that means little. The space between can be accessed from anywhere, but you must remember, if you are ever truly vulnerable to Chaos, it will be there."

"Can't you come with us?" I asked.

The Baron placed his hand against the door inside a door. Sparks flared around his fingers, making his skin translucent and his hand skeletal. The rings on his fingers glowed, and their edges softened like they were melting; the stones grew brighter, lit by internal fire. The Baron raised an eyebrow but didn't show any pain. Finally he pulled his hand away and blew on it gently.

"That is not one of my allowed domains," the Baron said. "Go. Free Anubis and return here through this door on the other side by saying the words on this page."

He twirled his hand, and a ragged piece of paper, yellow with age, appeared between his first two fingers. He held them out to me, and I took the paper. It felt delicate, like it would dissolve with a wrong move, and I was reminded of the fragments of paper that had fallen into my classroom. I had never translated the coded language. I hoped that wasn't going to bite us in the butt. I tucked the paper into my jacket pocket.

"The feathers will allow you entry, just like they do for their host creature. Don't get lost. Don't get found. But above all else, don't fail."

"How will we know how to free Anubis?" asked Lilith.

"With any luck," said the Baron, "he'll be able to tell you himself. Now go."

I glanced at my friends. Lilith and Crowley looked determined, but Zira looked like she was going to be sick, and Aleister looked way too excited about finally not being left behind.

I placed my hand against the door inside a door, and rather than the sparks that had surrounded the Baron's hand, my hand simply pushed the door open.

With a deep breath I pushed the door open wider and stepped through.

# THIRTY-NINE

I wasn't sure what I'd expected. Had I tried to imagine the space between worlds, I probably would have imagined the horror of nothingness we had seen out the windows of the Beadle's Tavern that wasn't. Thankfully, I didn't really have time to consider that before stepping through, or I probably wouldn't have moved.

The space between was a riot of colors and shapes and movements, or at least the echoes of those things. I turned as a translucent figure ran past. It was obvious that the person wasn't here, that it wasn't a strange being or soul but merely the representation of one. It was like the realities of other worlds were leaking into the space between and filling it with something, anything.

Sounds of music and voices overlapped with random noise and colors and images to make a world that was chaotically busy and beautiful. The ground was simultaneously glowing moss, and grass, and marble, and stone, and I knew that shouldn't make any sense, but it seemed normal, the way dreamworlds seemed normal.

Which was probably a good thing, because the floors weren't the only things that followed dream logic. Where we stood now wasn't a never-ending open space like Purgatory; it was mazelike, as the neighboring dimensions encroached on each other. The walls were a constant motion of whatever those surrounding worlds contained. The sky was the same as the ground, a blur of black and fire, swirls of stars on a baby-blue sky, with sparkling clouds and a ball of fire, all at the same time.

An animal of some sort ran across the sky upside down, and I wondered if ground and sky were relative.

"Whoa," Aleister said.

"Wow," echoed Zira.

"Well," Crowley said, looking around. "He's not here, so I guess we move."

"Which way?" Lilith asked.

There were options, certainly, but only one of them had a sparkling trail leading the way. I pointed. "That way." I tried very hard to keep the "obviously" silent.

"How do you know?" Lilith asked.

Was she serious? How was it not obvious to our always-on-top-of-things Intelligence? But when I looked around, everyone was staring at me, waiting to hear my reasoning.

"The path," I said.

"All the paths look the same," Crowley said.

"Uh, no, they definitely do not," I said. "C'mon, seriously?"

But everyone just looked at me like I was crazy.

"You can't see that?" I said bluntly.

"See what?" Crowley asked.

"There is literally a glowing trail leading the way," I said.

"There is literally not," Crowley said.

I huffed out a disbelieving laugh, but nobody else seemed to think there was anything unusual about what Crowley had said.

"How did you know that the griffin and fire weren't real back there?" Lilith asked, a calculating look on her face.

"Dude, that's right," Aleister exclaimed. "You totally knew!"

"I mean, I could just see it," I said.

"Well," Zira said. "Maybe we can figure out the why later and save Anubis now. Does that work for everyone?"

"Yeah."

"Yes."

"Let's go," I said, but why could I see things that apparently no one else could? Had Morgan done something to me? Were the glamours more than just fashion?

Morgan had become a person I trusted, who understood me when no one else seemed to understand. If they were using me . . . No.

I couldn't be distracted now. I had to hope that whatever I was seeing was leading us the right way and wasn't instead part of a plan in which I had inadvertently become a pawn.

The sparkling path led us between worlds in a twisty, winding route, and I was forcibly reminded of the Baron's warning as I felt eyes on me. We were never closer to Chaos than in the space between. I shuddered. With any luck, we'd be out of here before it took notice.

One more twist, and there he was: Anubis. He was sitting in a magically conjured golden chair, somehow looking both regal and irritated at the same time. Red chains wrapped around his arms and legs, attaching him to the chair, while a black cloth was tied across his eyes. I felt like, for a being with pure sight, the blindfold was adding insult to injury, but I was certain it wasn't just an ordinary blindfold. It had to be doing something, but it definitely wasn't stopping him from seeing us.

"A little assistance," he drawled. "If you please."

"Yes," I said. "Of course."

My stomach twisted as I approached, afraid that Anubis would use his abilities on me. I had no desire to know what was inside my heart, and even less desire for someone else to see.

"How do we undo this?" Aleister asked, tugging at a red chain that didn't budge.

I untied the blindfold, trying to be respectful and not touch the fur at the back of his hound head, and pulled it off, only to reveal another blindfold beneath. Or should I say, the same blindfold beneath, because as soon as I'd pulled the blindfold free, it had disappeared from my hand and appeared back on Anubis's head.

"Well, that didn't help," Crowley said.

"Indeed not," Anubis said, unamused.

"Who did this?" I asked. *How did they do this?* was what I wanted to ask.

It was a known tenet of how everything worked that Anubis had true sight. If that sight could be compromised . . . if there was a way around it, things could fall apart very quickly.

"I don't know," he said. His voice was even more irritated, if that was possible. "There was a flavor of mayhem and cold beauty before everything went dark."

"You can't see anything?" I asked. "Because I kinda thought you could."

"I didn't say I couldn't see anything," said Anubis. "I said everything went dark."

"Oh," Zira said, which just about said it all, really.

We exchanged confused looks and a few noncommittal shrugs. Anubis sighed heavily, and even though his eyes were covered, I knew he was rolling them at us.

"Mayhem" and "dark beauty" went with Faerie like "pretentious" and "boring" went with Heaven. Then of course there was the fact that glamours were being used, and the Order of Puck was involved, and while I hadn't clarified whether that was strictly a faerie organization, we knew at least one of their members was. But why would they do this? What were they hoping to achieve?

And what about the timing? Was the mixer actually a trap?

Oh, brimstone. My parents were never going to let me leave the house again.

# FORTY

re there no adults that could help?" Anubis asked. "I
do have a poker game to get to."

"Oh, you already missed that," said Aleister.

"WHAT?!" snapped Anubis.

"I'm sure there'll be more," Zira squeaked.

"That's not possible," Anubis muttered.

"More games are always possible," Aleister said.

"Not that," growled Anubis. "That I could have missed it
without noticing the time had gone by. *That* is impossible."

"Well, the Baron told us you missed a game," I said.

"You spoke to the Baron?" Anubis asked sharply. "And he
said I missed it?"

"Uh," I said, and then shrugged. "Yeah."

Anubis growled another, "Impossible," but it sounded less confident.

"If I can ask," Lilith started, "why are you so upset about that?"

"Yeah," Aleister said. "I get being bummed, but—"

"Sight," Crowley interrupted. "When things went dark."

"Exactly," Anubis said. "My sight is used to determine justice, but that's simply how I use it to support the balance. That's not the limit of its power. Time does not pass without my knowing."

"Huh," I said. What else could you do with pure sight?

My pondering would have to wait, because the fact remained that we were in the space between, with the god of death tied to a chair by missing captors who could be literally anywhere, with the *loa* of the dead waiting for us to bring his poker buddy back. Meanwhile our parents were in a potentially collapsing pocket dimension with their sworn enemy-allies.

So, yeah.

"How do we get you out of here?" I asked, feeling the panic rise in my throat like a scream.

Removing the blindfold hadn't actually removed the blindfold, and the chains seemed to be the same. At least

I thought they'd be the same. We hadn't been successful in even getting a grip on them at this point.

"If my sight were restored, I'd be able to tell you. Alas . . ."

Great. No problem, then.

And I still felt eyes.

Something was watching us.

I looked around, but I didn't see anyone. Then again, I knew Anubis could see us. He just couldn't *see* us. Maybe Anubis was the one making me feel like I was being watched. Maybe I was being paranoid.

A dark shadow caught my eye, and I turned my head to the right to see the tail end of something large slowly passing by. I shivered, remembering Baron Samedi's warning that we were most vulnerable to Chaos here. I was still wrapping my head around the fact that Chaos was a real being and not just a concept, but I still didn't want that confirmed. If seeing was believing, this was something I was willing to take on faith.

The shadow disappeared, but I still felt like I was being watched. And why was Anubis alone anyway? Did kidnappers often leave their abductees unguarded? Shouldn't there be someone here? And if they weren't here, what were they doing?

"We need to hurry," I said.

Everyone stepped closer, and Crowley sparked his magic

so that red haze swirled under his hand and over the bindings holding Anubis to the chair. Zira began to glow, and apparently that wasn't just something Cassandra had done for effect.

I stepped back to get a bigger view. The chair, chains, and blindfold had been conjured, but something had been done to Anubis to make everything go dark. Was it the blindfold I couldn't remove? If it was, how had his captors taken him by surprise?

My heart raced. Did I hear footsteps in the distance? It was hard to tell, with everything else going on. The space between was anything but empty or still. I forced myself to breathe. Focus. How could we free Anubis?

Wait . . . what was that? I crept closer. One of the chain links was different.

"Hold on," I said. "I see something. I think I found the weak link."

"Where?" asked Aleister. "I'll break it."

"Right here," I said, pointing to a link in the center of a crisscross pattern.

The link I had noticed glowed a slightly clashing shade of red, and when I looked closer, I saw that the different color was partially because of gold script written along the surface. It was too small to read, but I was betting that if I could, it would be the same script that had fallen into my classroom, the script Morgan had told me was Elvish. Did Morgan know more than they had let on?

Could Morgan be involved?

I brushed off the thought, and the stab of pain at the possible betrayal.

"See it?" I asked.

"No," Aleister said. "But let me try anyway."

Aleister put his hands on either side of the link, and a faint glow emerged between his fingers as he tightened his grip and pulled. The chain link began to stretch.

"It's working!" Lilith said.

In an enormous flash of light, the link broke, and Aleister fell onto his butt. For a moment I thought he had done it. After all, he was on the ground with a chain in each hand. But when I moved my gaze back to Anubis, he was still bound tight to the chair.

"If it were a simple matter of strength, I would have done it myself," Anubis said.

Then he cocked his head to the side in apparent thought. In a sudden movement he turned that hound head to look directly at me.

"Why did you think you found the weakness? What did you *see*?"

I knew instantly that when he said "see," it was significant, and for a moment I didn't understand what he was asking. But then I did. I'd seen the link in the chain, the same way I'd seen the sparkling path and known that the griffin flames weren't real. For some reason I was seeing things that no one else was. I remembered Uriel making a snide comment about the glamour leaking into my brain, and I scowled.

"One of the links looked different from the others," I said, somewhat helplessly. "The color was slightly different and there was tiny golden script in some Faerie language, Elvish, I think."

"More," Anubis demanded.

"I don't—"

"Keep looking," Anubis said. "I need to know what you see."

"Okay," I said. The link was the only weird thing I had noticed . . . No, wait. I had just taken things for granted. I had to stop assuming that everyone saw things the way I did. "The chair is conjured. It's elaborate with carvings like a throne, but it's not real."

My friends mumbled surprised responses.

"What?"

"Wait . . ."

"Not real?"

Apparently, my thought process was correct. What was obvious to me wasn't to them.

"Keep going," said Anubis, still staring at me with blindfolded eyes. Was the blindfold getting less defined?

"There are red chains wrapped around your arms and legs and across your chest, but there are also chains on the ground where Aleister tried to break them. The chains on the ground didn't take anything away from the chains still on you. There's a black blindfold across your eyes, but . . ."

"But what?" asked Anubis.

"But it's getting lighter," I finished, because as I explained away more of the glamours, the fabric became more and more translucent. I was even beginning to see more of the Jackal's face, or at least the glowing golden eyes. I wasn't sure I wanted the blindfold to be totally gone, to be honest.

"Yes . . . I *see*. . . . What else?"

As I spoke, things changed. Chain links disappeared, only to reveal other symbols. The chair's elaborate carvings revealed themselves to be sigils and words in different languages. And while I still seemed to be the only one able to see the glamours, once the new details emerged, everyone else seemed to be able to see them as well. It was like speaking the truth had made things visible.

Lilith and Crowley moved closer, and while Lilith muttered translations, Crowley ran his fingers over grooved sigils.

"Someone's coming," Aleister announced. His wings flared, and my stomach twisted.

"I can almost see the way to open the binding," Anubis said.

A voice behind me spoke. "Well, then it's a good thing we've returned."

# FORTY-ONE

Zira made a sound suspiciously like "Eeep," and I distinctly heard an irritated growl from Anubis before he cut off the sound and fell back into bored nonchalance. My voice faded as I turned.

Well, we didn't have to wonder if the red-eyed fae was involved. The question was, How many more were involved and how far did this go? Because there was no way Anubis had been captured by only three people. Right?

The fae I had followed was there; her red skin and red eyes were still partially hidden by the dramatic black cloak she wore—the black cloak I had caught glimpses of at home. Beside her were two other people, and I didn't need Morgan to identify them as high-court. After meeting Morgan and Rowan, it was obvious.

"Why don't you step away, children?" suggested the tall figure to the left, casually standing with his hands in the pockets of his tailored jacket. "I assure you, we have no intention of hurting Anubis. He's immortal. He'll be fine there forever."

"This is no place for children," said the red-eyed figure. Her voice didn't match her appearance at all. It was high-pitched and light and, dare I say it, childlike. Her forked tongue flicked between fangs for just a moment. "Though when Chaos rises, here will be everywhere and nowhere, so perhaps leaving and staying are not so different."

Okay, Crazy.

"Anubis has to be freed," I said cautiously. Maybe I wasn't dealing with evil people. Maybe we were dealing with people who weren't all there. "His imprisonment is already causing problems."

"Indeed," Red Eyes said. "There must be a fall before the rise. It's only logical."

"Yeah," I said. "See, I have a problem with both of those things, actually."

"Chaos can't rise," Aleister scoffed. "That would be the end of everything. Forever."

"Yes," said the third figure, who had been so far silent.

"Do you have any idea how infuriatingly boring forever is?"

"You *want* creation to end?" Zira asked. "But why?"

"Have you seen creation?" the third figure asked. She was dressed in a gown of iridescent fabric that flowed like water. "It's atrocious, filled with selfish, awful beings who perpetually act in boring predictability."

"But you'll probably stop existing," Zira said. "In any form."

"It's time," said the cloaked figure. "Life and death are all the same, being and unbeing."

"What our delightful friend Ophelia means is that this is a failed experiment," said the tall one in the jacket. "Another creation will come, one that perhaps is better . . . kinder . . ."

He paused like he was lost in thought or memory, before shaking his head. "Or maybe we'll all perish in a primordial ooze of making and unmaking. Isn't that correct, Cordelia?"

"Either way is fine," said Cordelia, the one in the stunning gown.

"Yes, as I said, Forrest." Ophelia shrugged. "It's all the same."

"Well, I'd like to skip both of those options," Crowley said.

"Yeah," I said. "Me too."

"And you're all in agreement with that, are you?" asked the one who must have been called Forrest.

"Uh, yeah," Crowley said.

"Definitely."

"Yes, please."

"Oh dear," said Ophelia.

"Indeed," said Forrest.

"Shall we, then, Forrest? Ophelia?" Cordelia asked.

"I fear we must."

And then the red-eyed Ophelia moved faster than I thought possible in a leap that took her to the edge of a dimension high above us. Her cloak dropped to the ground, revealing large leathery wings as she hung impossibly upside down, clinging to something unseen. Her eyes glowed for a moment, and then the dimensions around us grew dark and wavered. I knew they weren't really disappearing, but I didn't think everyone else did.

And then she started to sing. The sound echoed in my head, making my skull vibrate. Her voice made the world waver, and from my friends' reactions, I could tell I was only feeling a part of the horribleness. Zira started to cry.

Cordelia started making hand gestures that caused the sleeves of her iridescent dress to sway and dance unnaturally in the air. Forrest started tracing shapes on the ground with his foot, and I would have been insulted that he couldn't be bothered to even take his hands out of his pockets, if I hadn't been so panicked by what was happening.

Anubis was still restrained, my squad was panicking, I had no idea what to expect from Zira, and we were facing full-grown and seemingly very powerful fae, at least one of whom I was pretty sure was completely off her rocker.

"We have to free Anubis *now*," I said, but my squad was covering their ears and not hearing me. "Hey!" I shouted, shoving my elbow into Crowley's side. He looked up, a pained expression on his face, his hands still over his ears. What was I going to do?

The air was becoming oppressive, and the space between was growing darker while ominous shadows moved in the bordering dimensions. The creepy not-singing was still ringing in my skull, but as uncomfortable as I was, I knew I was lucky that I wasn't bearing the brunt of what was happening. I was somehow sheltered from the full effect. Not only that, but I knew that much of what was happening wasn't real, something my friends weren't able to understand.

My squad was suffering, and I was frozen, and failing again. Was it my destiny to fail?

# FORTY-TWO

I can almost see," Anubis said, bringing my attention out of my own head. His voice was a constant growl, making the words difficult to understand, but it was something I could focus on. Something that I could use to keep trying. "With your assistance I can break the binding. Just . . . a little . . . more."

"Crowley," I said, my voice breaking on his name. "I need you."

"Dude . . ."

"Whatever you're feeling, it seems worse than it really is," I said. "It's not real! You have to snap out of it."

Suddenly there came a feeling like movement over my

feathers and skin, like unseen fingers in the dark. I shuddered, but the responses from my friends were so much worse. They screamed.

I spread my wings like I could block whatever the fae were doing to my friends, and to my surprise it seemed to work. The shadows cast by my wings somehow made the space lighter, brighter, and although I could still feel the movement at my back, covering my friends somehow seemed to spare them the effects. Crowley sighed in relief, while Lilith and Aleister slumped, apparently thankful for the break.

Zira tried to copy me by spreading her wings to frame Anubis, but where my wings seemed to act as a barrier, her wings had no effect. Why? Was it because I was a power and she was a seraph? But if that was the case, why were my friends so affected?

Zira's wings slumped, and Aleister pulled her closer, under the protection of the shadow of my wings.

Wait, Zira was a seraph . . . a burning one.

"Zira," I said. She looked up, panting and sweaty. "Can you brighten this place up?"

There was a reason the seraphim were called "burning ones," and I had already seen some of that with Zira. We needed a reprieve. We had no chance of winning without

Anubis. We *had* to free him, fast, before the fae changed tactics to something a little more physical.

"I can try," Zira said, shaking her head in an apparent effort to clear her thoughts. She fluffed her wings, letting the feathers straighten.

"Ohhh, childrennn," sang Ophelia from above us. A chill ran up my spine that had nothing to do with faerie magic.

"I don't like her," Zira said. "Okay . . . here goes. Let there be light."

Zira lit up like a fireball, gradually at first so that her skin glowed bronze, and then brighter and brighter. I averted my eyes as Zira burned with celestial light and pushed the darkness back. Lilith and Crowley scrambled closer to the throne Anubis was still bound to. I was going to have to close my wings and help.

I wasn't sure how this new truth-speaking ability of mine of was helping Anubis, but it *was* helping. There was no doubt that the blindfold was fading. If it were gone completely, I knew Anubis would regain his sight and we would have a powerful ally.

And we *needed* a powerful ally.

My wings were just starting to close when Aleister's eyes widened. He took a deep breath, and I barely heard the "Look out!" before he was leapfrogging over me and launching himself into the air. I caught myself a split second before my face hit the ground, and I rolled onto my back to see what had sent Aleister into attack mode.

Aleister's wings flapped as he grappled in midair with Ophelia. She giggled as they fought, but at least the singing had stopped while she focused her energy on Aleister. Unfortunately, Forrest had decided to take his hands out of his pockets and used them to summon a sword. Not for the first time, I wished I already had my halo. The razor-sharp blade would have come in handy right about now.

I jumped to my feet just in time to avoid the swing of the blade. It was sharp, as evidenced by the clean cut through my coat. Brimstone! I loved that jacket, but thankfully, I was pretty sure that was as far as the blade had gone. At least I didn't feel any pain, and I supposed that was the important thing for the moment.

I was in defense mode, dodging and staying out of range of the blade, but this was most definitely a temporary answer. This was not helping Anubis. I knew I had to take the sword away, but what good was that going to do when he could just conjure another one?

I glanced over, and Zira was still keeping the darkness and magic at bay, but Cordelia was taking an interest in her. Zira looked decidedly panicked at the attention as Cordelia circled like a predator. Lilith and Crowley were starting to argue, with frantic gestures and pointing at various sigils on the chair and chains, and Anubis was still bound.

"Brimstone," I exclaimed as I barely twisted away from a dangerously close swing.

"We need you," Lilith yelled.

"A little busy!" I yelled back.

"Get unbusy!" yelled Crowley.

Aleister and Ophelia flew through the air in a haphazard tumble, slamming into the edge of one dimension and sending a wave of color and images splashing outward like a not-so-physical wave. The dramatics caught my opponent's attention, and I seized the moment. I rushed toward him and got inside the range of the blade before he could recover. I might not have had my own halo yet, but thanks to Aleister, I had been training in hand-to-hand combat since before I could fly.

# FORTY-THREE

al!" yelled Lilith. "We need you to tell us which of
these sigils are real!"

"You'd better hope I never weigh the scales for your house
of stupidity," snarled Anubis toward the iridescently clad fae.

Cordelia laughed. "Oh, my dear hound, you can retire
your scales. Those days are over."

I had almost managed a joint lock on my cursing opponent,
when my cut jacket became a hindrance, tangling around me
and ruining my finesse. I shrugged it free and created some
distance. I had to help Crowley and Lilith, but I couldn't help
from here.

"What . . . ," Forrest said, crouched and breathing hard.

I followed his gaze to see a glowing form beneath my sleeve. I pulled the sleeve up; the tattoo Morgan had placed on my skin was glowing silver. Was that what was allowing me to see through the glamours and spell work?

Morgan had said something about the tattoo. What had they said? I couldn't think clearly.

Forrest stood but didn't approach as I backed toward where Anubis was still held captive. Aleister, too, had backed away from his own fight. A few feathers were twisted out of position and his back heaved as he breathed hard. Zira's light was starting to waver. If we were going to do anything, it had to be now.

"Where?" I asked, flicking my eyes to where Lilith and Crowley were focused. There were sigils all over the chains and throne, but certain parts of the magical markings glowed differently, like some lines were false. "All of them are real, but most are wrong."

"Explain," Lilith said.

So I did. As I explained which lines were false, Crowley used his magic to highlight the true parts until the images began changing. I looked back as I spoke, and the fae still kept their distance like it was irrelevant whether we succeeded or not. That was worrying.

"Ahh," Anubis said. "Much better."

The blindfold was now gone, and though Anubis was still bound to the chair, he leaned forward as if he would pounce. The gold light from his uncovered eyes was bright, and wisps of steam emerged from either side as if his gaze burned. I was glad that it wasn't directed at me.

"Now I see the way free."

"You're too late," giggled Ophelia.

"Purgatory has fallen," Forrest said.

"It's nothing personal," Cordelia said. "It's just time."

I could see the Jackal's grin from where I stood, and for the first time our enemies looked uncertain.

"You, magician, do as I say," Anubis said.

As Anubis gave Crowley instructions, Forrest whistled a complicated melody. There was a shudder around us, and a large shadow glided overhead, drawing my gaze. The chains were beginning to drop strand by strand, but the magic was slow. Anubis's sight had returned, but there were still barriers in place that he couldn't free himself from.

The situation required help.

Which was why they had brought him here and left him alone where, even if he could see the way, it would be impossible for him to break the binds. Even as powerful as Anubis was, he couldn't do this alone.

Crowley and Lilith managed to get Anubis's arms free,

but as soon as they did, Cordelia began to cast a complicated piece of magic that just spelled trouble.

"You might want to hurry, guys," I said.

Crowley muttered under his breath while Anubis directed him. Zira had dropped the glow—making it harder for him to work—but only because the fae seemed to have switched gears. Zira looked helplessly between Crowley and Lilith.

I understood the feeling. Whatever Crowley and Lilith were doing to free the rest of Anubis from the conjured chair, there was nothing I could do to help. I wasn't a magic user. And worse yet, I didn't have a weapon to try to fight physically. The sword had disappeared as soon as I had gotten away from Forrest.

And then suddenly Ophelia shifted her feet, sweeping one leg out in a circle on the ground, which raised a wave of disruption into the sky between them and us. Whatever it was, whatever it looked like to my friends, it looked very real to me. This wasn't just a glamour. This wasn't just to confuse the senses. This was doing something . . . something big.

Suddenly the wave of disruption erupted upward and scattered down every pathway available between worlds. It snaked and curved in splitting vines. Another rumble. Another waver in reality. And the chains around Anubis fell away.

Anubis rose, the chair crumbling into pieces like gemstones falling into a pile. He snarled and a snake-topped staff appeared in his hand. Finally. We had some help. He held up his hand, and a glow of gold light spun into a ball as Anubis gathered and formed magic.

The fae didn't look nervous, though, and I suddenly realized that they honestly didn't care. Their intention wasn't to kill Anubis or to even make it out of here alive. If Anubis ultimately killed them, it didn't matter to them. Their plan was just to disrupt the balance and stall while Chaos seized its moment.

They didn't want anything.

They didn't care about living or even defeating us. Even what they were doing here was just a stalling tactic. If Anubis went home, he could attempt to stabilize Purgatory. If we left, we could warn Heaven and Hell. But the longer it took the more systems could be affected, the more cracks could form. They didn't need forever. They just needed right now.

My stomach sank. We had to get out of here. But how? Were they going to have to die?

Could I kill a fae?

Could I kill anyone?

# FORTY-FOUR

I didn't think I could kill them. It wasn't like humans, where we knew where they would go. Moving on from the mortal plane was no big deal, but I didn't know what happened to faeries when they died.

But as it turned out, it didn't matter anyway.

Anubis set the ball of magic flying, and as it neared the fae, it grew and expanded into a disc of gold spinning like a halo. But before it could do whatever it was going to do, a tentacle as black as the void emerged from a path and reached out and touched it. As soon as the tip of the tentacle made contact, the disc shattered into shards of gold that went flying.

"Down!" I yelled.

We hit the ground, pulling our wings tight to our backs to avoid the flying shrapnel.

"We have to get out of here," Lilith said.

"Yes," Crowley agreed. "Anubis is free, and we are way outclassed."

"What is that tentacle thing?" Aleister asked. "It destroyed Anubis's attack."

"It didn't destroy it," Zira said. "It unmade it."

"What?" Aleister asked.

Zira gestured around us. The pieces of the spell had broken further apart, crumbling into sand that disappeared.

"Unmade it," I repeated, and looked back to where another tentacle had joined the first. Ophelia was giggling. "The Baron said if we were ever going to be vulnerable to Chaos, it would be here. I thought he meant not to get caught by whoever had taken Anubis—"

"But," interrupted Lilith, "maybe that's not what he was talking about."

I had a bad feeling about what those tentacles belonged to. We had to leave.

"Okay," Zira said. "We have to get out of here. If we can get a message to our parents or someone . . ."

Anubis was raising more of his power and looked to be setting up another attack. He didn't look worried, but he was also the only one who could set Purgatory to rights. What if it wasn't just the fae he had to beat? What would happen if Anubis fell?

"What's going on with your arm?" Lilith asked.

The tattoo was glowing so brightly that the design was visible through my shirt. I pushed up the sleeve. The tattoo glowed and shone like melted silver.

"Faerie magic," Crowley said.

"Protection," I said without even thinking about it.

Morgan had said the tattoo was a symbol of protection against magical attack, *If you believe that sort of thing*. He had said it like a throwaway phrase, but Morgan was often falsely light. The symbol *was* protection. It was why I had been able to see through the illusions and wasn't affected by the attacks from the Order of Puck trio like my friends were.

"I guess Morgan's on our side," I said. Thank Lucifer.

"Then why aren't they here?" Lilith demanded. "Why did they leave this in our hands?"

"We can't worry about that right now. We have to go," Crowley said.

"Anubis has to come too," I protested.

"I'll be right behind you," Anubis growled, still battling against the fae.

"Good enough for me," Aleister said, jumping to his feet. "Which way, Mal?"

I got to my feet and took one last look at Anubis. He turned for a second so that one gold glowing eye went right through me. I swallowed and searched for the sparkling path between worlds that I had followed before. It was harder with the spaces less defined, but I knew I'd be able to find it. Morgan might not have been there, but they had given me the tools to stand for myself.

"There," I said.

We ran, chased by an ominous cry of, "You're too late!"

The divisions between worlds were less clearly defined than when we had arrived but were still holding. Ophelia had to be wrong; we couldn't be too late. We just couldn't.

But there were so many worlds that worked together to hold the balance, and the wrong souls had already ended up in Heaven and Hell. Purgatory was overrun, which affected the land of the dead, which affected the mortal coil. . . . I ran faster.

We arrived at the door inside a door, and I reached for it, only to have my hand pass through it. For a second I panicked.

"The page," yelled Lilith.

Right, the words. Of course!

I went to pull the page from my jacket pocket, but I quickly came to the terrible realization that I had abandoned the jacket in the midst of the fight.

"No," I said. "No, no, no. It's not—"

I had put the page in my pocket—the one thing the Baron had given me, our way home that I had been trusted with— and I had completely forgotten about it. What had I done?

"It's okay. It's right here," Aleister said. "I grabbed it from your jacket."

Aleister shoved the page at me.

A shadow slithered nearby, and I couldn't stop myself from looking. I didn't know what it was like to be unmade, and I didn't want to find out. I looked back at the page, mentally promising never to complain about buying Aleister ice cream again. The words were written in scrawled neon green against the worn yellow page, and it took a minute for my eyes to adjust.

"Oh, heavenly light," gasped Zira. "Something's coming. Hurry!"

I placed my hand on the door. "'Papa Legba, open the door! Open the door, Atibon, for us to pass now! Papa Legba, open the door!'"

The light glowed around my hand, and the doorknob— which only seemed to exist on this side—grew more solid. Zira screamed, and Aleister shouted. I said the words again.

Crowley shouted something in Enochian, and a purple burst of light lit the space around us. A flash of movement caught my eye, and I looked up to see something emerging from the space above, a dark darker than anything I had ever seen before slithering toward my head.

*Please!* I screamed in my head while my mouth repeated the words to open the door. For a second I swore I was looking into Morgan's eyes, and then a howl rang out, and the sounds of horns and shouts filled the air.

And then from one dimension to the next and through the space between, what could only have been the Wild Hunt barreled through. And even though I had nowhere enough ego to think the Hunt had come to our defense, it didn't matter, because whatever those shadows were, whether the tentacles belonged to Chaos, as Zira had suggested, or just an ancient beast, they found the Hunt much more interesting. Inches from my head the tentacle withdrew, all of them withdrew . . . no, not withdrew, changed focus. And followed the Hunt.

In an inane moment I wondered why, if we were finally in the same space as the Hunt, I wasn't feeling the urge to follow. When I looked to check on my friends, Zira and Aleister had already taken flight to join, but before I could even object, Lilith and Crowley grabbed them and yanked them toward the door. I saw the longing on their faces just as I noticed that the doorknob was solid. I grabbed it and my hand did not pass through.

The noise from the Hunt almost drowned out the screams of the fae behind us. I turned the knob and pulled the door open.

# FORTY-FIVE

We tumbled through the door back into that world of death, which was far more alive and real than anything in the space between. We were panting and sweaty and our clothing was the worse for wear, but the Baron jumped up from where he was waiting, a look of concern and then disappointment on his face.

"We freed him," I said.

"He said he'd be right behind us," Zira said, looking at the once-again closed door with concern.

"It was the Order of Puck," Lilith said. "They . . . I think they just wanted everything to end."

"Immortality is hardly for everyone," the Baron said. "Though that is little excuse."

"I don't think they were . . . all there," Aleister said, which was honestly more diplomatic than he usually managed.

"I didn't think people actually worked for Chaos," I said. "They were definitely trying, though."

"There are always some. These sound more like opportunists than true followers."

"What's the difference?" Lilith asked.

"From your description," the Baron said, walking directly up to the door, "these fae wanted to help Chaos rise to end everything, and they knew, like we all do, that the balance keeps Chaos locked away. Chaos was just a means for destruction. There are others . . . closer to the entity itself . . . the ones who speak to it and listen to its whispers . . . the ones who worship Chaos and believe it must be restored to its rightful place."

He placed his hand on the door, but like before, sparks formed around it and his bones became visible through his dark skin.

We exchanged worried glances. What was taking Anubis so long? Had he been overcome by the fae? By those tentacles? By something worse? If he didn't come back, Purgatory would fall. What would we do?

And then the door opened.

Anubis strode through the opening, and the Baron's shoulders slumped just the tiniest amount with relief. Anubis's gold eyes surveyed us all, and the blazing glow dimmed. I wasn't sure his hound head was capable of smiling, but he appeared to be pleased.

"Ah," Baron Samedi said. "You are late."

"So I've been informed," Anubis said. "I'll have to win your money at the next game, but for now I fear that though I have cleaned up one mess, I have yet another to deal with."

"Good riddance," the Baron said. "And indeed, you didn't have to make my work harder just to get out of losing. Please, fix the result of your slacking off and you can inform me of your misadventure later."

Anubis placed a hand on the Baron's shoulder for just a moment and then looked at us. "Thank you, children. I'll *see* you again."

We nodded.

"Wait," Aleister called. "How do you play poker with your sight? Isn't that cheating?"

Anubis's tongue poked out for a second in the same way that Damien's did when he was happy, before the god of death cleared his expression to something more regal.

"I would never," he said, and then Anubis disappeared.

The Baron shook his head. "He's a vicious cheater."

I huffed out a surprised laugh and felt myself start to relax. We knew what had caused the instability, and Anubis had resolved the issue. At least he had taken care of the three we knew were involved. There was no telling how much further the Order of Puck went, and how large its influence was. In any case, that information could be relayed to the adults, and they could take care of it. They would hunt down the rest of the order and make sure they couldn't complete their mission.

We were safe and the Baron had promised to get us back. I just had to hope that the mixer hadn't collapsed on everyone inside the pocket dimension.

"Your celebration is continuing," the Baron said as if reading my mind, and before Lilith went beyond taking a breath to ask a question, he continued, "Everyone is fine. The pocket dimension was stabilized. Time works differently in those worlds, and I would wager they haven't yet noticed you've gone missing. I will send you all back."

The Baron paused and cocked his head. A moment later we heard the commotion that must have drawn his attention.

"Good, we wanted to see him!"

"Seriously, if you had just listened . . ."

"But that's okay. I get it; trust has to be earned."

Between the trees and their hanging moss, the fog swirled with the movement caused by whoever was coming. The voices were familiar, but I couldn't place them right away, and I really hoped I was not going to be dealing with my classmates here. If the rumors were bad now, I didn't want to see what they would be like after being caught here with a seraph, all of us looking the worse for wear.

A group of the gede, followers of Baron Samedi, made their way closer. They were dressed much like the Baron, but there was no competing in the aura of power. Whoever was yelling was in their midst and wasn't quite visible, but the looks of annoyance on the faces of the gede told an entire story.

The two in the front parted as they emerged from the trees, and my mouth dropped open in shock.

"Baron!" cried the very familiar human. "We need your help!"

"Sean?" I exclaimed, while Crowley simultaneously said, "Charity?"

"Mal?"

"Crowley!"

Sean looked as shocked as I felt, but after a brief look of surprise, Charity smiled brightly, bringing out dimples on her dirty face. She waved frantically, and Crowley lifted a hand, looking shell-shocked. Sean gave a pained smile, and just that little bit sent the bats fluttering in my stomach.

"Sir," said the gede to the right. "These humans were the ones who were causing the disturbances. What should we do with them?"

"Please," Sean said, turning his head with some effort, as his body was held still between his captors, to face the Baron. "We were just trying to get your attention. That mess is not us. Tell us what's happening. We thought for sure you were hurt, but . . ."

"Why did you think that?" asked the Baron, though his expression said he didn't want to hear the answer.

"The dead . . ."

"They're rising," Charity said.

"And that's not all," Sean said. "People aren't . . . not that we want them to necessarily, but . . ."

"They're not dying," Charity said. "Which in theory sounds great, but it turns out it isn't really."

"Where did you see this?" Baron Samedi asked.

"New Orleans," Sean said. "It's a city in—"

"I know it well," the Baron interrupted.

"Now that Anubis is back," I said, cautiously inserting myself into the conversation, "shouldn't that be fixed?"

"Yeah," Lilith said. "Once he corrects Purgatory, that should stop the effect of the delay here and there."

"Yes," said the Baron, but he was frowning.

"Maybe you could try digging," Zira suggested. "I know Anubis hasn't been back long, but surely things should be better."

The Baron studied his shovel leaning up against a tree, and my stomach got that uneasy feeling it gets when you know things aren't going to go the way you want them to, but you're not sure why. He took solemn steps and retrieved his shovel. He chose a spot, near a babbling brook, and struck the dirt. He dug; the lush soil was deposited on the ground next to where he was digging. One shovelful, two, three . . . and the Baron stepped back.

I held my breath, staring at the hole. No one moved. And for a moment I thought it would be okay.

And then the soil burbled up, slowly but surely filling the emptiness meant to call someone home.

There were gasps all around, except for the Baron, who just straightened resolutely.

"I believe it's time for a visit to New Orleans," murmured the Baron.

"Thank you," Sean said solemnly.

As relieved as I was to see Sean and Charity alive, it didn't lessen my concern. Things were stabilized for now, but this wasn't over. Even if Purgatory was back in order and there were no more wrong destinations, the fact that the land of the dead was affected meant there could still be issues that would have ripple effects.

For so long we had been operating as distinct entities, as if our actions didn't rely on or affect others. But we were all in this together.

"What does it mean?" asked Aleister.

"It means," said the Baron slowly, "that there is a traitor in my midst."

The gede shared terrified looks, which were no doubt reflected on our own faces.

"I think we might have some ideas," offered Sean cautiously.

"Or," said Charity, "at least ideas about where to start."

"Show me," said the Baron. "But first I must send these children back."

"Wait!" I said. I quickly glanced at my squad, who were looking at me with ready, knowing expressions, while Zira looked on, vaguely traumatized. My squad nodded, and I knew we were once again in agreement.

I turned back to Baron Samedi, his followers, and our wayward humans, and gave my most confident smirk. "Do you need our help?"

# ACKNOWLEDGMENTS

Writing a sequel, especially one to a debut, is much harder than I expected. I've heard so much amazing feedback to *Grounded for All Eternity* that I admit I felt the pressure!

I wanted Mal's story to continue, and for those who loved the first to love this one just as much. I wanted to give readers a deeper look into Mal's world and expand on the universe it exists in, while still keeping to those messages of being true to yourself. About growing and doing what's right and finding out who you are and where you fit.

And let's be honest, when your teen sends you text messages while they're reading your book wanting spoilers and loving your characters and then complaining about the lack of merch when they finished reading? Yeah, that's the best feeling in the world, and also really makes you not want to fail on the sequel. Samantha, I hope you love this one just as much.

As always, a finished book is very much an effort by a whole bunch of people! Thank you, as always, to my agent, Victoria Wells Arms, who is always the best cheerleader and support system in this crazy publishing endeavor.

Thank you to my editor, Kristin Gilson, for always understanding what I'm trying to do with my story and for being as excited about the introduction of the Baron Samedi as I am! I love that you get it. Thank you for all your hard work.

Thank you to everyone at Aladdin/Simon & Schuster who has put time and effort into making this book a real and wonderful thing! There are so many of you, and your work does not go unnoticed. Thank you to my publicist, Nicole Valdez, for all your efforts to get *Grounded* in front of eyes!

A HUGE gigantic thank-you to the indie booksellers who have been so supportive! And to all the booksellers I've visited where I signed books only to hear that you had read the book and loved it. Thank you to Donna at the Eloquent Page, who hosted the book launch for *Grounded*—you're the best.

Thank you to all my writing community friends, especially K. Callard, Ally Malinenko, Lora Senf, and everyone at Spooky Middle Grade.

And most importantly, thank you so much to everyone who read *Grounded for All Eternity* and reached out to me, left reviews, made fan art, and told people about it. Thanks for reading and for your continued support. See you next time!

# ABOUT THE AUTHOR

Darcy Marks is a lifelong reader who learned to walk quite well with a book in front of her face, thank you very much. She lives in Vermont—with her husband, three genre-defying kids, and a very needy cat—where she writes rebellious fantasy books for kids. When she's not reading or writing, she explains math and science to lawyers as a forensic toxicologist and uses her several black belts to help smash the patriarchy with the Safety Team.